the Dead Kid

DETECTIVE AGENCY

Dial M for Morna

EVAN MUNDAY

ECW

Published by ECW Press
2120 Queen Street East, Suite 200, Toronto, Ontario, Canada M4E 1E2
416-694-3348 / info@ecwpress.com

Library and Archives Canada Cataloguing in Publication

Munday, Evan, author
Dial M for Morna / Evan Munday.
(Dead Kid Detective Agency series)

ISBN 978-1-77041-073-2 (pbk.)
Also issued as: 978-1-77090-418-7 (epub); 978-1-77090-417-0 (PDF)

I. Title. II. Series: Munday, Evan. Dead Kid Detective Agency.

PS8626.U54D52 2013   jC813'.6   C2013-902468-9

Editor: Erin Creasey
Cover and interior illustrations: Evan Munday
Cover and text design: David Gee
Typesetting and production: Carolyn McNeillie
Author photo: Jenna Wakani
Printing: Friesens   5   4   3   2   1   •

The publication of Dial M for Morna has been generously supported by the Canada
Council for the Arts, which last year invested $20.1 million in writing and publishing
throughout Canada. We also acknowledge the support of the Ontario Arts Council
(OAC), an agency of the Government of Ontario, which last year funded 1,681
individual artists and 1,125 organizations in 216 communities across Ontario for a
total of $52.8 million, the Government of Ontario through Ontario Book Publishing
Tax Credit, the OMDC Book Fund, an initiative of the Ontario Media Development
Corporation, and the Government of Canada through the Canada Book Fund.

Printed and bound in Canada

Call me, maybe.

– Carly Rae Jepsen

1

Radio-Free Sticksville

Nobody could replace Mr. O'Shea. Until someone did.

October Schwartz encountered said history replacement, Ms. Fenstermacher, in Sticksville's public library one Sunday afternoon, while October was doing some prep work in advance of raising her five dead friends.

October knew why *she* was spending the day in the library, but she couldn't fathom why Ms. Fenstermacher was spending her Sunday with hundreds of books and dozens of severely outdated computer terminals. Wasn't that like a police officer spending his day off fingerprinting his loved ones?

"October!" Ms. Fenstermacher called as loudly as the regulations of the library would allow and waved both hands at chest level like she was treading water.

October had really wanted to hate Ms. Fenstermacher: it would have been so much easier for her cognitive processes if this new teacher had been someone despicable or even someone forgettable and bland. That Mr. O'Shea was replaced wasn't overly surprising in itself. With a French teacher suddenly dead and a history teacher imprisoned, Sticksville was *the* place to be for the ambitious yet unemployed high school teacher that November. (Spoilers follow if you haven't read the first book.) See, after October Schwartz's history teacher, Mr. Page, accidentally (but heinously) killed her French teacher, Mr. O'Shea, Sticksville Central High School was scrambling to find non-murderous replacements for both teachers.

The instructor they found to replace Mr. O'Shea, victim of the fall's most horrible crime (so far), had made little impression on October. Mr. Martz was an older gentleman, about the age Mr. O'Shea used to be, who was neither significantly endearing nor unsettling.

Her new history teacher, however, was another story. And though Mr. Martz had replaced Mr. O'Shea in job title, Ms. Fenstermacher seemed like she might one day replace Mr. O'Shea (if such a thing could be done) as the teacher who could be considered some sort of friend.

But October had been burned by pleasant teachers before; after all, the last one turned out to be homicidal, even threatening October with an antique bayonet. The trouble was, October couldn't help but find Ms. Fenstermacher anything but . . . well . . . kind of awesome. Still, October couldn't shake the thought that some dark twist hid behind this awesomeness: there was a distinct possibility Ms. F. was a teen-detective-killing robot sent from the future only posing as a history teacher.

Okay, so it's a recognized fact that teachers, as a rule, are never going to win any Teen Choice Awards. But check this evidence: (a) Ms. Fenstermacher's hair was dyed nearly as black as October's, (b) she wore thick-framed glasses like she was Rivers Cuomo or Buddy Holly or someone, and (c) she referenced *Battlestar Galactica* in October's class three times in her first week of teaching.

In short, Ms. Fenstermacher certainly wasn't going to be mistaken for Mr. Santuzzi, October's less-than-awesome math teacher who ran classes like a boot camp, any time soon. October looked up from the historical atlas of Sticksville spread across the study group table and returned the wave as noncommittally as possible. Unfortunately, October's half-hearted gesture was encouragement enough: in moments, Ms. Fenstermacher was standing at her shoulder.

"What brings you to Sticksville Public Library this dazzling Sunday afternoon?"

Let's assume that was an ironic usage of the word dazzling. Though the weather forecasts had called for overcast skies, chilly temperatures, and light rain on that November Sunday, the Weather Gods had exceeded all expectations and whipped up a truly miserable afternoon. Outside the floor-to-ceiling library windows, it looked like sewer water was being hosed down from the rooftops (which was probably not the case).

"Oh, stuff," October answered.

Of course, by "stuff," she meant "some last-minute research on Sticksville in the early twentieth century and the MacIsaac family in particular because I've slacked off all month and I'm raising a few friends from the dead tomorrow night so we can figure out who killed one of them."

Y'know, *stuff*.

"Don't let me keep you from your stuff," Fenstermacher said, eyeing the historical atlas with curiosity. Finally, a teacher in Sticksville with a sense of personal space. "I've got movies to borrow. I just wanted to say hello."

With that, Ms. Fenstermacher — clearly vying for cool grownup status, and in a much more ham-fisted way than Mr. O'Shea ever had — departed for the DVD section, leaving October to her historical cartography. And not a moment too soon: the instant her new history teacher had left, October Schwartz uncovered what she'd been searching for the past hour: the address of the boarding house where the living version of Morna MacIsaac had done that living over a hundred years ago.

October hadn't dedicated as much of her free time over the past month to historical research as she'd originally planned. As you may recall, the whole mystery of Mr. O'Shea's death was solved by thirteen-year-old October Schwartz with the help of five dead Sticksville children. Those five dead children were from five different, far-flung eras of Canada's past, and each of them had no idea how they died. In fact, they all had significant gaps in memory around the days leading up to their mysterious (and, let's assume, tragic) deaths. After the dead kids helped October figure out the mystery behind Mr. O'Shea's death, she agreed to help them solve the mysteries of their own deaths in return. She had decided to start with Morna MacIsaac, the dead girl whose family immigrated to Canada from Scotland in 1910.

October hadn't seen or heard from the dead kids since Hallowe'en. The basic rule (and *yes*, dead kids are stuck with rules, too) was that they could only be raised during a full moon and would only remain among the living until the next full moon. Now, the full moon was here (at least, it would be when it got dark), and so was the narrow window during which she could raise her dead partners again. She was glad to have at least one shred of valuable information she could present to Morna when she resurrected her, alongside her ghostly compatriots, Cyril Cooper, Tabetha Scott, Kirby LaFlamme, and Derek Running Water. She didn't want to look like a *total* slacker.

Returning the atlas to its spot on the dusty shelves, October wondered if there was a way she could bring even more evidence to the dead kids — get a little extra credit, for lack of a better term.

"Ms. Fenstermacher," she called, making — against her better judgement — that same treading water motion. "Ms. Fenstermacher, would you mind helping me?"

A stack of DVD cases under her arm, Ms. Fenstermacher strolled across the library and sat down beside the wide-eyed girl dressed all in black.

"You need help with something?"

"Do you know where I'd find old newspapers? From 1914, say?"

"I'm not sure. This is my first trip to the Sticksville library, but there's probably a microfilm station where you can look at old newspapers."

"Microfilm?"

"Let's find a librarian."

☠

Ms. Fenstermacher yanked open a metal filing cabinet. Inside, rows upon rows of small paper boxes rested like little white chipmunk coffins. (Actually, it's probably better if you don't visualize dead chipmunks.) Faded stickers were affixed to each one, printed with dates and *The Sticksville Loon*.

"If a newspaper page hasn't been digitized," Fenstermacher explained, "it's likely you can find it on microfilm: small photos of some of the oldest newspapers that can be blown up in a projector. What date are you looking for?"

"Uh, December 1914," October answered, remembering the end date on Morna's grave marker. "I'm making a family tree for my dad. Y'know, as a birthday present." October smiled at her effortless deception. Gullible Ms. Fenstermacher didn't realize her dad's birthday wasn't until March.

"You're in luck then. Looks like you'll just need this one film," Ms. Fenstermacher said, collecting a little white box from the cabinet. She walked over to what looked like an ancient television/microscope hybrid. "It's just like loading film into a projector. Or like threading a needle."

Ms. Fenstermacher extracted the shiny snakelike black coil from its container, and October nodded at her teacher's comparison to two things she'd never done in her life. Seriously, Ms. Fenstermacher might as well have said it was just like churning butter. Luckily she was more than pleased to spool the microfilm herself.

"It's all loaded now," she declared, turning the machine on. The front page of a *Sticksville Loon* from 1914 glowed wanly from the viewer. "You can advance through the pages with this knob, and use these dials to zoom and focus. Give it a spin."

October sat cautiously in front of the monolithic device and began to advance through the ancient reproductions of *Sticksville Loon* pages, her eyes roaming the screen for any mention of the MacIsaacs. Ideally, Ms. Fenstermacher would have returned to her DVD search at this point, just so October didn't seem like a complete ghoul, trolling the library for tales of murdered children, but, as the terrible weather outside acknowledged, this was *not* an ideal situation. Apparently, October's history teacher wanted to make sure she got the hang of the microfilm reader first.

"You know, if your dad's family is from Sticksville, you might want to drop by the Sticksville Museum," Ms. Fenstermacher suggested, leaning on the desktop. "I volunteer there in my spare time; it has loads of records and photographs. The museum is in the old Cooper House."

"Cooper House?" Ms. Fenstermacher couldn't be talking about the former residence of her dead United Empire Loyalist friend, Cyril, could she? October couldn't think of that now; she had to focus on the microfilm.

"Mm-hmm. Drop by after school some time."

"Well, this could take a while," October hinted.

"Hey, there's something interesting," Ms. Fenstermacher exclaimed, not getting the hint at all.

The something interesting was the front page of the *Sticksville Loon* October had stopped on. The headline screamed *Chinese Saboteur Nabbed in Sticksville!* A quick scan of the front page told October a Chinese resident in the boarding house was arrested for attempting to bomb a Canadian military base, Fort Hannover. The article was interesting itself, what with all the Chinese sabotage, but the accompanying photo really struck October — a portrait of the residents at the boarding house where the saboteur was found. Just under a dozen people, including, October immediately recognized, a healthy and breathing Morna MacIsaac.

"I think we have a few pieces at the museum on that sabotage case."

"Ms. Fenstermacher, how do I print this page?" October asked.

"Print? You can't print it. It's not like a computer," Ms. Fenstermacher explained. "You'll have to write the information down."

"But what if I want that photo?"

Ms. Fenstermacher was stumped. "Cheese and crackers. What if I take a picture with my phone and email it to you? Would that work?"

"I'd be forever in your debt, Ms. Fenstermacher," October said. "You need photocopies made, coffee brewed, whiteboards cleaned — just name it."

October eyed the plain wall clock above the library's checkout desk. She was running out of minutes before her dad expected her back at home. The address she'd found in the atlas for the Crooked Arms boarding house wasn't but a twenty-minute walk from the library, but that was probably twenty minutes she didn't have. (And yes, the Crooked Arms is the name of the boarding house where Morna MacIsaac had lived. It may sound made up, but it's a totally legitimate boarding house name.)

October thanked Ms. Fenstermacher and returned to her group study table. She pulled her black umbrella from her backpack, and exited into the cold, filthy rain. In just one night, she would raise the dead kids from the grave again, and together they would all investigate this Crooked Arms place.

☠

Where are my manners? I apologize — we just leapt into the fray (if a public library could ever be described as a fray) without so much as a welcome. So, welcome, dear readers, to the second adventure of the Dead Kid Detective Agency. *Ta-da!* You can expect the same kind of madcap exploits featured in book one — our plucky heroine with a penchant for black eyeliner and her five most deadest BFFs uncovering dark secrets that will rock the quiet town of Sticksville to its secretly rotten core and doing so in the zaniest possible manner. There may even be a few flashbacks in which we will peep in on Sticksville a hundred years in the past. Won't that be thrilling?

And if you are concerned, having been introduced in the first few pages to another friendly teacher, that dear Ms. Fenstermacher will end up impaled by a chalk pointer or crushed by a toppled basketball net four chapters from now, have no fear. I wouldn't do that to you two books in a row, would I?

☠

The next afternoon, Mr. Santuzzi dismissed his second-period math class with an ominous warning: "This Thursday is our unit test on the Pythagorean theorem. Don't let it be your last."

Their last test on the Pythagorean theorem? Their last test ever? Was capital punishment now on the table for math class? Had it ever really *not* been on the table in Mr. Santuzzi's class?

The questions were endless, so the cryptic threat stuck with October all the way to the cafeteria, where she met with the two friends of hers who still had heartbeats, Yumi Takeshi and Stacey Whatshisface. Yumi was pretty much the only girl at school who wore more black and heavier makeup than October, and Stacey was her tall, awkward sidekick. The month between that fateful Hallowe'en night when Mr. Page was arrested and now had not witnessed any spike in the trio's popularity. They remained about as desirable to most classmates as a case of back acne. They sat isolated at the final outpost at the edge of the misfit cafeteria table, like astronauts in a capsule from which mission control had cut off all communication.

Yumi and Stacey were attempting to rein in massive grins when October sat down across from them. They weren't a humourless bunch, but smiles of that magnitude were cause for some alarm.

"What?" October demanded, picking a label off her apple with her ragged black fingernail. "What did I do? Did I get eyeliner all over my mouth again?" Yes. That had happened. Two weeks earlier, October's "Zombie Tramp" nickname was briefly replaced by "The Bearded Zombie Tramp."

"No. Nothing like that," Stacey insisted.

"Who's got two thumbs and a radio time slot?" Yumi asked. She jammed her thumbs toward her face and exclaimed, "This girl!"

Yumi and Stacey folded into the cafeteria table with laughter.

"I don't get it," October said.

"You're sitting across from the new DJ of Radio Sticksville High," Yumi said. "I'll be playing all your favourite hits — or, more accurately, all *my* favourite hits — for my adoring cafeteria audience every Tuesday and Friday lunch hour."

"Since when does this school have a radio station?" October asked. A fair question since they were currently seated in a completely music-free cafeteria environment.

"We're starting up Radio Sticksville in December. The radio station equipment has always been here," Yumi explained. "There just weren't any teachers willing to supervise."

"And who's supervising it now?" October asked, chomping down on her Red Delicious. "Not the guy with the sideburns who teaches tech?"

"No," Stacey said. "It's your hot new history teacher."

This just proved to October that Ms. Fenstermacher was becoming much too cool for her own good. She really needed to tone down the whole hip teacher act — perhaps she could develop a weird facial tic or wear sweaters from Northern Reflections.

"She's not that hot," Yumi argued.

"She is — and I don't make this designation lightly — a *stone cold fox*," Stacey rebutted.

"That's great, Yumi. How did you get the DJ job?" October asked, ignoring the total pervosity Stacey was currently demonstrating.

"They had a meeting about the radio program and announced they wanted a grade nine to DJ one of the time slots. I had the best music selection."

"You were the loudest," Stacey corrected.

"Yeah, yeah. Listen to your Walkman while I perfect my DJ name," Yumi said.

As instructed, Stacey returned to his ancient Walkman while October and Yumi brainstormed the ideal DJ moniker. By the end of lunch hour, they'd narrowed it down to two choices: DJ Yusless and DJ CD-Ramen, though they agreed the latter might be kind of racist. Who should interrupt this pivotal decision-making process but Mr. Schwartz, arriving without warning or apology in the cafeteria doorway.

"Heads up, October," Stacey warned, pulling out his earbuds. "Dad alert."

The warning came too late. Mr. Schwartz had already beelined to their loser table, and pretty much every other table with any level of social standing degenerated into giggling, finger-pointing, and general derision for October and her whole rogue dad predicament.

"October!" Mr. Schwartz exclaimed, brushing his chalky hands on his brown slacks. Do people still say slacks? That's what they were, in any case, so they should. "I'm so glad I found you."

"Dad," she stage-whispered through clenched teeth. "Could this not wait until after school?"

"Sorry, pumpkin," he said, almost as if he were taking some perverse pleasure in his daughter's suffering. "But that's what I need to talk about. I have to stay extra late today for volleyball. Our girls are on a roll. We could make it to the championship!"

"That's great, Dad. Really." She wanted to be proud of him, but more importantly, she wanted him to be gone. She directed her dad to the door with a dramatic roll of her harshly outlined eyes. "I'll see you later tonight?"

"Your friend Ashlie Salmons is really a phenomenal player," he continued, an unstoppable embarrassment machine. "She's going to take us to the regionals, I'm sure."

October no longer wanted to be proud for her dad. *Her friend Ashlie Salmons?* Since October had moved to Sticksville this past summer, Ashlie Salmons had done everything short of poisoning her. October nearly blew apple chunks all over her dad's chalk-streaked shirt. Instead, she merely frowned and arched her brow.

"Okay. I get it," Mr. Schwartz relented, finally clueing in. "Dad. School setting. Bad idea. I understand. See you at home."

He tried to exit as speedily as possible, but the damage had been done. It makes no difference how quickly you drive away once you've caused a multi-vehicle accident.

"That was unfortunate," October said.

Stacey and Yumi made facial expressions that were all like, *Tell me about it.*

"Tell me about it," said Ashlie Salmons, sidling up to October's cafeteria bench. "Doesn't your dad care about your social status? Wait, is there any social status lower than Zombie Tramp, even?"

Ashlie brought a manicured finger to her lip, as if she were actually considering this taxonomical quandary. Beside the dishevelled trio, with Yumi and October clad in unwashed black clothing and Stacey in the mismatched thrift-shop mess he was wearing, Ashlie looked like another species in her perfect jumper, grey leggings and trademark oversized belt.

"Uh —" Yumi started, either to answer or to deliver a stinging comeback.

"Don't even start with me, Kung Fu Zombie Tramp," Ashlie barked. "You're already on my list for stealing that radio time slot. It should have been Devin's."

"You're still seeing that guy from Phantom Moustache?" October asked, referring to Sticksville Central's band du jour.

"Like he'd ever leave me," Ashlie answered. "With DJ Kung Fu Zombie Tramp at the mic instead of Devin, we'll have to listen to funeral marches twice a week."

Like a cat who had tired of playing with her food, Ashlie Salmons drifted back toward her usual table. The surprise chat with Ashlie was traumatic enough, and on another day, October's dad's visit might have crushed her spirit completely, but she was unflappable this Monday. This Monday was November 28, the first day of the full moon. The first day (according to the dead kids' own extremely unscientific reckoning) that she could summon them back to the mortal plane or wherever it was where she and Ashlie and her dad and the members of S Club 7 lived, assuming they're all still alive. After tonight in the cemetery, good times were going to roll. Crime-investigation good times.

"What are you up to tonight, Schwartz?" Yumi asked. "Want to come over to my place and listen to some funeral marches?"

"You know me," October said. "I love me some dirges. But I've got to get some work done on this thing." With that, October lifted the battered composition book she kept with her at all times, the one labelled *Two Knives, One Thousand Demons*. "These demons aren't going to stab themselves to death. Someone's got to write it down," said October, succinctly explaining the writing process. "I'll be in the Sticksville Cemetery until it gets too dark to see."

The bell rang and October started packing up her things for music class.

"If you get bored," Yumi said, "just give me a call."

"On what phone?" The three friends passed the soda machine where just a month earlier, Mrs. Tischmann had misplaced her wooden leg.

"Yeah, I need a cell," Yumi added. "Life would be so much easier."

"Don't look at me," Stacey said, feeling the keen weight of conversation upon his shoulders. "I'm still working with a Walkman."

☠

Half a day later, Mr. Schwartz was sound asleep, unable to inflict much in the way of embarrassment in his near-catatonic state, and his daughter, now quite adept at sneaking out, was standing in the middle of a clearing in the Sticksville Cemetery, that same *Two Knives, One Thousand Demons* notebook in her outstretched arms. Overhead, the trees, shorn of all their leaves, looked like skeletons reaching up to the sky, grabbing at the full moon like it was a Frisbee at some skeleton ultimate tournament. The entire cemetery — from the majestic, show-off tombstones that towered far above October's height to the lowly paupers' graves marked only with a rough-cut stone — had a bluish, deathly sheen. But it's not all that unusual for a graveyard to look a little deathly.

October was lucky she'd worn her black peacoat, because it was positively freezing in the graveyard. October (the month) had been cold enough to make her consider un-friending her ghost neighbours; could she really visit the dead kids night after night in the middle of December? Maybe she could sneak a space heater onto the cemetery grounds somewhere, hide it behind a rarely visited tomb.

The cold was only a minor deterrent, though. October was warmed from top to tail by confidence. (Figuratively, of course. Confidence produces no heat energy whatsoever.) Once she read the mystical phrase she had somehow accidentally written into her still-unfinished demon-slaying epic, her dead friends would be with her. She'd tell them about the Crooked Arms, ask Morna about that Chinese saboteur, and investigative hijinks would ensue: clues would be discovered, suspects would be interrogated, property would be damaged (let's be honest), and in no time at all, they'd solve the mystery of who killed Morna MacIsaac. A few sub-zero degrees on the thermometer wasn't going to slow her down.

October thumbed the lined pages of the composition book until she reached the reanimating verse. Watching as the vapour escaped from her mouth in the frozen air, she drew in a deep breath and recited the words:

> As Nature turns twisted and dark,
> To this dread graveyard I donate my spark.
> As tears begin to blind mine eyes,
> The innocent young and the dead shall rise.

Then nothing — absolutely nothing — happened.

☠

Ouija Board
to Death

So, I broke the dead kids. Apparently.

The next morning, Mr. Martz stood at the front of the class in his suede brown suit, running through yesterday's *très* easy French assignment, while I tried to figure out how exactly I'd broken them. Truthfully, I'd only raised them from the dead once, and I'd kind of taken it for granted I could recreate my results. I had figured it would be kind of like flipping a dead-undead light switch. And last night it wasn't like I'd only spoken the stupid apparently-not-that-enchanted words once. I had flipped that light switch up and down a dozen times. Tried a few different voices, closed my eyes while I chanted, even stuck myself with my Cure pin thinking a blood sacrifice might do the trick. I sucked my sore thumb in French class, puzzled by the complete lack of ghostly activity in the cemetery.

My failure obsessed me through both first period and Mr. Santuzzi's class. I rolled it around in my head like a marble. Since simply saying the words wasn't enough, how could I bring my dead friends back to life — or back to Sticksville, at least? I didn't know anything about resurrecting people or contacting ghosts; the first time had been a complete accident. I only had one ace — not even an ace; more like a ten — up my sleeve, and it involved the folded printout of that *Sticksville Loon* front page in my bag and the tendency of my two living friends to not ask prying questions.

When I arrived at our usual lunch table, Yumi and Stacey were studying pages and pages of notepaper spread all over its surface. It looked like they were planning a land invasion of Europe.

"October," Yumi barely glanced up from the handwritten lists that blanketed the table. "Good. You can help us. We're trying to figure out which songs to play on my inaugural radio show. Stacey and I have it narrowed down to just over two hundred."

"When did you do all this?"

"Stacey came over last night. We brainstormed."

I eventually found a space among the lists to set down my lunch. In the middle of a difficult debate Yumi was having with herself over whether she should play something from *The Crow* soundtrack or if that was just too obvious, I rudely interrupted with my dead kid problem, albeit in a sideways manner.

"What do you guys know about 1914?"

"I know it has nothing to do with what songs we're going to play on Friday," Yumi replied. "Focus, October!"

"Wait, *we*?" Was I going to be a DJ, too? The flattering thought almost made me blush.

"Yeah. There are two microphones in the DJ booth. Stacey's going to be my radio sidekick."

"Stacey?"

Far be it from me to question Yumi Takeshi's plans, but Stacey was barely verbal. I'm not sure what the captain of the silence team was going to add to DJ Yumi's radio fun hour.

"What happened in 1914?" Stacey asked, determined to prove me a liar about his non-verbal tendencies.

"Oh, it's just part of this dry history project Ms. Fenstermacher assigned." I dug into my bag and laid my folded printout on top of the list named *Songs with Hurt in the Title, Part 1*. The picture quality wasn't going to win any awards, but Morna MacIsaac could clearly be seen, along with several other residents of the Crooked Arms.

"Who are those people?" asked Yumi.

"I don't know. People from 1914 Sticksville, I guess." Playing dumb for effect.

"Some of the people look kind of familiar," Stacey added.

"Ms. Fenstermacher says I have to write a biography of one of them. They all lived in the Crooked Arms."

"I would *kill* to be in Ms. Fenstermacher's class," Stacey announced.

"And what is the Crooked Arms?" Yumi asked.

"An old boarding house on the other side of town."

"October," Yumi said, in rational Yumi mode, "you know we're friends. But my knowledge of Sticksville history? Not the best. Plus, I've got crazy serious radio programming issues to sort out right now. Maybe Stacey can help you out here. He's the one who's seen this photo before."

"Is it from a history textbook or something?" he asked.

A few aisles up, Ashlie Salmons was feeding Devin McGriff gravy fries like he was a star performer seal at MarineLand, and her plate of fries was a bucket of herring. Despite my overwhelmingly negative feelings toward Ashlie, at least she'd always seemed self-sufficient. Leader-like, even, in a repressive dictator kind of way. Watching her dote on Phantom Moustache's lead guitarist while her usual followers — Goose Neck, Novelty T-shirt, and the little girl with the big laugh — looked on made me throw up in my mouth a bit. Or maybe that was just from the way Devin McGriff ate gravy fries.

"Can we get back to sorting?" Yumi said. "I've only got three days until the show. And what do you want us to do about these super-dead people? You want to borrow my library card?"

"Okay, I get that history is boring," I said, shaking away thoughts of Ashlie Salmons' well-being. "But I had this idea: the Crooked Arms still exists, though it's sort of . . . kind of . . . condemned. What if the three of us took my Ouija board to the old, possibly haunted Crooked Arms?"

So, yes, that was my plan. Since the dead kids didn't seem to be in the Sticksville Cemetery where I first found them, maybe they were at Morna's place. And if my usual invocation wouldn't work, maybe a good old-fashioned spirit conjuring would. I knew Stacey would do pretty much whatever Yumi and I did, provided he didn't have drum lessons. But I wasn't sure if I'd hooked

Yumi with the promise of a haunted house. She'd encountered some real-live ghosts before — namely Morna MacIsaac and Kirby LaFlamme — and had dealt with it unproductively by screaming like a banshee. At the same time, she *did* like all things dark and scary, and she'd practically begged me to show her around the Sticksville Cemetery behind my house. A séance at a spooky old boarding house could go either way.

"Do you remember last month, when a ghost attacked me at Mr. O'Shea's old house?"

Attack was a pretty huge exaggeration, but I did remember. "Yeah."

"So that's going to be a hells no," and with that, Yumi flashed me the peace sign and gathered all her playlists and books to head for class.

Try as I might, it seemed I was doomed to fail at having living sidekicks. My Ouija board and I would be flying solo at the Crooked Arms that night.

☠

My Ouija board, though technically a board game from Hasbro — the same demonic occultists who brought you Pokémon and My Little Pony — is in reality (or at least, according to me and a lot of other experts) a surefire way to communicate with the spirits of the dead. To be honest, I'd never really used it before, because you're supposed to do it with a few friends, and those had always been in short supply. But after I watched that old movie *The Craft* and saw those wicked high-school witches set the heart-shaped pointer on that board of letters, numbers, and simple answers, it had jumped right to the top of my theoretical birthday list. I was kind of excited to use it. And even though I was forced to use it alone, I had high hopes it would have a million times more spirit-contacting power than, say, Boggle.

This was the plan:

1) Break into the Crooked Arms.

2) Use Ouija board to contact spirits of dead kids.

3) Ask dead kids how to properly resurrect them.

4) Go home. Later, do said thing to raise dead kids.

No sweat. Except, I was sweating. And given I wear a lot of black and am not going to be mistaken for an Olympic gymnast any time soon, that wasn't strange. But I was sweating more than I'd consider typical. I had no idea if using a Ouija board at Morna's old boarding house would do anything at all. After tonight, we were into waxing moon territory and I'd be unable to raise the dead kids until next month's full moon. There was no real Plan B in this situation.

The Crooked Arms was at the sad end of a sad street named Turnbull Lane. The surrounding neighbourhood wasn't one I'd been to often, and my dad frequently warned me to avoid the area. More buildings were abandoned and falling into disrepair than weren't. However, I was determined to become familiar with it, if this was Morna's old stompin' (and dyin') ground. I trudged through the mud puddles from the weekend's rainstorms, passing deserted storefront after deserted storefront.

At Turnbull Lane's end stood the Crooked Arms, facing an empty garbage-strewn lot. Three storeys tall, I could see where the building had picked up its name. The original carpenters must not have had any levels or T-squares or whatever. Really, the wind seemed to be the only thing keeping the clapboard walls from toppling over. I wondered how Morna could have grown up here, if it had been as dilapidated when she'd slept inside. And it turns out I wasn't even kidding about it being condemned: I noticed a large sign planted in the brown grass and weeds that revealed the house was scheduled for demolition early in January.

Getting into a soon-to-be-demolished building proved difficult. I had to hop over piles and piles of junk, and not just newspapers or plastic bottles — rusted old tricycles and wooden skids — things I was pretty sure I'd need a tetanus shot for if I stepped on them. Even the porch itself was a minor obstacle, with its rotted wooden boards encircled by a plastic orange fencework that warned of the ghostly walk-up's looming demolition.

Significant warning signs aside, I knew I had to get inside the Crooked Arms to try contacting the dead kids through the

Ouija board. Scary as the crumbling façade might have been, I'd been through worse. Heck, I'd been threatened by a crazed teacher at bayonet-point. No old house was going to scare me away. If I wanted the Ouija to work, I had to go inside. Inside was where the spirits would be, in theory.

I had to hoist myself (and my backpack) over the orange faux-chain-link plastic fence, tumbling over it like an overfed hamster escaping its terrarium. Next I proceeded to the Crooked Arms' front door, which to my surprise was slightly ajar. I'd kind of expected a lock on the door — that I'd need to break a window or shimmy down into a storm cellar — but instead I could just stroll right in. I tiptoed across the threshold, completely terrified that someone could be inside waiting for me.

"Hello?" I sputtered. If there was someone inside this deathtrap of a boarding house who planned to turn me into a lampshade or something, I'd rather know sooner than later. Not that a guy who turns people into lampshades is necessarily going to identify himself right away.

Every time I think I'm pretty clever and a semi-decent detective, something happens to prove just how wrong I am. Exhibit A: I forgot to pack a flashlight. In the gloomy dark, I could barely see a thing. I stood there for a full three minutes until my eyes began to adjust and I could identify some shapes in the shadows. Luckily, breaking and entering during a full moon provided some natural light. A short front hallway opened into a little lobby-like area, complete with front desk and grandfather clock, both festooned with cobwebs like tinsel around a Christmas tree. I'm pretty bad at judging the age of things, but I'd say everything inside the boarding house was a million years old. From the front lobby, heavy wooden doors led to separate rooms in both directions, and dead ahead, a wooden staircase, with steps collapsed and some altogether missing, led to the murk above. The strangest thing (aside from how many spiders now seemed to live in the building) was that all the furniture I could see — the desk, the clock, an armchair, even an umbrella stand by the stairs — was tagged with an orange receipt of some kind.

Were these things being sold before the place was demolished? Who would buy this collection of what seemed — neat grandfather clock aside — like future garbage dump material? Despite the solid pile of dust that coated nearly everything, I could see that I wasn't the only recent visitor: there were footprints of dress shoes in the dust on the wooden floor. A small pile of broken bottles had accumulated in the corner opposite the front desk, and above those shards of brown glass, a message in a deep red: *Asphodel Meadows*.

"What's Asphodel Meadows?" I asked no one in particular. You might find when there's no one else around, you start talking to yourself. Especially in the dark. I'm pretty sure it's totally normal. The two-word phrase wasn't the only writing on the wall. Above a vintage, candlestick-shaped telephone on the front desk, three numbers had been written with a shaky hand: 735. I couldn't have imagined a more cryptic room if I'd tried.

I glanced up the staircase, which ascended into charcoal darkness. If I had to guess how high it went up, I'd probably say forever, though from outside, the Crooked Arms was only three storeys tall. Rather than travel upstairs, to greet whatever weirdness might be waiting for me, I figured the first floor was

25

as good a place as any to conduct my séance.

Setting my backpack against the wall, I dropped to my knees and placed the board on the floor. The Ouija even gave that waxy new-board-game crack when I unfolded it. Placing the heart-shaped planchette in the middle of the board with my

shivering hands, I began my séance of one. But before anything could happen or I could think of the right question to ask, my mind clouded over with a million worries: Should I have lit candles? Does a Ouija work with only one person's hands? Should I be clearing my mind? (Fat chance of that happening.) Worries aside, nothing would happen if I couldn't even decide on a question. I inhaled sharply and just asked something really basic.

"Is somebody there?" I asked.

The planchette, to my total surprise, began to hum beneath my fingers, which I held very gingerly over its surface. I felt a prickle of terror travel up my arms. I'm not sure what I was expecting — this was what I wanted to happen, right? Before the indicator could slowly coast in one direction or another, the phone rang.

That's right, the million-year-old phone, caked in dust, rang.

The Ouija planchette stopped humming. Unfortunately, the phone didn't stop ringing. I scrambled to my feet and stared at the ancient telephone. Who could be calling here? If I stared at it long enough, would it just stop? Apparently not. On the tenth ring, I wrapped my sleeve around my hand and lifted the phone's receiver. Holding the base to my ear, I kept the mouthpiece far enough away from my lips (I hoped) that my hyperventilation couldn't be heard.

"Is this October Schwartz?" a woman's voice echoed.

I wasn't going to say anything. Just listen. It could be the police, looking to identify the intruder, and I didn't want to volunteer any information about myself.

"Is this October?" it asked again, the voice a sandpaper whisper. How did she know my name? "Write."

There was something weird about the voice. I couldn't hear any background noise. Just the woman's voice on its own.

"Wait, what? Who is this?"

"You must write!"

"Who are you?"

And the telephone line went dead.

3

Every Day I Write the Book of the Dead

In retrospect, I probably should have tried calling that voice back. I'm not sure if *69 works on those old pre-touchtone phones, but I could have tried. Instead, spooked as I was by receiving a late-night phone call from some mystery writing coach, I scooped up my bag and the Ouija board and charged out of the Crooked Arms as fast as my legs would take me. Returning to the Crooked Arms, ever, didn't seem like an option. Was the voice on the phone a ghost? A friend of Mr. Page out for revenge? These were questions I didn't really feel like investigating.

One outlandish thought was that the voice on the telephone was one of the dead kids trying to contact me. I'm not sure if a telephone is traditionally used as a conduit to the world of the dead, but I suppose it's possible. No more implausible than a board game, really. But the voice definitely wasn't Morna's or Tabetha's. So who was commanding me, October Schwartz, to write? And why?

Sweet (or creepy) as it was that the spook-tacular phone-caller wanted me to write, it wasn't going to help me bring the dead kids back the mortal plane or cross over or whatever, which was my primary concern at the moment. Completing work on my book, *Two Knives, One Thousand Demons*, was kind of a back-burner thing.

The next morning, I sat in front of my locker door, peering into my schoolbag, the glossy edges of the Ouija board visible beyond my binder and math and French books. Only one night of full moon left, and I didn't have the slightest idea of how to raise my friends from the dead. That, and I now had a stalker with phone access to the Crooked Arms.

Stacey Whatever and Yumi Takeshi stopped by my locker a few minutes before I had to leave for Mr. Martz's French class.

"How was your night?" Yumi said, trying to kick her loose shoelace on top of her foot. "You work on your history project?"

"Uneventful." Really now, I couldn't tell Yumi and Stacey about the mystery voice. They were spooked enough that I even wanted to visit the Crooked Arms.

"You didn't go to that boarding house?" Stacey asked.

"No," I scoffed. "That would be . . . like . . . really danger-ous if I did."

"So, Schwartz," Yumi changed the subject, "is your music class going to be part of the school's holiday pageant? I asked Stacey, but he never knows what's going on."

Sticksville Central High School had a long tradition of holiday pageants — an annual festive parade of humiliation where various music and drama classes and semi-talented teachers and students performed seasonal songs and skits. I say *seasonal*, but I'd surprised if this year's show featured any non-Christmas content. Maybe they'd roll out Mrs. Tischmann to explain Hanukkah and how a dreidel works, but even that seemed unlikely. Of course, all this information came not first-hand, but from Mrs. Tischmann, our music teacher, and from Yumi's cousin, who once witnessed Clark Clarke-Henning break a decorative oversized candy cane over Mr. Santuzzi's skull during a performance of the "Ukrainian Bell Carol," an act for which he allegedly was expelled and then disappeared.

"Our class is supposed to play a couple songs," I said. "Mrs. Tischmann loves that stuff. I think I have to put holly on my trombone or something."

"Sounds dire," Yumi said.

"Yumi's drama class is in the pageant, too," Stacey said.

"That's *my* news, Stacey," Yumi pouted. "But he's right.

We're doing a way-abridged version of A Christmas Carol. I really wanted to be that Grim Reaper guy at the end . . ."

"The Ghost of Christmas Future?" I said.

Yumi cringed at the word ghost.

". . . but Mr. Lavender assigned us roles and I'm Tiny Tim. Tragically."

"It's a big part," I said. "I mean, I don't think the Grim Reaper even gets any lines."

"Yumi's Tiny Tim because she's the shortest girl in the class," Stacey whispered to me conspiratorially.

"Shut up! Or you're going to need crutches to get around."

"Don't worry," I said, trying to ease the rising weird Cold War–level tension between the United States of Yumi and the United Soviet Socialist Republic of Stacey. "Tiny Tim's a cake role. Plus, you get the final word."

"I do," she admitted. "Whatever, I'm just glad we're not doing the stupid nativity scene."

"October would have been cast as one of the oxen." It's like Ashlie Salmons had been skulking around the corner, just waiting for one of us to feed her a setup like that. "Or did they have pigs in the manger, too?"

Yumi shot a death stare at Ashlie, who was clearly in the festive spirit early, candy-caned from her red tights to her red-and-white striped dress. It wasn't even December.

"October, Stacey," Yumi smiled dramatically. "I believe you've met my co-star."

I'd forgotten Yumi and Ashlie had drama class together. How unbearable that period must be for her.

"You'll be playing a tree?" Stacey asked, causing Yumi to nearly spit.

"I'm the Ghost of Christmas Past — an important role. I would have been given a bigger part, but I'll have to miss a few rehearsals because of volleyball. My boyfriend is in the pageant, too. Devin convinced the principal to let Phantom Moustache play a song."

"And you'll be playing Christmas Past because you're so much older than your classmates?" I asked, like a total jerk.

"Ah," Ashlie remarked, seemingly surprised by our three-pronged attack. "Mocked by the tween."

Ashlie Salmons had been left back a grade. I had skipped one. It was kind of a thing.

"I'd love to stay and chat with you deadweights," she said with a purposeful turn, "but I just remembered I have a boyfriend who's much more pleasant to talk to. And look at." With that, Ashlie marched down the music hall in her red ballerina flats, head held high.

"I liked her a little better when she didn't have a guitarist boyfriend," I decided.

Yumi was torn. "That's like choosing your favourite type of papercut."

☠

My entire day at school had been spent theorizing what that phone call at the Crooked Arms meant. I also debated if I should tell someone about this magical phone call. Would anyone understand? Maybe I could tell someone who barely knew me, like Ms. Fenstermacher. Speaking of my history teacher, if my dad held a gun to my head and asked me what we'd talked about in history class that afternoon, I couldn't have told him. The only thing I had thought about was that phone call commanding me to write. Luckily, my father isn't nearly as homicidal as that, and history doesn't seem to interest him much. Instead of holding a gun to my head that night, he served me dinner: a father favourite of turkey breast and assorted vegetables. I found myself half-hoping (against my better nature) for one of Dad's depressive episodes: when Dad was down, we ate Chinese takeout.

He'd been coaching the Sticksville Central girls' volleyball team to victory after victory, which seemed to be helping with his clinical depression. It was also affecting his wardrobe: Dad sat across from me at the dinner table in his grey Sticksville Central High School T-shirt and navy gym shorts. Whenever he ducked his head to take a bite of dinner, the silver whistle still around his neck nearly dipped into his vegetables. I felt like I was going to get called on unnecessary roughness during dessert.

"The holiday pageant is coming up," he stated.

I didn't think there was an answer to that.

"Are you doing something in the pageant?"

"My music class is playing a few songs," I said, separating the peas and beans from the carrots, which had all been jumbled together.

"Great. I can't wait."

"You're going to the pageant?"

"Of course."

I felt bad, and averted my eyes by staring at the cubed carrots. My dad confused me. He did all the right things dads were supposed to do — without question or debate, even — but still, he embarrassed me, and still, he couldn't get out of bed a couple days a month like a normal person could. I hated that I was ashamed of him, given all the ways he tried to help. Maybe there wasn't anything wrong with my dad; maybe everything else was wrong.

"You know," he said, mouth full of turkey. "The girls' volleyball team is doing very well."

"Okay . . ."

"It would mean a lot to me if you came to a game." Then Dad did something like that, which reminded me he was far from perfect.

"Dad, Ashlie Salmons will be there," I whined. "She's the closest thing a real human being has to an arch-nemesis."

"And she'll be playing a volleyball game. How can she antagonize you from the volleyball court?"

"She'll find a way."

"If you came to a game, I'm certain we'd win. I'd have my good luck charm in the crowd."

Ugh, Dad. *Ugh.*

The other night in bed, after I first came to the ultra-troubling realization that I might not be able to bring the dead kids back — at least not for another month — I reasoned it wasn't so bad, because (a) tomorrow was December and it'd probably be too cold (and possibly snowy or slushy) to be spending late nights out in a graveyard or running around town, breaking into boarding houses, and such-like. Maybe it made sense to limit raising the dead kids to April through October, treating them like an amusement park. And (b) I could spend my December not worrying about what sociopath killed a nice little Scottish girl in 1914 and focus on happy holiday times with my dad and new friends and new town in the present day.

But over our sad turkey and vegetables tonight at dinner, I remembered what Christmas with my dad was like. Presents were in short supply, which had bugged me as a kid — two books for Christmas? — but that didn't matter so much to me now. More of an issue was Dad's mood during the holidays. People always forget that if you don't have a lot of family or friends, or if you have a wife who mysteriously disappeared without explanation, or if you have clinical depression, or all of the above, the holidays can be really unpleasant. All that festive cheer just highlights how alone you are. Or at least, that's what Dad told me every Christmas Eve, so you can see how un-merry my Christmas usually was. Typically, it involved a dark conversation with my dad about holding onto friends, trying to accept what you had and who you were and inevitably it drifted into talk about my mom.

Without fail, we'd watch *It's a Wonderful Life* on Christmas Eve. I feel like Dad really identified with George Bailey, except for that part at the end when (spoiler alert!) George's friends and family all come together to help him out with the money that was stolen. In Dad's version, I'd probably show up with fifty cents and that would be it. Understandably, he always ugly-cried his eyes out at the end, and I'd run into my room so I could cry alone.

Happy Holidays from the Schwartzes!

Christmas was coming, and not only was the goose getting fat (who eats goose for Christmas anymore?), but I was reminded that part of the reason I was resurrecting the dead kids, trying to solve their mysterious deaths, was so they could eventually help me find my mom. Not that finding my mom would help my dad. I wasn't so naïve that I didn't realize his depression was a medical thing, something that couldn't be fixed by a kiss from his true love. But it couldn't make things any worse. Could it?

I swallowed another forkful of assorted vegetables and asked to be excused.

☠

Dad fell asleep on the couch that night to *How the Grinch Stole Christmas* (original, good version), a disturbing sight because — as I've pointed out, despite all this yuletide talk — it was technically still November. The early bedtime meant he was super tired, which made it easy for me to slide open the glass kitchen door, tiptoe down the back porch, and open the iron gate that connected our backyard to the Sticksville Cemetery without disturbing him. (I know. It's creepy, but it's cool. I got over it a long time ago.) Against my better judgment (which some might argue I don't even have), I decided to follow the phone lady's instructions and write. Maybe it would help; after all, I'd been writing in the cemetery when I first raised the dead kids. At ten o'clock, I had a flashlight trained on the composition book open in my lap and I was seated where all this occulty business had begun in September — on top of the young United Empire Loyalist Cyril Cooper's grave.

In case you didn't know, I'm sort of a writer. Not necessarily a good one; I'm a writer the way someone who does the electric slide at a wedding is a dancer. Mr. O'Shea thought I had some talent, but he was probably the only one in the universe and now he was very much dead. The book I've been writing, *Two Knives, One Thousand Demons*, is a harrowing tale of horror and survival featuring Olivia de Kellerman and her one-woman, two-knived war against legions of demons raised by one misguided father in an attempt to resurrect his dead child. Sounds boss, right? All I needed to do was finish it.

I hadn't been to the cemetery to work on the novel for a month, having abandoned it completely in favour of taking down notes about what had happened during my adventure with the dead kids. But that didn't materialize into a story either, so there I was in the graveyard with two books — dead kids and dozens of demons — doing my best to procrastinate on both. Still, the voice on the phone had told me to write; there was a very slight chance that writing could bring back the dead kids, so that's what I did.

The one time I had successfully raised them, I'd written a section about raising someone from the dead, then read that section aloud, so that's where I started. I quickly penned a new scene in which Olivia practiced an arcane blood ritual to raise dead warriors to aid her in her war for humanity's survival and then I read the scene out loud.

Nothing.

I embellished, providing more ridiculous detail:

Olivia de Kellerman slid the ceremonial dagger across her right palm, the crimson blood forming a channel along her heart line. She moved her hand in a slow circle in the air, the blood dripping in an oblong oval in front of the tombstone.

Olivia shut her heavy-lidded eyes and began to call the undead warriors by name:

"Arise Cyril! Arise Tabetha! Arise Kirby, Morna, and Derek!"

Nothing again. I stood up from Cyril's grave and glanced around. No signs of any dead kid activity. Could someone have prank-called a condemned boarding house? At the edge of the wooded area, I pawed through a few shrubs and trees, but the only thing moving in the cemetery appeared to be me. The scene I was writing and reading out loud didn't really work in the novel; it's like the ghost world could tell I was faking it. To be honest, I don't really remember if anything unusual had happened the time I'd been successful — was there an eerie sound? An electric current sizzling the hair on the back of my neck? (Not that I have a lot of that — I keep a clean, elegant back-of-neck.) If there had been any such sign, I couldn't remember it. The dead kids had only revealed themselves — and reluctantly — days after I had accidentally raised them by reciting that made-up spell.

That gave me an idea.

What if I had been speaking the correct words the other night, but I just needed to actually write them down again? Dropping to the ground, I scribbled the words to that distraught father's spell in the composition book once more, then read them aloud for my non-existent cemetery audience:

> As Nature turns twisted and dark
> To this dread graveyard I donate my spark.
> As tears begin to blind mine eyes,
> The innocent young and the dead shall rise.

When I felt something push against my bum, I knew my hunch had worked. I clambered to my feet to see the earth where I had been sitting — just in front of Cyril Cooper's tombstone — pulse like it had a massive heart that suddenly began beating. I cleared my notebook and pens from the area and within seconds, white knuckles, then a full hand emerged from the ground. The hand gripped the earth like it was putting on its boots and the ground was a sturdy friend's shoulder. It heaved itself upward and the body of Cyril Cooper broke

37

through the topsoil, dirt and bits of grass cascading down from his tricorn hat and ceremonial drum. He hoisted himself fully out of the ground, then got to his feet and dusted the caked dirt off his pantaloons.

"October!" he exclaimed, shaking off his tricorn. "How have you been?"

Seeing Cyril rise from the grave, clawing his way out of the ground like a brain-thirsty zombie was something new. Speaking wasn't really an action I could perform just yet. The other dead kids — Tabetha Scott, Morna MacIsaac, Kirby LaFlamme and Derek Running Water — bounded out from the little cemetery forest and smiled.

"Okay, we're here, we're here," Kirby muttered. Though Kirby had never been my favourite of the five dead kids — probably due to his general unpleasantness and unlikeability — my heart just about exploded through my rib cage to hear his sardonic voice. But my heart was also currently exploding from fear, since Cyril had just pulled himself out of his own grave just two steps from my face.

"She did it!" Morna shouted with joy.

"How is she?" asked Derek, the most recently deceased of the bunch.

"I am not sure," Cyril said. "She seems healthy enough, but unable to speak."

"Great. Is she going to be dumbfounded every time she raises us from the dead?" Kirby complained. "I thought we were over that."

"Sorry," I said, finally regaining the ability to speak. "Sorry, but I wasn't expecting that. Cyril, clawing his way out of the grave. I — look at this mess."

A small crater dotted the cemetery in front of me, and sod and grass had been flung every which way.

"Oh, it's fine," Cyril said repeatedly, kicking a pile of dirt back into the Cooper-sized hole he'd left. "See."

"Oh my." Tabetha, escaped American slave and Underground Railroad refugee, smirked. "You did that whole risin' from the tomb thing? That's jes' mean, Cyril."

"What?" I said.

"Ye could have appeared like we did," Morna chided.

"It was to provide a sense of drama!" he defended. "I was just having some fun with the living girl!"

So Cyril *chose* to dig himself out of the grave like some sort of terrifying pirate-costumed prairie dog. Maybe just to see if I'd pee my pants, which (full disclosure) I nearly did. Already, raising the dead kids seemed like a bad idea.

Cyril apologized: "I didn't need to do that. My real body — or what's left of it — is still down there. See?" With that, he passed his ghostly arm through mine, which was still shaking a bit.

"That was a close one," said Derek. "I didn't think you'd raise us in time."

"I was worried, too, but I figured it out. Thanks to your help."

"Our help?" Kirby asked. "Whatever do you mean?"

"The phone call." *A-duh.*

"Listen, October," Kirby explained. "I realize you don't

know much about being dead, but you don't get to make telephone calls from the afterlife."

"Then who called me? Someone told me to write." As disturbed as I had been to receive a phone call from beyond the grave, it was more disturbing still to realize the dead kids had nothing to do with it.

"We didn't do it," Morna said, scanning the graveyard with her wide, shockingly white eyes.

"So, some stranger called me at Morna's old house, knew my name, and knew how to raise you from the dead?!" I shouted.

"Troubling," Kirby admitted.

"Troubling?!" I shouted again. "Cyril's pantaloons are troubling. The fact that Derek was buried in a black T-shirt is troubling. This is full-blown *alarming*, Kirby!"

"Well, where is this telephone?" Derek asked, glancing down at his black T-shirt in embarrassment.

"Telephone?" Cyril asked.

"I'll explain later," Morna whispered.

"At the boarding house where Morna used to live. I'll show you later. For now, I'm just glad to have you back."

"It's nice t' be back, in the land a' the livin'!" Tabetha stretched her arms to the night sky.

"But I don't understand," I said. "Why did I have to write out the words again? I thought that saying them out loud was what brought you or summoned you or whatever."

"We thought so, too," Cyril said.

"Maybe because you wrote the words that raised us, there's some kind of mystical power in the writing itself," Derek theorized. "There are a lot of Mohawk legends about the power of writing. Usually in a negative context, though . . . that's why Mohawk is mainly an oral tradition. But maybe there's good power, too."

"I guess if I ever figure out who called me, I can ask her," I said.

"It's nice t'see ye," Morna said, breaking into a sidelong smile.

"You, too, Morna."

"What's new?" Derek asked.

"Not much. It's colder, not that you can feel it. I have a couple new teachers to replace the dead and arrested ones. And my dad's now best friends with my enemy, Ashlie Salmons. I'd ask you the same, but I guess you've just been dead."

"Ashlie Salmons?" Tabetha asked. "She the one Morna here thrashed with a newspaper?"

"Yeah," I said, savouring that fond memory.

"Have ye found anything," Morna asked, studying her clasped hands. "Ye know . . . about my . . . ye know."

"Hold on now," Tabetha interrupted. "Let's do this proper-like. Truth or Dare!"

☠

"Truth," I started, pointing to Morna MacIsaac.

The dead kids had seated themselves in a wide circle in the cemetery clearing, just underneath a large, gnarled tree. Morna sat directly across from me.

"Did you pee your pants when Cyril climbed out of his grave?" Kirby interjected.

Cyril couldn't help but snicker into his fist.

"*No.* You wish. And that doesn't count — you interrupted Morna," I said indignantly.

"Thank ye."

"Truth. Again. Hit me."

"Have ye found anything about how I died?" she asked, try-ing not to sound too desperately hopeful.

"Actually, yes."

Distorting the timeline a smidge, I described how I'd dis-covered Morna's old boarding house, how it was scheduled for demolition, and how I'd discovered a newspaper story on a scandal at that same boarding house that must have hap-pened just days before she died. I scrambled to my bag, which I'd left leaning against the back of Cyril's gravestone, and pro-duced the printout of that *Sticksville Loon*'s front page. Morna, becoming momentarily corporeal, took the printout in her bony white fingers and studied the photograph. She couldn't read (nor could Cyril or Tabetha), but she could identify the people in the image.

"Your turn, Morna," I said.

"Truth," she answered, distracted by the photograph.

"Do you remember this scandal at all?" I asked. "Could it be connected to your death?"

"This is my home," she pointed to the Crooked Arms in the photograph. "And that's me. And me mum an' dad . . . one of me brothers. That's Nessie who lived upstairs and the landlord, Mr. Rasmussen. Mr. Sundbäck, the inventor. And that's Sam, who lived across the hall."

She said her housemates' names aloud, like she was rediscovering them in her mind, the way I'd slowly been able to remember what all my old *Magic: The Gathering* cards did when I'd unpacked them after our move to Sticksville.

"Says right here that Sam was a saboteur," Kirby said, reading over Morna's shoulder for the group. "He was going to use a bomb on Canadian troops about to ship out for World War I."

"Do you remember any of that?" I asked Morna, hoping this would be way easier than it wound up being.

"No, I know all these people, but I don't remember Sam being arrested," she said, as if trying to recall the details of a vivid dream. "The last memory I have — before I died — is of m'brother, Rory, becoming a soldier and leaving for Fort Hannover."

When exactly Morna's memory stopped, I couldn't be sure, but given there was no brother of fighting age in that photo (unless the Canadian military recruited eight-year-olds in 1914), she must not have remembered the day the photograph was taken or any days afterward.

"Wait a second," I said. "Do any of you remember, say, the day of your deaths?"

None of the dead kids were quick to respond, but the general consensus was a mumbled *no*. This whole hazy memory gap of a couple days around their deaths was going to be problematic, I anticipated, to my figuring out who or what killed them.

"We may need to ask someone for help," Cyril sagely advised.

"Help?" I coughed. "Where are we going to get help? Everyone from 1914 is dead!"

☠

For Whom the Alexander Graham Bell Tolls

The following evening, a crisp Thursday, the determined and mostly courageous October Schwartz decided to visit her new history teacher, Ms. Fenstermacher, at her second job, docent at the Sticksville Museum. Unprepared to return to the Crooked Arms and its eerie telephone just yet, October figured she could search the museum for some clues to this Crooked Arms scandal that just slightly predated Morna's death. So, just before she was expected home for supper, October walked downtown to the Sticksville Museum, which coincidentally had been built inside what remained of the old Cooper House. As in, the former home of one (now dead) Cyril Cooper and his family.

Downtown Sticksville was something of a tangled spaghetti pile of streets. Nothing seemed to go north or south, east or west. By the time October pressed through the museum's front door and activated the electronic chime, she'd gotten lost three times. October walked through the front corridor, which was lined on either side with large windows and poorly illustrated books of Sticksville history. The corridor opened up into a large hexagonal lobby, with stone floors and rooms in all directions. Against the wall directly opposite the corridor stood a glass case with a miniature village depicting Sticksville, circa 1783. On either side of that case were doors leading to a kitchen and dining room furnished in late 1700s décor; to her right was a large display entitled Sticksville at Wartime.

"Welcome, October!" came a voice from her left. Seated behind a small desk was Ms. Fenstermacher, beaming in her horn-rimmed spectacles and plaid shirt. Behind her was a large placard illustrated with "Famous Sticksvillians," whoever those might be. "It's nice you came by. Have you been to the Sticksville Museum before?"

"No," October admitted.

"An influential family of shipbuilders named Cooper used to live in this historic house, in the late 1700s. The first generation of Coopers to live here actually had a son about your age who mysteriously died in Sticksville's shipyard one night."

"Really," October said, maintaining her cool and trying not to look like she'd been talking to that kid's ghost last night. She also tried not to notice the fact her history teacher was regaling her with weird tales of child murder the moment she walked through the museum doors. "I think I've heard something about that."

"Did you just come by to check out the museum?" Fenstermacher asked. "Or is there something in particular I can help you with?"

"Actually, I'm really interested in this," October gestured to the Sticksville at Wartime display. "Remember how you helped me find that article about that Chinese saboteur? Do you know if there's anything at the museum about that? My dad's family tree present is getting more elaborate."

"Hmm," she mused, pushing her fingers against the side of her forehead as if she might be telling October something telepathically. (If Fenstermacher were indeed a telepath, how cool would that be? She'd be a real asset to the Dead Kid Detective Agency.) "If there's anything on hand here, it would be in that display. Let's check it out."

Her Mary Janes snapping against the stone floor, the history teacher guided October over to the war-themed display. She peered into the glass case and tented her fingers.

"The display only seems to have that same newspaper you found on the microfilm."

"I have the photo you emailed me here. I printed it out," October said.

"Ooh, let's see."

As October retrieved the printout from her backpack, Ms. Fenstermacher couldn't help but notice the Ouija board jammed in between her math text and the *Two Knives, One Thousand Demons* composition book.

"Ha, I used to have one of those," she said, either impressed or amused.

"Oh?" October played dumb.

"Until quite recently, I was really into that kind of stuff — I could read your tarot cards or your tea leaves. I had books that showed you how to remove evil spirits that would, y'know, sit on your chest while you slept."

At first, October felt Ms. Fenstermacher was trying to shift gears from Coolest Teacher of the Year to Most Bananas Teacher of All Time. Ghosts sleeping on your chest? But then October realized (a) she had spent her previous night playing Truth or Dare with a bunch of ghosts, and (b) the information that Ms. Fenstermacher was some kind of lite dabbler into the spirit world could come in handy.

"Yeah?" October said, feigning interest, which was masquerading as real interest. (It's complicated.) "But you lost interest in ghosts and psychic stuff?"

"Sort of. I still have all the books and cards," she said. "It's funny. Sticksville was once kind of a hotbed of occult activity."

"What do you mean?"

"I mean in the 1700s, the townspeople alleged a male witch lived in town, and not just some old guy who made herbal remedies and stuff. They claimed he had powers and communed with the Devil, the whole nine yards."

This may be the only time you ever hear "communing with the Devil" included as part of "the whole nine yards." But then, October was talking with Elvira, Queen of Grade Nine History.

"You're kidding." All of a sudden, October's friendship with five dead kids no longer seemed so out of place.

"No, it's in most of the records from the time. Here, look at this miniature village of Old Sticksville," Ms. Fenstermacher walked October over to the tiny 1783 recreation, which looked like a miniature train set, sans train. "See that little skinny house on the far right? All by itself? That's where the 'witch' lived. A guy named Crisparkle."

October studied the miniature town, tried to make sense of where the skinny house was in comparison to the Cooper House. "That's in my friend Yumi's neighbourhood."

The skinny little house seemed too small for a person. More like a porta-potty than a house, but then, this was a miniature village. The houses weren't necessarily to scale.

"Sorry, I've sidetracked you," Ms. Fenstermacher said. "You need information about things that happened over a hundred years later. And you need actual facts, not rumours and speculation about witches."

"Um, yeah. About 1914 and a place called the Crooked Arms."

"Making some kind of description for every year in your dad's family tree? Well, this display won't be much help. But I think we do have some records on that boarding house. Wait down here. Some of our files are upstairs."

Ms. Fenstermacher bounded like a history-loving jack rabbit up the staircase to the right of the miniature village to retrieve information about Morna's old boarding house. As soon as she'd reached the top of the stairs, all five dead kids bounded from the far wall into the museum lobby in one jumbled pack.

"I thought she'd never leave," Kirby exhaled.

"What are you all doing here? It's barely even dark! You're going to get me in trouble!" October whispered. "Ms. Fenstermacher, like, reads tea leaves and stuff. You just know she'll be able to see ghosts!"

"I know. Crazy broad," Kirby said. "What was all that talk about witchcraft?"

"I remind you, for the hundredth time, you're a ghost."

"Nevermind the witches," Cyril marvelled. "We're in my old house! It looks very different, but this is my house!"

"It's a museum now, Cyril," Derek said.

"You famous or somethin', Cyril?" Tabetha asked.

Cyril, meanwhile, was moving around the tables and lifting the pictures off the wall to see if he could find anything he remembered from the house.

"Cyril, stop touching things!" October spat. "You should all leave. I'll meet you at the graveyard later and tell you what I learn."

"No," Cyril insisted. "We're going to hide in the kitchen while your teacher tells you all about where Morna used to live."

"I might remember something important," Morna suggested.

"October!" Ms. Fenstermacher called from the office upstairs. "I'll be down in a sec."

October exhaled heavily enough to fill three party balloons. "Okay, okay. But can you please hide now?"

The dead kids leapt into the shadows of the poorly lit circa 1783 kitchen just in time. Ms. Fenstermacher was galloping down the stairs as the last of them, Tabetha, disappeared into the shadows. Waving a teal three-ring binder in her left hand, the history teacher announced, "Here's our Who's Who of the Crooked Arms in 1914."

Now bear with me. We're going back in time, just like in that delightful song by Huey Lewis and the News (or one of their delightful songs — I'm partial to "The Power of Love," too), to Sticksville, November 1914. Sticksville nearly a hundred years ago looked quite different. Sticksville Central High School, which October attends and Mr. Santuzzi terrorizes and Mr. O'Shea died in, had yet to be constructed. And while the Sticksville Cemetery did exist, the row of houses that now border it, including the Schwartzes', did not.

Turnbull Lane, where the Crooked Arms is located, did exist, and even then, it was an unfortunate type of street. The kind you wouldn't stroll down at night unless you had to, or unless you liked the idea of being knocked senseless by a sack full of doorknobs and robbed of your possessions. (Most people aren't into that.) The dirt road was lined on either side by drinking establishments and tenement housing, and though you'd find horses and carriages (and even the occasional new fangled automobile) on some of the more affluent roads in Sticksville, nearly everyone travelled on foot over Turnbull Lane.

One tenement house stood out from the rest, positioned at the very terminus of the lane, less like an actual dwelling, more like a monument to bad carpentry. That building, as if you hadn't already guessed, was the Crooked Arms. Home, for four too-short years, to Morna MacIsaac.

The Crooked Arms was unusual, even if it were not for its isolated location on the street. The building was imposing; regardless of the less-than-professional quality of the house's construction, the architecture of the building itself did lend the Crooked Arms some measure of grandeur. The rentals were surprisingly affordable; given the location and a distinct lack of amenities, the landlord was forced to keep the rent low. The residents of the Crooked Arms comprised a motley crew: people without much money who could manage without certain amenities. Amenities that included, in 1914, a telephone.

"Looks like the Crooked Arms first got a telephone installed in 1914," Ms. Fenstermacher said, flipping through the pages of the binder. "And when they did, they started making a registry of all the boarders in the house. All their names and occupations are here."

"Wait," said October. "They only got a telephone in 1914? Wasn't it invented way before that?"

October, as it happens, was right. Though Canadian Alexander Graham Bell had invented the telephone in Brantford decades earlier, in 1875, and though hundreds of Canadian families and businesses had been using telephones for years, its arrival could still be a special occasion in a smaller town like Sticksville in 1914. Morna MacIsaac was the first of the dead kids to ever use a telephone.

ALEXANDER GRAHAM BELL

"They were late bloomers," Ms. Fenstermacher said. "The original phone number here was 735."

"Only three digits?"

"That's all they needed back then."

October, bright person that she

is, made a connection between the Crooked Arms' phone number and that 735 written on its wall, though why it was written so manically, she couldn't guess. Maybe there was someone living in the Arms named Asphodel Meadows, too?

"So who lived there in 1914?"

Ms. Fenstermacher went through the three floors from bottom to top. "Kasper Rasmussen, landlord, first floor. Gideon Sundbäck, famous inventor, also first floor. On the second floor, we have the MacIsaac family: William, Margaret, and three children, Rory, Morna, and Boyd."

October now knew Morna's entire family by first name. Seemed strange given she would never ever meet them and they'd been dead for a hundred years. It was a bit of a shame. Morna was such a pleasant person; October figured meeting her entire family would have been nice.

"Also on the second floor, Sam Cheng, laundry owner."

That must have been the saboteur from the newspaper article. Laundry owner? More like Chinese demolitions expert!

"On the third floor was Roxy Wotherspoon, schoolteacher. She's also Sticksville's very first suffragette, October."

A quick history lesson: in 1914, women weren't allowed to vote in Canada, in either provincial or federal elections. (Not-fun fact: women weren't considered persons under Canadian law until 1928.) The movement to give women the right to vote (or suffrage) was well underway, with statue-worthy women like Nellie McClung and Ella Cora Hind making some progress in Manitoba. In Sticksville, Roxy was something of a one-woman show, so she'd often take an early morning train trip to Toronto to meet with Dr. Margaret Gordon and the Toronto Suffrage Society for the occasional march or demonstration to demand the vote for women.

"And rounding out the building," Ms. Fenstermacher continued, "is Dr. Alfred Pain, doctor and *Titanic* survivor. Another celebrity in the house! I bet you didn't know Sticksville had a *Titanic* survivor, did you?"

October grimaced a smile, though the thought of being a celebrity by avoiding terrible disaster kind of made her feel ill.

"And that's it?"

"That seems to be the entire house," Ms. Fenstermacher said, flipping back and forth through the binder for effect. "At least, it was at the time of the photograph."

"Ohhh," came a groan from the kitchen.

"Did you hear that?" Fenstermacher whispered.

"Hear what?" October clearly lied. She recognized the voice of Morna MacIsaac. Who else besides the dead kids would be in the kitchen?

"I'm going to go check it out."

Luckily for October, the dead kids were smarter now than they had been on their first case together. By the time Ms. Fenstermacher illuminated the kitchen display, all the dead kids had scurried out the door or through the walls into the backyard. Still, Ms. Fenstermacher opened the cauldron over the fire and searched all the closets, just in case there was an intruder (or chest-sitting demon) hiding inside the museum. Upon finding nothing, Ms. Fenstermacher was satisfied she'd imagined the sound. October thanked her and set out home for dinner.

☠

In the Sticksville Cemetery that night, the excitement was so thick, you couldn't even cut it with a knife — that's how thick it was. It would likely require some sort of blowtorch or laser. October sprinted into the clearing at the centre of the graveyard where she'd often met the dead kids.

"Morna! Morna!" October shouted as loud as she could without drawing any attention from the houses nearby (including her own). "Are you here?"

The Scottish girl from the early 1900s popped up behind a

weathered tombstone and raised her hands in front of her, as if October were about to rob her at gunpoint. (Which was, let's admit, pretty unlikely.) The other dead kids emerged from the forest.

"Morna, there you are," October huffed. "Did you hear Ms. Fenstermacher? Do you remember a Sam Cheng in your building? He was the saboteur from the newspaper."

"I do. I remember Sam," she said, biting her lower lip. "I'm starting to."

"Can you remember anything else about him, Morna?" Cyril asked.

October and the dead kids had surrounded Morna from every direction. In other circumstances, such an arrangement could even pass for fun. Say they were all at a nightclub and they'd circled Morna MacIsaac to spotlight and witness her incredible breakdancing. But alas, none of the kids were old enough to enter a nightclub and Morna had died at least sixty years too early to know much about breakdancing. As it was, having her friends all around, interrogating her about memories she barely had, was intimidating. She began to fluster.

"I don't know . . . I just remember Sam an' . . . blood," she exclaimed. "So much blood!"

The forecast for Sam Cheng's innocence was not looking good.

☠

5

Broken Telephone Pictionary

Friday was one of Dad's bad days, clinical-depression-wise. The good news was those bad days had become rare in the past month. The bad news was that their relative infrequency didn't really make coping with them any easier. Particularly when they happened on a school morning and I was kind of working on a streak in the not-showing-up-super-late-every-day department.

I'd been trying to stay ignorant of as much volleyball stuff as possible, but, given that I lived with the girls' volleyball coach, I was semi-aware that tonight was some kind of big game and whether Sticksville Central went on to the regional championship largely depended on the outcome. And I'm smart enough to understand that depression isn't like eczema, so take it with, like, a spoonful of salt when I say the high stakes of the upcoming volleyball match caused Dad's mental illness to flare up.

So, T-minus-forty-minutes to school's start and my dad, science teacher Mr. Schwartz, was still in bed, staring at the ceiling. Only with some quick thinking on my part did we manage to get both of us out the door and at Sticksville Central in time. While putting together lunch in the kitchen, I rifled through the drawers until I found the long matchbox with a red bird on the cover. I grabbed a chunk of yesterday's *Sticksville Loon* and stood on a chair just underneath the smoke detector. Depression or not, that alarm was much too annoying to just lie in bed and ignore. Plugging my ears, I stuck a match.

55

Apparently, the school's volleyball dominance wasn't going to help with my dad's depression as much as I'd hoped. I wished there was some way I could help my dad — y'know, something better than pulling the fire alarm on him — but for the moment, it was all I could do.

☠

I daydreamed my way through that morning's French class. Well, it wasn't totally a daydream, but, like, a daydream planning session. Now that all signs pointed to Sam Cheng being Morna's blood-soaked killer (ew), what was my next step? There was no way he was still alive, and if I found his grandchildren or whoever, what good would that be? Supposedly, the dead kids would remain ghostly corpses until they found justice for their deaths, but how was I going to arrange that? I had so many questions about the dead kids and the process of solving the mysteries of their deaths. So many questions, in fact, that a full five minutes passed after the second-period bell before I realized I was still sitting in French class staring at the blackboard.

"Ms. Schwartz," Mr. Martz called. "Ms. Schwartz, *réveillez-vous*! You'll be late for your next class."

Coming to, I apologized to Mr. Martz (*Excusez-moi!*) and left him in the dust as I hightailed it to Mr. Santuzzi's. (I don't really know what "hightail" means, but I swear I've heard it used in this context before.) It was too much to hope that Mr. Santuzzi was late for his own class; he kept a strict regimen, like he was still doing military service. Probably kept his calculators clean like they were semi-automatic pistols or combat boots.

At the math room door, I silently depressed the door handle and nudged my way in, like I could somehow sneak into Mr. Santuzzi's class while sweating and panting from my sprint across the school. No such luck — Mr. Santuzzi was planted at the front of the room, introducing some guy who looked like a sleazy bank teller. Like a bank teller who held dog fights in the vault after his co-workers had left for the day.

"And this vampire-in-training," bellowed Mr. Santuzzi, gesturing toward me with his meaty hand, "is Ms. October Schwartz."

The math class laughed. Ha, vampire jokes for the goth girl. Very original, Mr. Santuzzi. With a sense of humour like that, you could have a job as a gravedigger.

"You'll get to know her, Mr. McGriff," he continued. "She's fond of giving *creative* answers on her math tests."

Cripes. Mr. Santuzzi *still* wasn't over that time I'd called him a jerkwad and stuff on my quiz. It had been almost two months. Get over it! Mr. Santuzzi rarely smiled — didn't want to unsettle that serious moustache — but the corners of his eyes crinkled in memory of that memorable quiz. As I took my seat, I wondered who the joker being introduced to the class was when Mr. Santuzzi read my mind.

"Ms. Schwartz, as I've already informed the portion of the class who managed to arrive on time," he said, adjusting the buttons on his seafoam green vest, "this is Mr. McGriff. He's doing his teacher's degree at the University of Western, and as part of his studies, he'll be assisting me for the next month or so."

"It's okay, October," he said. "I used to be a little goth, too."

More laughter from the classroom, even from my traitorous and asthmatic neighbour, Myra Entwhistle. McGriff seemed about as goth as an ice cream sundae. Mr. Santuzzi now had an assistant. I assume he was there to lighten Santuzzi's workload so he could focus full-time on committing atrocities in his fashion and upon his students.

This new teaching assistant McGriff was all gussied up like he was attending his dad's third wedding, but his gelled hair and Timberland boots were pure high-school thug. He didn't look much older than Stacey. He certainly wasn't taller. I know it's wrong to judge people based on their appearances. (Happens to me all the time.) But something about McGriff set off my Spidey-sense.

"Some of you may recognize Mr. McGriff," Mr. Santuzzi said, helping me make the connection that should have been obvious. "He was a star player for Sticksville Central's baseball team for years, and continues to play at Western. His younger brother is a fellow student of yours."

Devin McGriff's brother. So this was the sibling of the demon-witch's boyfriend.

Eager to share my math war stories with Yumi and Stacey, I rushed to the cafeteria, only to find our usual table empty. I sat down with my lunch unopened and patiently (I thought) await-ed their arrival, but they didn't show. Only their voices did.

"Good afternoon, Sticksville Central!" shouted Yumi Takeshi's boisterous high-pitched voice from the cafeteria's P.A. system. "We are DJ Yu-sless and Stacey Kasem, and this is our first-ever radio show! We hope you mark this historic occasion in your sad little diaries!"

Then the P.A. blared forth with an uptempo punk anthem from Bad Religion. Not, in my humble opinion, a bad start to Yumi's high school radio career. All that planning paid off. Fur-thermore, I could see some of the people in the cafeteria were getting into it. Could this radio thing make Yumi and Stacey popular? If they became popular, would they still eat lunch with me? And was Stacey's last name "Kasem"?

An unintended consequence of Yumi and Stacey's radio time slot was that I was now eating lunch alone at the outcast table. To compensate, I positioned myself close to the Dun-geons & Dragons guys (but not too close), so it *almost* looked like I was eating lunch with them and stared straight ahead at my food while I ate. As I worked through my spartan lunch — sandwich, (Spartan) apple, pudding cup — I could feel the atmosphere of the cafeteria begin to sour and turn against the musical selections DJ Yu-sless was subjecting them to. Things turned when Yumi played Nick Cave's funereal "Red Right Hand" and only worsened when she followed up with a very long interlude by German robotic techno pioneers Kraftwerk. Not only was she playing bands that nobody knew, those bands were playing music they hated. Additionally, Yumi filled the space between songs with some of the most boring information ever: "Did you know Kraftwerk's studio telephone had no ringer? Callers were instructed to phone the studio only at one precise time each day." Stacey said absolutely nothing.

Things got ugly very rapidly.

"We have our first call-in request!" Yumi shouted throughout the cafeteria at the end of the Kraftwerk song. "Hello, you're on the air with DJ Yu-sless and Stacey Kasem."

"Yeah, this is Devin McGriff?"

At the other end of the cafeteria hall, I could see him and the other members of Phantom Moustache huddled around his cell phone.

"Devin McGriff, from local rock band Phantom Moustache?" Yumi said, clearly relishing her power as radio DJ. "Do you have a request?"

"Yeah," Devin snickered. "Why don't you and your loser friend jump in front of a truck?"

Faced with such hostility, Yumi promptly hung up and, not missing a beat, turned on Van Halen's "Jump." I was, frankly, amazed at her cleverness in the midst of such hate. Van Halen didn't change anything, though. The component parts of Phantom Moustache were rolling on the cafeteria benches with laughter at their amazing prank.

One of the problems with Radio Sticksville was that the DJ booth had a large window that overlooked the school's main atrium, and this atrium was where your high school social status overachievers — your star athletes, your charismatic young felons, your rich dunderheads — dwelled. It was also, coincidentally, where presents were slowly being collected for the school toy drive at the foot of a leviathan Christmas tree. (Bolted to the atrium's raised level and secured with cables, it nearly reached the skylight.) At any given moment, the radio DJs could see everyone in the atrium and vice versa. So when the mob grew unhappy with DJ Yu-sless's musical selections, they knew where to direct their anger.

By the time I'd finished my lunch and exited to the atrium to check on Yumi and Stacey, it was too late. A crowd had gathered round, yelling insults at the DJ window, unable to get through and forcibly remove the two of them. Someone had mashed a carton of gravy fries on the window and, while I stood there in shock, Devin McGriff appeared, Ashlie Salmons at his side, with a bottle of ketchup he'd lifted from the cafeteria.

"The school refuses *me* a radio spot and give us this *garbage* instead!" he shouted, clearly outraged by Radio Sticksville's lack of meritocracy.

He walked over to the DJ window, uncapped the plastic ketchup bottle, and aimed it directly over where Yumi's face was, on the other side of the three-inch-thick glass. Slowly, carefully, in bright-red ketchup, he wrote "YU SUCK." The group of irate students applauded, but I couldn't help observing that Stacey and Yumi wouldn't be able to read it from their angle. Inside the booth, they seemed both unsettled and confused.

A shout in the atrium broke up the applause. Everyone turned to see Mr. Santuzzi, his massive arms folded across his

not-inconsiderable chest.

"Mr. McGriff," he shouted. "To Principal Hamilton's office *immediately*. There are more constructive ways to express your disapproval."

Devin McGriff, ketchup bottle in hand, slinked past Mr. Santuzzi, his head held low like someone had stapled his chin to his collar.

"Your brother, Skyler, will hear of this, too."

Skyler? Devin's older brother was named *Skyler* McGriff? His name sounded like a brand of ski jacket.

"The rest of you, scatter!" he shouted. "If you have a problem with the radio show or the radio station in general, you can make a complaint to Ms. Fenstermacher."

Though I wasn't one of the window vandals, I, too, scattered. I wanted to talk to Yumi and Stacey about their show, but I figured I could do that at the end of the day. If they were smart, they'd wait until the fourth-period bell rang to sneak out of the radio booth as quietly and inconspicuously as possible. So as to avoid a riot.

☠

"Have a great weekend, history buffs," Ms. Fenstermacher said sarcastically, let's assume. "Remember that we start your oral presentations about the Great Depression on Monday."

While the rest of the class filed out to fun and death-free weekends, I lingered to ask Ms. Fenstermacher about the fate of Sam Cheng.

"Thanks for coming by the museum yesterday," Ms. Fenstermacher said, organizing the items on her desk.

"Yeah, about that," I said. "What ever happened to that Sam Cheng guy? The saboteur?"

"Well, he was arrested," she said, standing erect and looking skyward. "Come to think of it, I don't know what happened after that. He probably spent most of his life in jail. But I can check for you."

"You wouldn't mind?" I asked.

"Not at all. I'll be at the museum tomorrow, so I'll see what information they have on hand."

"You're working at the museum on a Saturday?" I was offended on her behalf.

"Yes, October. History never sleeps."

I suppose Ms. Fenstermacher thought that would make a cool catch phrase, and I guess it would be okay for something like the History Channel or some documentary, but she said it when all I asked was if she was working on Saturday. It was kind of weird.

"Well . . . thanks."

When I caught up with Yumi and Stacey at their lockers just after my chat with Ms. Fenstermacher, we held a little bit of a post-show post-mortem.

"How did you think it went? Honestly," Yumi asked. I could feel invisible tractor beams shooting from her dark eyes, demanding the truth.

"How do *you* think it went, Yumi? They threw gravy fries at you!"

"But did *you* like our show? Did you like the music?"

"Yeah, I did," I said, though in the chaos of the ketchup incident, I didn't even really listen to the second half. "But you don't have to worry about me."

"First show: rousing success!" Yumi blurted, fists to the air. She high-fived the much-taller Stacey. "You're our target demographic, Schwartz."

Yumi was freaking me out. Could she not sense the scorn coming from everyone toward her? Ashlie, Devin McGriff — even Mr. Santuzzi didn't seem to be a fan.

"Stacey, is your last name Kasem?" I asked.

"October," Yumi sighed. "It's a joke. Like Casey Kasem?"

That didn't help me understand the joke.

"One of radio's most famous DJs? The voice of Shaggy in *Scooby-Doo*?"

No help.

"I can't believe you don't know my last name," Stacey said, wounded.

"What is your —"

"Do you have any constructive criticism?" Yumi interrupted, locking her locker and pulling on a black parka that seemed to envelop her like giant blob.

"Well, the parts in between songs were a little . . ." I hesitated. "Dry? It could be less informative, more fun. And Stacey should say something!"

Stacey looked like he'd been tasered in the chest.

"More fun," Yumi reiterated, slinging her bag over her shoulder.

"Yeah. Maybe tell a few jokes?"

☠

The dead kids didn't know I'd return to the Crooked Arms that night. I wanted to see if the phone would ring again, just one more time on my own. Maybe I could discover who was calling and how she knew so much. I was planning to bring them to the boarding house eventually; Morna used to live there and she deserved to see it. But tonight, I needed to do this by myself.

I skulked down Turnbull Lane, attempting to be as inconspicuous as possible. The collar of my black peacoat was turned up and I kept my chin to my chest. I even doubled-down on the eyeliner I was wearing, which made me look a bit like a raccoon or a superhero. Either way, I was above the law tonight. After clambering over the orange fencing and crawling through the open front door, I found the lobby of the Crooked Arms undisturbed since I'd last been there. *Asphodel Meadows* was still emblazoned on the wall. The old grandfather clock still stood at attention like one of those guards at Buckingham Palace. Most importantly, the phone was still there, gleaming in the dark room.

With great deliberateness, I quietly crossed the room to face the 735 on the wall. Upon closer inspection of the phone on the desk underneath the numbers, I could see the smears where my sleeves had wiped away the thick dust. (I should probably have washed that sweatshirt afterward.) So, there I was, staring at this old phone, with no idea of how to make it ring. Should I have brought the Ouija board again? I could barely tell the thing on the desk before me *was* a phone: it was a pot-metal black thing that looked more like a small lamp. A wooden base held up the phone's mouthpiece, a small metal funnel thinger, and a small horn connected by a metal coil that rested in an attached hook. There weren't even numbers to press or a rotary dial to turn. I was stumped.

If there had been numbers or some way of calling a number, I'd have tried 735. I mean, it was written on the wall just above the telephone and was, according to Ms. Fenstermacher, the phone number of the Crooked Arms. But how could I call that number? Feeling extremely stupid, I picked up the candlestick telephone with my bare hands this time and listened. There was no dial tone; the phone was completely dead. Nevertheless, I lifted the mouthpiece and spoke into it.

"Seven. Three. Five?"

I kicked myself for not sounding more confident, but I *was* saying numbers into a long-disconnected telephone in a condemned building. Confident was one thing I was not. So, I was more than surprised when I heard the telephone connect with a slight hiss.

"Hello, is someone there?"

Nobody answered, but I felt like someone was on the line.

"Who are you? Why are you helping me?"

Again, no answer. Just a low hiss in response.

"I know you're there," I said, sounding way braver than I was feeling. "I'll tell the police about this."

I have no idea what the police would do about mysterious phone calls on long-dead telephone lines, but I made the threat nevertheless. It had the desired effect.

"No," the voice said.

"Who are you? You told me how to raise the dead kids. Can you tell me who killed Morna?"

"You're looking at the wrong person," the voice said in its laboured voice. It almost sounded like it hurt for the person at

the other end of the receiver to speak.

"Tell me where to look. Anything!" I was desperate. Clearly. I was possibly talking to myself on a vintage phone.

"This must remain a secret. Do not tell anyone."

"Okay," I said, though this was some cause for worry. Could I not even tell the dead kids? They'd have to know about this phone. They already did, kind of. "Okay, fine."

"Secret."

"Yes, just —"

And that's when Alyosha Diamandas, real estate agent at large, barged through the front door with a fist full of orange tags. A cold wind followed him and hit me square in the cheek to announce his arrival.

"Little girl," he shouted, more annoyed than enraged. "What are you doing on my phone?"

☠

Lying Inside a Broken Phone Booth with No Money in My Hand

Late that Saturday night, indignity of all indignities, I was driven home by Sticksville's creepiest realtor, Alyosha Diamandas. He and I had a bit of a history, as he had shown me Mr. O'Shea's house under false pretences, and he'd had a few run-ins with my dead friends. Steering his rusted-out yellow Yaris through the quiet night, he kept shifting his beady-eyed gaze over to me and all I could say was "Sorry" over and over again. Apparently Alyosha was the one who'd been tagging all the furniture and appliances inside the Crooked Arms. He'd bid on the contents of the soon-to-be-demolished boarding house and won, and was slowly tagging and collecting all the old furniture to furnish the properties he was attempting to sell.

He turned his eyes from the road again to look at me — the vandal, the trespasser — and his centipede of a moustache twitched above his lip.

"Look, I'm sorry," I said.

"Yes, very sorry," he said, gripping the steering wheel like it were a venomous asp about to strike. "You could have damaged those antiques. I do not understand why you children are always breaking into places."

Though I was a little unimpressed by him referring to all that junk in the Crooked Arms as antiques, I just shrugged. "Sorry."

"I just hope nothing was too badly damaged. You wrote

that on the walls, too? That *Asphodel Meadows?*"

"What, no? That was there when I got there." Something still bugged me. "So, that telephone. It's still connected?" I asked. "It still has service?"

"Mm? What?" he said while executing a right turn. "Little girl, that phone is a hundred years old. Why would I, or anyone, pay for service?"

"But . . . but the phone was plugged in," I insisted. "Are you sure?"

"Of course I'm sure."

This was terrible news. Apparently I was talking to myself via an old phone. I was listening to voices in my head. More urgently, I was only a couple minutes from home and had no idea how I'd explain my visit to the Crooked Arms to Dad, or why I wasn't home around midnight. I only hoped I could convince Alyosha to drop me off without coming inside. I really wanted to avoid a conversation between my dad and Alyosha Diamandas about my curfew. After all, Alyosha Diamandas thought he'd met my dad already, when I'd tricked him into showing me Mr. O'Shea's house, but it was really just Stacey in a false moustache. That would be difficult to explain. Luckily, Diamandas was eager to return to cataloguing his many treasures and let me out at the end of my driveway. So I was safe, this time.

☠

Next week, we were fully into December, which meant — *quelle surprise* — it was so cold that I wanted to set myself on fire. Thus, my boss black peacoat got a lot of action, which led to a pretty weird exchange with my dad on Tuesday morning. Here's how the convo (conversation, that is) went down:

Dad strode into the kitchen, still putting on his plaid tie, which he typically only wore on Robbie Burns Day or other Scottish celebrations. "Rowdy" Roddy Piper's birthday and things like that. I was just about ready to leave for school when he noticed my fashionable outerwear.

"Is that your mom's coat?"

"Dad," I said. "Mom's been gone for eleven years or something. Where would I find her coat?"

The black peacoat was part of a particularly triumphant weekend visit to Value Village, courtesy of Yumi's dad (and his car). Not only was this kick-butt coat acquired, but also an *Escape from New York* T-shirt, Snake Plissken and all.

"Oh," Dad said, a little shaken. "I must be confused. Your mom used to have something like that. Though I guess it would be too large for you."

One, I thought that was pretty kind of my dad, suggesting Mom's coat would be oversized on me. I wasn't a hippo, but nobody would be putting me on the top of a cheerleading pyramid any time soon. Two, it was way weird that Dad was bringing Mom up in casual conversation all of a sudden. This was the man who liked to pretend she'd never existed, and aside from the ankh necklace I always wore, the only item of my mom's still in the house was supposedly a framed photograph my dad kept.

"Sorry, Dad. It would have been nice if it was her coat, though. Mom must have had good taste."

The weirdness obsessed me in a minor way as I cut through the cemetery and walked to school. But it didn't last long. I was more obsessed with finding out about this Chinese saboteur Sam Cheng and whoever was on the other end of the mystery phone. And after what was to come during Yumi and Stacey's lunch-hour radio show, all other thoughts were kind of obliterated.

☠

Since Yumi and Stacey had started ditching me during Tuesday and Friday lunch to be radio disc jockeys, I had become more aware than ever that the Sticksville Central cafeteria was a shark tank and I was only so much bloody chum. I had to be careful to avoid the watchful gaze of Ashlie Salmons and her band of not-so-merry women. More importantly, I had to be on guard for Devin McGriff and his fellow Phantom

Moustache band members. After losing the radio slot to Yumi, Devin had been very vocal about his hatred of my friends and me, and the other members of Phantom Moustache — Preston Sinclair, Tyler Young, and the undeniably cute but terrifically dumb lead singer Boston Davis — had joined him in solidarity. If Devin McGriff had become a Sticksville Radio DJ, they would have (sort of) been DJs, as well. And they could have played Phantom Moustache tracks in the cafeteria. Theoretically, this would have quadrupled the Phantom Moustache fan base, but given their talent, this plan could have just as easily backfired.

To make a long story short (too late, I know), I had to avoid looking anywhere near the guys in Phantom Moustache, even if they happened to be busy making a sign at their table that said *If Terrible Music Had a Name, It Would Be Yumi.* It's like they were preparing for an anti-pep rally or something — they had markers and Bristol board and everything.

The P.A. popped and I cringed. Already I was bracing for the worst — the last time around, everyone in the cafeteria was *surprised* to find they loathed Yumi and Stacey's radio show; this time, they were *prepared* to hate it. However, today's programming proved difficult to hate.

"Good afternoon, Sticksville Central!" Yumi Takeshi's strident voice reverberated off the painted brick walls of the cafeteria. My fellow students turned at their benches toward the closest speaker, ready to be displeased. "We got a lot of . . . uh . . . *constructive feedback* about our last show, so we're doing something different this time around. It's a period-long musical tribute to everyone's favourite rage-fuelled math teacher, Mr. Santuzzi!"

A couple people snickered; a few others looked to their friends to see if this actually could be happening. Was it all some bizarre dream? Personally, I thought I had temporarily lost my mind — always a concern. Yumi was a mad genius! Was she really going to devote her entire radio show to making fun of the school's most universally feared and disliked teacher?

"Without further ado," Yumi's voice trumpeted, "I present

to you our mash-note mix-tape to Mr. S. You love his tight seventies wear, you love his Fu Manchu moustache, you love his general air of menace. Now you'll love his favourite songs, as compiled by yours truly, DJ Yu-sless and my good friend Stacey."

"I helped," Stacey mumbled.

The P.A. system began to play the theme song from *Hair*, a not-so-subtle reference to the widely held belief that Mr. Santuzzi had no hair of his own, that his scalp was covered with a lacquered, ill-fitting carpet sample. When Yumi followed it up with The Village People's "Macho Man," some people were literally on the floor, trying and failing to stand under the gravitational pull of such incredible hilarity. And neither Yumi nor Stacey even *had* Mr. Santuzzi as a teacher. Their experience of him purely came through me and Yumi's cousin (who had Santuzzi rumours to spare). By this point, I had already decided this was the greatest day at Sticksville Central High School. Ever.

As Yumi's set began to wrap up, I threw out what remained of my lunch and travelled to the atrium to witness Yumi and Stacey in their natural environment. No one was vandalizing the window; people in the atrium applauded after each song. A couple fans were bowing in deference. Both Yumi and Stacey, crouched in the radio booth, had wide smiles plastered across their faces. They'd brought the entire school onto their side, and only at the expense of one diabolical math teacher.

"Thank you, thank you. You've been a great audience. This is our last song," Yumi called, now more like a carnival barker than that friendless Asian goth I'd met a couple months ago.

"Thanks," added Stacey. (Okay, maybe she had *one* friend when I'd met her.)

"Now, I'm not saying Mr. Santuzzi's a creep . . ." she began. "But I'm pretty sure Radiohead wrote this song about him."

The opening notes of Radiohead's "Creep" tinkled into the atrium and cafeteria, and almost the entire school roared like a particularly enthusiastic crowd doing the wave. At first, I was like, who are all these people singing along to "Creep"? I thought Yumi, Stacey, and I were like the only ones at school who even knew who Radiohead was, but my admiration for Yumi's brilliance overwhelmed my disbelief. And when I say they played "Creep," I mean the real, non-radio-edit version, venomous profanity and all. That was like a double whammy of insubordination.

Four minutes of F-words later, the song faded out and Yumi and Stacey emerged from their radio booth like conquering heroes home from a war. The gathered masses in the atrium erupted in applause; it was as if Yumi had just slain a dragon by raising thousands of dollars for bone-marrow research. But the triumph didn't last.

"Miss Takeshi!" Mr. Santuzzi bellowed from the other end of the atrium. People's heads started to turn domino-style back toward the authoritative voice. How did Mr. Santuzzi know Yumi's name? Did he memorize the entire school roster, just in case any of the students ever tried his patience?

"Your radio show. Hi-*laaaaar*-ious," he said, his coal-black eyes nearly melting Yumi's face from her skull. "To the principal's office. *Now.* Your radio career is being strangled in the crib."

That was, I thought, a weird and graphic metaphor for him to use. Stacey and Yumi looked at each other, completely unsure of what to expect next.

"Bring your lanky friend, too." Apparently Mr. Santuzzi

didn't know *everyone's* name. And I wasn't sure he was allowed to comment on a student's lank, but he was probably too peeved to care, having just listened to a full hour of radio mockery. "I'll get Ms. Fenstermacher, and we'll all have a little chat."

Yumi and Stacey loped down the atrium toward the front office, and Mr. Santuzzi glared at various rubbernecking students until they vacated the area. I was a little concerned I'd never see the two of them again.

☠

Thankfully, the two of them reappeared at the holiday pageant rehearsal after school. Whatever happened, it couldn't have been too severe because there was Stacey Whatshisface, pounding on the timpani drums during our run-through of "God Rest Ye Merry Gentlemen" like he was hammering those dead gentlemen into their coffins. I was excited Mrs. Tischmann had decided we were playing that song because (a) it's about as dark as Christmas songs get, and (b) there's a pretty awesome trombone part in it.

I could tell by the verve with which Stacey hopped onto the drum kit stool that he was most excited about "Jingle Bell Rock," a song that is ironically as far from rock as humanly possible. That part didn't matter; Stacey got to play the drum kit. This was the moment drummers lived for, the reason they subjected themselves to triangles and tambourines and whatever those little things that looked like rainsticks were called: to sit behind that kit and pretend they were Animal from The Muppets.

As the "Jingle Bell Rock" thudded to a halt at the repeated cries of Mrs. Tischmann, she exhaled and decided, "Okay, that's enough for tonight." That was fine by me as I had to talk to Stacey, stat, to find out how Mr. Santuzzi had or hadn't brought down the hammer on their radio show. Mrs. Tischmann looked harried and scatterbrained as usual as I crossed the band room to reach the percussion row.

"So?" I said, shaking my trombone in an almost threatening

way. "What happened? Are you guys suspended?"

"No," he said, screwing or unscrewing something on the snare drum. "Mr. Santuzzi was pretty mad, but we're on probation or something. He and Ms. Fenstermacher are discussing it. But if we play any more swears on-air or whatever, we're kicked out."

"But that's *so* not fair!" I shouted, though, really, it was positively reasonable, considering Mr. Santuzzi.

"Principal Hamilton said it's fair," Stacey shrugged and stuffed his drumsticks into his back pocket. "C'mon, let's go find Yumi. Her rehearsal should nearly be over."

Yumi's drama class was also spending most weeknights practising their weird revision of Charles Dickens' *A Christmas Carol*. (In their update, Ebeneezer Scrooge was an internet millionaire and Bob Cratchit, his unpaid intern, fresh out of a computer science program.) Feeling a little awkward without our third Musketeer, Stacey and I walked over to the drama room, just as their rehearsal was ending. Yumi was folding up her prop wheelchair (part of the modernization of Tiny Tim, I guess) as we approached her.

"You escaped punishment?" I asked.

"Hey, Schwartz," she said, shedding the fingerless gloves of her costume. "Yeah, Stacey and I are safe — for now! But we'll see how long that lasts."

"What did Santuzzi say?"

"Oh, he was pretty angry," she said, leading us from the drama room to her locker. "I can't remember everything he said. Mostly he was just confused about why the two of us made a radio show about him, since he's never taught either of us."

Made sense to me.

"Are you two done carolling or whatever?" she asked. "Get your stuff and let's go. We have to find a phone to call Stacey's dad so he can pick us up."

After we suited up for the winter weather, we left school for the gas station about two minutes from Sticksville Central: the closest place that still had a pay phone. Given the unpredictability of our rehearsal schedule, Stacey's dad insisted we call him to get a drive home. But since none of us had cell phones and the school office was closed, we had to go wandering. Personally, I thought it was criminal to not have pay phones in the actual school itself, but apparently no one in the school administration cared what *I* thought. (This also explained why every classroom didn't have a mandatory cat mascot.)

The phone booth at the Otter gas station was like a beacon at the corner of the cold, dark intersection. Beyond, the nearby Heavendale Plaza had shut down for the night, but the light inside the telephone booth still flickered like a bug zapper — or more like the fluorescent lights in every mental institution in every horror movie. As uninviting as that was, the faster we used the phone, the sooner Stacey's dad would arrive in his Pontiac Sunfire and rescue us from the frigid wind. Was that too dramatic?

Well, if that was too dramatic, how about this? Stacey's dad never had the chance to drive us home that night, because we went home in a g.d. ambulance!

Stacey, Yumi, and I all crammed into the phone booth, reasoning that it must be warmer in there than outside. We were pressed up against each other and Stacy was just barely able to move his arm into his pocket (at least I think it was *his* pocket), take out the change, and dial his father.

Dial tone.

Two rings.

Then, "Hey, Dad?"

"Get your elbow outta my chest," Yumi whispered.

"Sorry. Dad?"

And then it happened, in less than an instant. A camouflage tarp dropped down over the sides of the booth. Out every glass window, all I could see were patches of green and brown. Then the booth started to rock back and forth, like a boat in a thunderstorm. I couldn't see a thing and my stomach lurched with each shift in the phone booth's direction. Stacey had sharp elbows, and he seemed to be jamming those elbows everywhere.

"Watch it!" I said, taking an elbow in the eye.

"Stop rocking the booth!" Yumi shouted.

"It's not me!"

"What is happening?" Stacey asked, with more calm than the situation called for.

"Open the door!" Yumi yelled.

But we were too late. The booth toppled over and suddenly my back was on the pavement, my shoes were in the air, and shattered glass and camouflaged tarp filled every empty space in the booth. The sound it made was like a thousand light bulbs bursting in unison. My face felt broken open, I couldn't move my legs, and I could feel liquid running down my arm. Stacey, who seemed to be the top of our teenager-and-glass layer cake, propped himself upright and pulled Yumi, who'd been mashed between us, out of the glass deathtrap. This freed my legs to the point where I could stand on my own.

Assessing the situation, my face felt bruised and my black peacoat was sporting a few unsewable holes. And that liquid running down my arm was my own blood, which was alarming to say the least. But my hand didn't look too badly cut. I wished I could say the same for my friends. Stacey's face looked like it had lost a fight with a cheese grater and Yumi's arm was hanging at a really stomach-churning angle. However, there was no sign of our attackers or anyone else. I half-expected a bunch of goons clapping when we emerged from the coffin of broken glass.

"What just happened?" Stacey said again, voice still calmer than I'd have liked.

"My arm *really* hurts," Yumi gulped, trying not to cry, I think, in front of the two of us.

Covering the crumpled phone booth was a military-patterned tarp. Though the fall had twisted and distorted its shape the message left in yellow spray paint was still easy to read. Splashed across the tarp, in bright block letters: *Go Back to China.*

Something told me Sticksville's ugliness was just beginning to bubble up to the surface.

☠

Big Trouble in Little Sticksville

October and her cafeteria tablemates looked like they'd survived a minor explosion. Stacey had white tape bandages speckled all over his face like a cut-rate mummy Halloween costume. Yumi spooned her instant noodles robotically into her face with her one working arm. Her other, wrapped in a black cast, was folded in a sling. October looked like a virtual paragon of health with just one swollen purple eye socket and bandaged hand. The three casualties sat quietly chewing and slurping their lunches, barely saying a word to one another. The mood in the Sticksville Central cafeteria that Wednesday afternoon was sombre, even in what was, for all intents and purposes, the high school gloom capital of the world.

Word about the phone booth hate crime bounced around the high school faster than a pinball, post-tilt. The office staff was notified, phone trees were activated, and Principal Hamilton organized an emergency assembly. More unofficially, the school's brightest and bravest gossips, true unsung heroes, began telling unfounded stories about the severity of the three students' injuries, the identity of their attacker(s), and the motivations behind the phone-booth tipping. By the time first period had started, no one, not even the clueless Mr. Martz, had to ask October why her eye was black and her hand wrapped in tape.

October, Stacey, and Yumi were all assigned a series of mandatory sessions with Dr. Lagostina, the school therapist. For

October, this was old hat. She'd been forced to do some therapy sessions with Lagostina earlier in the year, after getting into a few scraps with Ashlie Salmons. October wasn't worried about herself. The message on the camouflaged tarp made it clear that Yumi was the target of the phone booth attack. Stacey and October were mere collateral damage. She couldn't imagine the things Yumi must have been feeling.

Mr. Santuzzi's class had been pre-empted by the emergency assembly. While October appreciated any excuse to miss Santuzzi's math-adjacent punishment session, this assembly was of particular importance. Principal Hamilton was particularly incensed by the phone booth attack, and it was noticeable. While the students of Sticksville Central sat ashen-faced in the bleachers, Principal Hamilton prowled and bounded across the gym floor like he was performing the most terrifying floor gymnastics routine in history.

"This sort of racist intimidation and violence will not be tolerated against our students here at Sticksville Central High School," he insisted. "It's wrong, and you all know it's wrong. So if you know anything about who committed this heinous crime, I want you to speak to me or someone else in the school office. There's no honour in standing up for racist thugs."

For a few moments, Principal Hamilton stood stock-still at the basketball foul line. He scanned the crowd of students, eyes burning, nostrils flaring. One could be forgiven for thinking he was going to identify the culprits, right there during the assembly, just through sheer force of will and forehead sweat.

"Once we find who did this," he continued, "the police will be notified and the perpetrators will be punished to the full extent of the law. This school has no patience for this kind of behaviour."

But that was this morning. Things had calmed down (at least a little bit) by lunch. You could tell that people wanted to congratulate Yumi on her tremendous Santuzzi-themed radio program, but the rumours and assembly about last night's extreme hate crime made everyone who was not in that telephone booth a little cautious around her. A few brave people — mostly the art kids and punks — came up to Yumi with sentiments like, "Screw those people, whoever did it," which was nice, but probably rang hollow for Yumi. Unless you've been facing a smashed phone booth spray-painted with a message telling you to go back to China, it's probably pretty hard to even understand how upside-down Yumi's world had turned.

"I'm not even Chinese," Yumi said between mouthfuls of noodle. It was the eighth time she'd mentioned it today, as if the mix-up in cultural background were the worst part of it all. "My parents are from Japan. And I was born here."

Yumi's forearm had been broken in two places, but it was her sense of security that was most damaged in the attack. She'd even followed the ER doctor's suggestions and gone with a black cast so no one would even realize if nobody signed it. Both Yumi and October had been teased for being "Zombie Tramps" before (mainly by Ashlie Salmons), but Yumi had never been bullied for her Asian background. Perhaps, dear readers, we were naive in thinking she'd be free from that kind of thing in Sticksville.

"You okay?" Stacey asked. The glass had cut him over his lips, so it hurt him even to speak. Luckily for him, he was Stacey.

"I guess."

"Don't worry. We'll find who did this," October said. Already, she was plotting ways the dead kids could help her investigate last night's crime.

"Why are you always saying that?" Yumi said, nearly on the verge of tears. "Just leave it alone. Why do you always have to be all Hardy Boys about this? You said that about Mr. O'Shea and you got kidnapped."

"Sorry," October said. It was the words she used most frequently in recent days. Yumi had a point — October's mystery-solving often seemed to lead to some sort of personal peril — but being October, a stubborn, determined person, there was no way she could leave this alone. Not with the aid of five dead kids at her disposal.

Their uncomfortable cafeteria silence continued. Not that it was silent inside the cafeteria — two grade eleven DJs, Mike Kraminski and Vincent Schrader, were midway through their radio show and it wasn't half bad. But October, Yumi, and Stacey sat and ate like their lunch would be their very last meal. In short order, the three non-McGriffs from Phantom Moustache visited their table to disrupt the unearthly silence.

"Pretty rad facial scars, Stacey," Preston, the bassist, said. He put a foot up on the cafeteria bench, about two inches from October's thigh. Preston Sinclair looked like a yearbook photo from the 1960s from the neck up and he wore loafers in that way no other high-school boys do.

"You look like a boxer or something," Taylor Young, Phantom Moustache's drummer, added. He was a short, porcupine-ish boy with too much hair.

Since this was the first time ever anyone in Phantom Moustache had spoken to any of October's friends without making veiled threats, she wasn't really sure what was happening. Everyone seemed to be waiting for someone else to speak.

"Uh, thanks," said Stacey, wincing from the effort.

"Listen." Lead singer Boston Davis finally spoke. "We have a preposition for you."

"Proposition," October corrected.

"Whatever," Boston said, flapping his hand at our eyeliner-loving heroine in that "talky-talky" sort of way. "We couldn't help notice you're a drummer and you've got a pretty sweet radio show."

"So?" Yumi said, saving Stacey the pain of a response.

"So," Boston continued, glowering at Yumi. "Taylor here is grounded until the new year since his parents caught him in a makeout session with Wanda Pang, and we're playing a show at the holiday pageant. We need a drummer."

Wanda Pang was the only other Asian girl in the whole school, which meant she was probably feeling very paranoid after the phone booth attack. Taylor just shrugged.

"My dad is strict."

"Devin hates me — and Stacey by extension," Yumi pointed out. "He thinks we stole his radio show."

"Don't worry about Devin," Boston said. "*I'm* the lead singer. Don't you know how a band works?"

"Besides, he really only hates you," Preston helpfully added.

"Thanks."

"So, yeah," Boston said. "Just keep time and don't bring Yoko around and the job is yours."

He patted Stacey's shoulder like a gangster welcoming him to his protection racket, and all three band members returned to their usual cafeteria table, where Devin McGriff was seated with Ashlie Salmons' arms around his neck. However, the reference to the gifted Japanese artist often blamed for breaking up The Beatles left a bad taste — even worse than the cafeteria food — in our heroes' mouths.

"Her name is Yumi," Stacey said. "Jerks."

"That was kind of racist," October thought aloud. Perhaps this was just the kind of thing Principal Hamilton was talking about.

"*Whatever*. At least they didn't break my arm," Yumi said with a grand gesture to her sling. October wasn't so sure, though. If Devin McGriff hated Yumi for taking the radio slot, why couldn't one of his bandmates have been the person who overturned the phone booth? Aside from them, October didn't know of any enemies Yumi had.

"So, are you going to do it?" October asked Stacey.

"I don't know," Stacey said, at great personal cost to his face. "I kind of don't like those guys. *Ow*. Or their band."

"You should do it," Yumi said between shovelfuls of instant noodles. "You'll become, like, three million times cooler. Just don't forget us when you're at the top of the food chain."

☠

As a conclusion to the day's lessons about racial intolerance, Ms. Fenstermacher switched gears from their current history unit, the Great Depression, to teach a lesson about the typical Asian immigrant experience in early twentieth-century Canada.

"The other week, we talked about the building of the Canadian Pacific Railway," Fenstermacher reminded the class. It sounded like a lot more fun (or less depressing) than the Great Depression. "We talked almost exclusively about the positive impact it had on Canada as a nation. But did you know that railway was largely built by Chinese immigrant workers? Most of whom were mistreated, separated from their families, abused? Over six hundred Chinese workers died during the construction of the Canadian Pacific Railway. So many that the telephone was often called the 'crying line' in Chinatowns across Canada, because it only brought tragic news."

The story of the railway workers is truly awful, dear readers, and I really wish I could say it was completely uncommon in Canada at the time. But like George Washington before me or any man ensnared in Wonder Woman's golden lasso, I cannot tell a

lie. Canada was something of a hotbed of anti-Chinese sentiment in the early twentieth century. When Canada was building the Canadian Pacific Railway, they encouraged immigration from China, because they needed Chinese workers to toil on the railway and clear tunnels with dynamite (sometimes exploding themselves in the process) for very little pay. But once the railway was built, most Canadians didn't *need* Chinese immigrants any longer, so the government imposed a head tax. Any Chinese citizen who wished to immigrate to Canada could do so . . . for fifty dollars.

This fee was later raised to $100, which in modern terms is more like $10,000, and by 1903, the head tax was raised to $500! And even still, once they arrived in Canada, the Chinese immigrants often faced strict working rules and regulations to protect traditionally white-owned businesses like laundries. The country had a long history of anti-Asian sentiment, which Ms. Fenstermacher, usually not a real downer, revealed to her history class. By the time the final bell rang, October felt nearly as sick as she had seconds after the phone booth attack. Something was rotten in the town of Sticksville.

☠

The dense smell of teriyaki sauce hit October like a fist when she entered her house. Between volleyball games and holiday pageant recitals, October and her father hadn't eaten dinner at the same table too often lately. Whenever they did, the food tended to be things that were easy and quick to prepare — things like tacos or, in this case, stirfry. October offered to make dinner frequently, but her dad always declined. In truth, he probably just wanted to actually keep down the food he ingested. Cooking: not a life skill October currently had. This isn't *The Dead Kid Culinary School*, after all.

October waited outside the kitchen door and stared at the wall-hanging just to the left of the door frame — a weird German needlepoint behind glass — and hesitated before entering the kitchen. The German needlepoint was just one of the many odd decorations in her house she'd never questioned, like the lamp in the living room covered in seashells. She dreaded dinner because she knew her dad would want to discuss the phone booth again. October just wanted to forget it ever happened.

"Dinner's just about ready," Mr. Schwartz appeared at the door frame, scratching behind one ear with a wooden spoon. "Have a seat."

October took her place at the table and watched as her father ladled the teriyaki beef onto the pile of rice on her plate.

"Looks good, Dad."

Mr. Schwartz sat down across from his daughter and rubbed his hands together in a dramatic way. "Thanks. You know, we talked about this last night, but I want you to come straight home after school from now on."

"But —"

"Straight home. No more writing in the cemetery. No more cemetery at all."

As you might imagine, Mr. Schwartz hadn't been too thrilled to find his only daughter was the victim of an assault.

"What about the holiday pageant?" October asked. "I have to stay late for the music rehearsals."

"You can just wait at school after practice," he said. "I'll drive you home. I don't want you trying to find a phone to call Stacey's father."

October's dad had always been a bit overprotective. While he sometimes fell short in the providing dinner and not being clinically depressed departments of parenthood, being overprotective, he had mastered. And October could understand his concern. She was still sporting a black eye. However, October wasn't too thrilled to stick around until volleyball practice ended to get a ride home from her dad. Ashlie Salmons was often at those volleyball practices, being on the team and all, and we all know how October felt about her.

"But what about your volleyball practice?"

"You can wait," he said, stabbing his beef stirfry with his fork. "The practices don't run too long. Bring your book. You can write about Emily de Kandlestick."

"Olivia de Kellerman," October grumbled.

"Yes, her."

"Maybe you could just get me a cell phone for safety." October threw a Hail Mary pass, seeing if all this overprotectiveness could benefit her in some way.

"Sorry, kiddo. That's a negative."

"I just don't see why I have to wait around watching you teach Ashlie Salmons volleyball, when she's probably the one that tipped the phone booth."

Mr. Schwartz brought his quilted paper napkin to his face and wiped downward with great care, almost as if he were taking out dentures or something — which was strange as he was not quite old enough for that yet.

"Why would you say that?" he asked.

"What? About Ashlie?"

He nodded, napkin still gripped in both hands.

"Because she hates me! She hates me, she hates Stacey, she hates Yumi," October barked, outlining three solid reasons.

"October, I know you and Ashlie have had your differences in the past, but she's proven herself a valuable leader to our girls' volleyball team."

"Differences?!" October was truly offended. "Dad, Ashlie Salmons terrorized me when we first moved here! And I know she's your golden girl or all-star now, but she doesn't like me. Can

I be excused? I'm not hungry anymore."

October was still hungry, but she was also trying to make a point. Being righteous often means missing out on meals.

"Where are you going?" he asked as October brought her plate to the sink.

"To my room," she said. "Don't worry. I'm not going to the cemetery where your best friend Ashlie Salmons might crush my other hand."

October let the plate and fork clatter in the sink with such volume that it sounded like a microwave kicked down a staircase.

☠

That night, October lied to her dad on two separate matters. For one, she didn't honestly think Ashlie Salmons tipped the phone booth — at least not on her own. Ashlie was probably in the vicinity of a hundred pounds if you included her massive belt; there was no way she could topple October, Yumi, Stacey, and a phone booth together. She figured Devin McGriff was angrier at Yumi and much more likely to do it. (Though it was possible, October thought, that Ashlie *knew* Devin did it and loved him all the more for it.) For two, though October did immediately head to her bedroom after dinner, she'd planned to sneak into the cemetery at *some* point that night.

Luckily, the endless volleyball practices meant her dad was very tired and in bed by ten, so he didn't notice when October slid open the kitchen door, no matter how concerned he was for his daughter's safety. There was no real need for fear, though. In most situations, October's five dead friends could protect her just as soundly, if not better, than her dear old dad.

Given that she was bundled up in her peacoat and gloves, October thought she might be able to hide her injuries from the dead kids so they wouldn't worry, but she forgot about the holes the broken glass had cut into that peacoat and that half of her face was completely purple. Cyril was first to notice the roughed-up October Schwartz's entry into the graveyard.

"October! What in tarnation happened to your face?" he

shouted, drawing some attention to the bruises. Sometimes, readers, Cyril's old-timey slang really makes me laugh. I'm just waiting for him to shout, "Oh my stars!" In no time, all five dead kids were inspecting October's half-mauve face.

"Did you eat a pie too fast and injure yourself?" Kirby asked, who was really one to talk.

"Kirby!" Morna chided. "Wha' happened, October?"

"Who did this t'you?" Tabetha demanded.

"That's not all," October admitted, pulling off a glove to reveal her bandaged left hand. "Don't worry. It's not my writing hand."

"So, what *did* happen?" Derek asked.

"My friends and I were in a phone booth when someone tipped it over."

There was a collective groan of pure disgust from the dead kids, followed by Cyril asking, "Phone booth . . . ?"

"Like a little room in which you can speak to people far away," Derek explained. "Using a telephone. Remember that thing you yanked out of the wall at the police station?"

"Yes . . ."

"That was a telephone."

"But who did this t'you? Who should we give nightmares for the rest of their lives?" Tabetha was out for revenge.

"No one," October said. "I don't know who did this."

As much as the idea of dead children entering her assailants' bedrooms and haunting their minds forever made October smile, she had promised to figure out how Morna died first.

"It's cold out here," October said. "Can we go inside one of the tombs?"

Cyril and Tabetha ghosted through a large stone mausoleum's door, then unlocked and opened it from inside. (That's what we're calling it when the dead kids walk through walls from here on in. *Ghosting.* We all on board?) The tomb was slightly warmer than the outdoors, but the group had to leave the door open so October could still see the dead kids. They all huddled around the tomb's central stone coffin to decide their next move.

"We should find out who toppled that phone booth and *punish* them," Derek said.

Tabetha agreed. "Yeah. The sooner, the better!"

Morna looked forlorn, but she was also on board with this change of plan.

"No," October said, ever the martyr. "Morna, we're solving your murder first. That was the deal."

"But your booth-tipper is still on the loose," Derek protested. "Whoever caused Morna to die is long dead."

"Though I hate to admit there's anything right about Mr. Running Water, Derek is making a lot of sense," Kirby conceded.

"This is not about making sense. I'm talking to a bunch of ghosts," October reminded.

A heated debate followed about which mystery should be investigated first, with Tabetha and Derek championing the phone booth mystery and October wanting to stick to the original agreement and give Morna's mystery a fair shake. Morna herself remained quiet for most of the discussion. She didn't want to seem selfish, but it was obvious to all sides that Morna felt like she'd been pushed aside.

"Why don't we ask Morna what she would like to do?" Cyril asked. There was a reason he was unofficial leader of the dead kids. All their sunken, hollow eyes turned toward the Scottish girl in the moth-eaten gingham dress.

"Well?" said Kirby.

"It makes the most sense t'look inta the phone booth," she said. "I can wait."

"Are you certain, Morna?" Cyril asked.

"She said she was," Tabetha said.

"Yes."

"Listen, we can do both at the same time," October suggested. "We're smart, right? We don't have to decide one or the other."

Morna smiled a bit, but Team Phone Booth was already into Phase One of their crack investigation, and October hadn't even had a chance to find out from Ms. Fenstermacher what had become of prime murder suspect Sam Cheng.

"Okay, first thing, October," Derek began. "Take us to where it happened."

"Scene a' tha' crime!" Tabetha shouted.

89

"Why?"

"They always do it in the movies," Derek reasoned, though that didn't explain Tabetha's enthusiasm, since she'd died before film had been invented.

"And if the criminals have left any clues," Kirby added, "that's where they'll be . . . moron."

"Hey!" Derek shouted. He didn't properly appreciate Kirby's shaming.

The dead kids sealed up the cozy tomb and October guided them on a rare outside-cemetery field trip to the gas station near her high school. Since a full day had passed since the incident, most of what normal people would call "evidence" had been confiscated by the police. All that remained was a stump of phone cord and glass shards sprinkled like Parmesan cheese over a Caesar salad where the booth once was. Gone was the booth itself, the novelty racist message military tarp, anything that could have helped the dead kids' investigation. As the crack mystery team circled the blank space where a telephone booth used to be, tiny water crystals began to fall from the sky. The winter's first snow had arrived, and October Schwartz, unlike most kids her age, was scouring a crime scene with a bunch of dead kids.

"It's snowing!" Morna cried. From the sound of it, she was looking forward to days of skating and tobogganing. Kirby had other things on his mind.

"We'll have to hurry then. Before the snow covers any clues."

"What're we lookin' for?" Tabetha asked. "There's nothin' here."

"October said the tarp had been spray-painted with yellow paint," Derek said. "See if you can find a can of yellow paint."

"What about boot prints?" Cyril asked, lifting his tricorn hat and scratching his sandy blond hair.

"Good idea," Derek said. "Look for shoe prints. Or fingerprints. Or any kind of prints, really."

"I'm going to look through this bag of trash," Derek announced, heading toward the pile of garbage bags collected by the curbside outside the gas station. That was another good thing about enlisting dead kids to help you solve your mystery. Given they were all rotten flesh themselves, they didn't think twice about pawing through someone's mouldy leftovers and soiled diapers.

"Quiet," Kirby commanded, cocking his head to the side like a dog who's heard his own name. "Does anyone hear that?"

Of course they had all heard it: an engine accelerating, a car (or motorized vehicle of some sort) approaching in the night, though no one could spot headlights. The sound was too small to be a bus or pickup truck, but seemed too much for one car. Whatever it was, it was coming closer, and in a hurry.

"Maybe you should hide," October said. "What if someone sees you?" She always feared someone would see her socializing with her ghost friends, though it was physically impossible for most people to spot them. But a certain percentage of living people *could* see the dead, so it wasn't an unreasonable fear. Yumi had already proven she could see the dead kids. Sticksville's most dogged real estate agent, Alyosha Diamandas, too. As far as October could tell, Sticksville was filled with little Haley Joel Osments, honing their sixth senses, spotting dead people at every turn.

"Okay," Derek said, mid-garbage-rummage. "Everyone hide in the —"

But it was too late! A dark-coloured van appeared much sooner (and closer) than any of them expected, screeching to a halt in front of the phone booth's remnants. The side door clattered open and little cylindrical projectiles began firing out the van's side. October took a hit in the shoulder, then another in the shin. Was this a drive-by shooting? October couldn't help but think she was destined to die at this phone booth, one way or another, *Final Destination* style. Only fair, she figured, to go out like 50 Cent nearly had.

October toppled over onto the sidewalk and covered her face with her arms to shield it from the theoretical bullets, but peered through one eye to scope out the reign of terror spouting from the van. Her dead friends were taking shots, as well. Tabetha fell backward into some shrubbery; Kirby collapsed onto a half-fence at the gas station's perimeter. The barrage eventually ended and a head popped out the van's side to make sure October had been subdued. The face was covered in a blue mask. The person in the passenger side of the van was also, she noted, masked. The van was full of superheroes or Mexican wrestlers.

Apparently satisfied with their work, they slammed shut the van's side door and gunned the engine, hurtling down the street, still sans headlights. Someone was liable to get really hurt driving around that way, but given the recent drive-by, the van passengers didn't seem overly concerned with public safety. Considering October was not bleeding profusely and just badly bruised, she quickly determined she had probably not been shot. That was a relief.

The dead kids emerged from their respective hiding and/or collapsing spots and tried to figure out what had just happened.

"Do ye think they saw us?" Morna asked, rubbing her neck.

"I don't know if they saw us, but they certainly hit us," Kirby replied. "Accidentally or on purpose."

Derek hoisted himself from the garbage and walked over to where the rest of the team had gathered, looking at the little cylinders wrapped in brown paper littered all over the ground.

Snow had started accumulating, surrounding them with a wispy white powder.

"They're quarterth," Derek said, opening his closed fist to display a roll of twenty-five-cent pieces in his brown palm. He'd newly acquired a lisp after a volley of quarters had knocked out his two front teeth.

"What happened to your teeth?!" October was horrified.

"I think I thwallowed them," he said.

"They'll come back," Kirby said. "I'm ninety percent sure of that."

"Is everyone okay?" Cyril asked. "Aside from Derek, that is."

"October," Derek asked. "Why ith thomeone attacking you with quarterth?"

The obvious answer — they were cheaper than dollar coins — was probably not the one Derek was looking for.

☠

8

Yumi, Yumi, Don't You Lose My Number

"Stardate: December eighth. A thin cover of frozen water particles has covered the planet in a phenomenon the life forms here have dubbed *snow*," Yumi spoke into her new cell phone like it was a *Star Trek* tricorder. She was paused dramatically at the end of the arts corridor, one arm in her sling, the other lifting the flip phone to her lips, as if it were recording her weird space monologue.

Snow *had* fallen overnight. What started before last night's twenty-five-cent drive-by had continued overnight until all of Sticksville looked like it had one of those flimsy Styrofoam blankets. That blanket had dripped off my Chuck Taylors and collected into a cold grey soup in front of my locker. Braving the slush moat that had developed in the school hallway, I managed to cram in my schoolbag and lock it shut.

"Since when are you into *Star Trek?*" I asked.

"I'm not," Yumi said, snapping the phone closed like a bear trap. "Though Spock is kind of hot. Besides, you knew what I was talking about, so I could ask you the same question."

"You got a phone," I stated the obvious.

"Yep," she said, turning it over in her one unbroken hand like it was one of those magical Indian stones in *Indiana Jones and the Temple of Doom*. "And all it took to convince my dad was a swarming by violent racists. What a pushover."

Something told me Mr. Takeshi and the Sticksville Police

were on speed-dial on Yumi's new phone. Stacey Whatchama-callit showed up at that moment, also suitably impressed with Yumi's new acquisition.

"New phone."

"Yes, sir," Yumi replied, flipping the phone open and closed like it was a hangnail she couldn't leave alone. "Dad also registered me for self-defence lessons. So I'm set. Either of your parents encouraged toward a phone purchase after our beating?"

"No," I sighed. "My dad told me last night it's not happening any time soon. Instead, I get him as the Kevin Costner to my Whitney Houston for the rest of my high school life. But, like, without the romance."

"*The Bodyguard* is awesome," Stacey said, almost in his own world. "Yumi, we should play the soundtrack on the air one day."

"I'll think about it," she said. "If we're ever allowed on-air again. That's too bad, Schwartz, we could be texting like nobody's business. Sorry. How about you, Stacey? A phone in your future after your face got Freddy Kruegered?"

"My dad's still paying off his car phone. So, probably not."

I'll be honest. I'm not even sure what a car phone is.

"Well, whatever," Yumi said, shoving the phone into the pocket of her black jeans. "Whenever you two *do* get phones or whenever you need to call me, you can reach me at 868-5309. I've already determined that can be translated to TOTL-FOX, if you need a mnemonic device."

"I'll keep it in an important place," I said.

And on the inside front cover of *Two Knives, One Thousand Demons*, I wrote: YUMI — 868-5309.

Just as I was mentally applauding Yumi for managing to incorporate mnemonic into conversation *before* first period, Ms. Fenstermacher approached, dressed in an adorable polka-dot top thing and her usual thick-framed glasses. Seriously, if she hadn't been so awesome, I'd probably have hated her.

"Speaking of total foxes . . ." Stacey whispered.

"Oh, good," Ms. Fenstermacher said. "You're both here."

Apparently, Mr. Santuzzi had a talk with Principal Hamilton about his issues with a school radio show devoted to mocking him, and so the Radio Sticksville program was now under significant scrutiny. Everything that played over the P.A. system in the atrium and cafeteria had to reflect "the spirit and values of Sticksville Central High School," whatever those were. I mean, a teacher killed another teacher with a car, then tried to stab me with a bayonet — all within my first two months at this school. Not sure I'm all that gung-ho on promoting Sticksville Central values.

"What this means," Ms. Fenstermacher said, "is I need the two of you —all of the DJs — to be on your best behaviour. No making fun of the faculty, no curse words. Think you can do that?"

Stacey nodded like a bobblehead doll.

"Will it be like this forever?" Yumi asked.

"At least until I have that maniac Mr. Santuzzi off my back. Thanks for understanding."

Teachers at Sticksville didn't seem to feel any qualms about talking ill of each other behind each other's backs. Maybe that was another Sticksville Central value? We watched Ms. Fenstermacher mosey back down the hall in her Mary Janes.

"I guess I'd better head off to French class," I said.

"And I . . . will follow Mr. Fenstermacher," Stacey said, still speaking in short bursts because of all his facial cuts.

"Stop being gross." Yumi punched him in the shoulder with her good hand. "That said, I would gladly sit in on October's math class. She gets all the teacher luck."

This was news to me. Nobody was clamouring for a class with Mr. Santuzzi. "You would? You know Santuzzi probably despises you now for that radio show."

"Yeah, but Skyler McGriff is helping out in your class."

"Ew," I said, kind of horrified with Yumi. "Devin's brother? He's old. And what's the deal with his hair? He looks like he hits on waitresses at Applebee's."

"He's way hotter than his brother," Yumi insisted.

"They're like rotten apples and rotten oranges," I said.

Stacey just shook his head in disappointment.

As we walked to class, a thought occurred to me: Mr. Santuzzi hated Yumi's radio show. He was also ex-military and, if Yumi's cousin's stories were to be believed, had a bit of an uncontrollable rage issue. What if he totally Hulked out and flipped the phone booth by himself? It seemed too petty for Mr. Santuzzi, and it didn't explain the masked quarter-tossers last night, but I couldn't rule anything out. For the moment, I kept my theories to myself.

☠

During math class, I tried to see in Skyler McGriff what Yumi saw in him, but I just couldn't. I guess varsity baseball had given him strong arms, but that was about it. It was much easier to imagine him and Mr. Santuzzi getting along extremely well. Maybe Mr. Santuzzi had even hand-picked him for his class, being the most elite of total jock thugs. Yumi had terrible taste in guys, though, so I decided to stop wasting mental energy on it and instead focus on — not mathematics — but the ongoing saga of Olivia de Kellerman.

Though I'd always done relatively well in school, math had never been my strongest subject. But lately I found myself understanding it and able to get away with paying less attention in class. Shockingly, I was becoming a great math student (lateness aside). Maybe the rest of the class was getting dumber. Dangerous as it was to attempt anything besides schoolwork in Mr. Santuzzi's class, I had begun secretly writing passages — sometimes even just scraps of dialogue — for *Two Knives, One Thousand Demons*. I had to be careful, because my neighbour, Myra, was nosy, and Mr. Santuzzi (probably from days spent as a sniper or mercenary or something) could spot fun at a thousand yards. But my recent experience with magic phones, glass wounds, and van-based ambushes had inspired whatever storytelling organs existed inside me.

Mr. Santuzzi was going over the answers to a quiz on factorials, saying he hadn't seen so many failures since he visited the Coast Guard (must have been some army joke I didn't get), and I was deep into a battle between Olivia de Kellerman and a half-dozen demons at a public swimming pool. The leader of the small coven had cornered her on top of the high-dive board. On a side note, I was concerned about my title. Demons add up and I would be at one thousand before I knew it. Changing it to *Two Knives, Ten Thousand Demons* was looking like a necessity.

"Miss Schwartz," Mr. Santuzzi called out, his hawk-like eyes trained on my book covered in handwritten script, with clearly no math equations in sight. "What was your answer to question six?"

"Uh . . . correct?" I had stuffed my quiz into my bag earlier. It would have looked suspicious to retrieve it now.

"That may well be," he said, stroking his black moustache in an unsettling way, "but I'd prefer if you used my class for math study instead of writing love letters to Edward Cullen."

More unsettling than his moustache was the fact that Mr. Santuzzi knew a character's name from *Twilight*.

"Mr. McGriff, please confiscate October's book," he said, then turned back to the board. "You can get it back at the end of class, *if* I'm feeling generous."

There must have been a public execution I was unaware of, because Mr. Santuzzi was feeling generous. Before lunch began, he allowed Skyler McGriff to return *Two Knives, One Thousand Demons* to me.

As Skyler was handing me the composition book, he asked, "So, are you a writer?"

"I guess," I said. "I try."

"*Two Knives, One Thousand Demons* sounds pretty wicked," he said, thumbing through the pages. "I used to really be into horror stuff."

Okay, so can I get my book back, or are we going to reminisce about the person you used to be, teaching assistant?

"Hey," he said. "You wouldn't mind if I borrowed it, would you? Just overnight? I'm kind of interested in seeing what it's about."

This was becoming strange. Why was this university bro so interested in my book all of a sudden? Had Mr. O'Shea been re-incarnated as Devin McGriff's older brother? That would have been so heartbreaking.

"Well, it's about this girl who's got two knives and she has to fight off a thousand demons . . ." I delivered my elevator pitch.

"See?" he said, clapping the notebook shut. "Sold already. Sounds wicked. Say, I'm sorry to hear about that phone booth thing."

As depressed as I was to hear a full-blown hate crime down-graded to "phone booth thing," it was nice of Skyler to express the sympathy Mr. Santuzzi seemed to forever forget. "Oh, thanks. I didn't get the worst of it, though." I raised my left hand to display my recently changed bandages.

"Yeah, please pass my apologies on to your friend, Yumi," he said, gesturing with my *Two Knives, One Thousand Demons* book like it was now a natural extension of his arm. "She lives out on Klaxon Road, right? That's an unusual area."

"Mmm?" I said. I was too busy thinking how Yumi's head would explode when I told her that Skyler McGriff knew (a) she existed, and (b) where she lived.

"Have you heard about all the witch stories in Sticksville's past?"

"Oh, yes . . . the guy. Crisparkle."

"Yeah, just a bunch of stupid folklore," Skyler decided. "But, as I said, I used to be into that kind of thing. Speaking of which: your book. I'll bring it back tomorrow."

Somehow, over the course of my awkward conversation with Mr. Santuzzi's assistant, I'd avoided detention or punish-ment of any kind. How could I refuse?

☠

The dead kids wandered around the lobby of the Crooked Arms late that night, and I found myself watching the front steps as closely as a dog watches the door for its master. Alyosha

Diamandas couldn't interrupt us tonight; I wouldn't allow it. He already had a history with the dead kids that I was none too pleased to repeat. This time, however, I had remembered to bring along a flashlight, making it a bit easier for us to see inside.

My five friends were prowling around while I peered out the window, watching for any headlights on Turnbull Lane.

"Come away from tha' window," Tabetha shouted. "No one's comin' down this street. It's deserted."

"Last time, Alyosha Diamandas found me here," I explained.

"If he comes, we know how ta' handle him."

Reluctantly, I left the window to join the dead kids, who were already opening drawers in desks and cabinets, searching through all the dusty corners. Last night, after I had collected all the rolls of quarters (that's evidence, and good money) and Derek had given up the search for his front teeth, the dead kids and I started discussing Morna's mystery, and we decided we all needed to visit the Crooked Arms. For one, it might jog Morna's memory. After all, a little mention of Sam Cheng helped her remember the Chinese saboteur covered in blood. For two, I thought it was an outlying possibility that we could find some evidence related to Morna's death, despite the fact it had occurred about a hundred years earlier. (Most evidence, I guess, doesn't stick around for that long.) While Cyril and Derek went through the front lobby desk, Morna was stationed in front of the grandfather clock, staring up at its broken face.

"Do you remember something about that clock, Morna?" I asked. Maybe the grandfather clock held some clue to what happened here in 1914.

"I remember something about it," Morna said, slowly, deliberately. "Something inside the clock, maybe? I can't remember."

Cyril and Derek walked over from the desk to the grandfather clock, stopping on either side of its display window door. They slid their long, bony fingers under the edge and attemped to pry the door free.

"Outta my way," Tabetha grunted; she shoved the other

dead kids and me from her path and wrenched the front door entirely off the clock with surprising strength. The panel clattered to the floor but the glass didn't break. Alyosha Diamandas was definitely going to notice that.

"What's inside?" I asked, guiding the flashlight's beam inside the clock.

"Nothing," Cyril said. "The clock is completely empty. Maybe something happened to Morna while she was looking at the clock?"

"Was that any help?" I asked Morna.

"Not really."

Kirby asked me to shine my flashlight over on the far wall.

"Over there, October," he said. "What's Asphodel Meadows?"

This was the million-dollar question. "I was hoping Morna might know."

Morna contorted her lips and squeezed her eyebrows together. "Sorry . . . I don't know what those two words mean together."

Eyes cast downward, Morna MacIsaac shuffled over to the corner with all the broken glass and sat down, crossing her arms and legs over top one another. I was beginning to feel that investigating Morna's death was nearly as painful for her as the original killing itself. I crouched down beside her.

"Morna, it's okay if you don't remember anything," I said. I was going to put my hand on her shoulder, but I worried my palm would just pass through and I'd fall face first into broken beer bottles. "We'll figure this out. You don't need to force it or feel ashamed."

"What should we look fer next?" Tabetha shouted, still bent over, half-inside the grandfather clock.

"There's the telephone," I said, pointing the flashlight so it glinted off the metal receiver perched at the end of the desk.

"Oh, you mean the magical phone?" Kirby joked.

"Try it, smart guy," I said. "I swear, it works."

Derek picked up the antique phone and lifted the horn to his lips. "What thould I thay?" His front teeth hadn't grown back quite yet.

"The number on the wall. You have to access the voice by saying seven-three-five."

"Theven-thwee-five," he recited.

"Does he really have to be the one on the phone?" Kirby criticized. "He sounds as if he's had a brain injury."

Derek scowled at Kirby.

"No offence," he huffed as he squatted down.

We all waited in tense silence for Derek's next words. Unfortunately, those words were "Ith not working."

This was disappointing to say the least. If there was no more voice on the magic phone at the Crooked Arms, not only did it stall our investigation, it also made me look delusional in front of the dead kids. But I hadn't just imagined that voice, had I? I had another idea.

"Morna, you try it."

"Me?"

"The phone doesn't work," Kirby insisted.

"But if the phone is something, y'know, supernatural or whatever, maybe Morna needs to talk into it. She has the connection to this house."

"Worth a shot," Tabetha said.

Morna spoke the three numbers in her quavering Scottish accent into the phone, but the line remained dead. The dead kids were certainly starting to think I was hallucinating at best, or outright lying at worst.

"Somebody's imagining things," Kirby said.

"I swear, that phone told me how to raise you from the dead!" I protested.

"Great, maybe it will tell us which horses to bet on down at the track, too," Kirby said, not realizing there were no horse-tracks for about two hours in any direction from here. "Should I put twenty dollars on Shadowfax?"

Then I remembered the second thing the telephone voice told me: that I wasn't supposed to tell anyone about the telephone. Could the voice have forsaken me because I told the dead kids? They shouldn't even count, though; they'd been dead for years!

"Give me that phone," I said, swiping it from Morna's

hands a bit more forcefully than I'd intended. "Seven. Three. Five," I said.

A long pause worried me, but after about ten seconds of me trying not to look any of the dead kids directly in the eye, a familiar hiss popped into my eardrum.

"Hello?" I said. The other dead kids looked at each other in disbelief; I think they all thought I was pretending.

"You weren't supposed . . . to tell," the voice whispered.

"I know. I'm sorry," I said, trying to place the voice. What did Yumi's cousin sound like? "I thought my dead friends would be okay, but I realize now I was wrong. Can you help me find out who killed my friend Morna MacIsaac? She lived here about a hundred years ago."

"You've been looking in the wrong place."

"I know," I said. "You mentioned that. Where should I be looking? She really needs to know."

"Third floor," the voice rasped. "The room on the right. At the nightstand, under the floorboards."

With that, the hiss stopped, the line went dead.

"You really expect us to believe you were talking to some-one?" Kirby rolled his eyes.

"I was, and it told me where to look."

"Look fer what?" Tabetha said. "I don't even know what we're lookin' fer."

"The third floor, she said. The room on the right."

"Tha's Miss Wotherspoon's room," Morna remembered. (Finally, she remembered *something*.)

Lifting my arm slowly, like a magician pulling a rabbit from his top hat, I guided the flashlight to the top of the dark-ened, cobwebbed stairs.

"I'm not going up there alone," I said.

"Chicken," Tabetha spat. She tightened her boot laces and started up the creaky steps.

"Here, take the flashlight!" I called.

"Don't need it."

The other dead kids and I stood quietly in the lobby, listening to Tabetha's heavy boots squeezing tortured noises from the wooden floors. I gestured toward the stairs, inviting any of the other dead kids to join her, but they were sticking with me. The Crooked Arms was a creepy place, even if you were already dead.

A minute later, the sound of boots stopped. Total silence followed.

"What's happening?" Morna whispered.

"I don't know," I whispered. "Why are we whispering?"

As our brief exchange ended, Tabetha let out a blood-curdling scream above. I'm not sure why sound curdles blood (does it do that to milk?), but that was an issue for another time. Perhaps a really inspired science project. I'd never heard Tabetha scream in terror before and it was truly disturbing. The whole building felt like it dropped ten degrees in temperature.

"Tabetha?!" I called out, but immediately after the scream, the rhythmic sound of her boots returned, so we all figured she must be okay. That is, until we realized the sound wasn't her boots.

As the slow drumbeat of thuds increased in volume, an object came into view at the top of the stairs, bouncing down in a series of high arcs. The object was Tabetha Scott's severed head, the eyes wide and blank, thumping down from the third floor and landing, finally, right between my black Chuck Taylors.

"Gahhh!" I have never yelled so much in my life. Even when I first met the dead kids, even when Cyril dug himself out of his grave. I immediately bolted for the front door, but Cyril and Derek held me back. Clawing at their shoulders, trying to break free, I was turned around by the two dead kids so I again faced the disembodied head of Tabetha. The head then blinked and broke into a massive smile.

"Gotcha!" she said.

I nearly punted Tabetha Scott's stupid head through the window.

"I will murder you and never stop murdering you," I muttered to Tabetha's smiling face. The other dead kids laughed like hyenas on nitrous oxide. Their high-pitched laughter made my normally pale face turn hot pink, even the side that wasn't bruised.

Once I'd forgiven my dead friends — which I wasn't even willing to call them at that point — for their unfunny nightmare-material practical joke, we all ascended the stairs to the former room of Roxanne Wotherspoon to look for, well . . . I wasn't quite sure. The voice never said *what* we'd find near the night-stand, under the floorboards, but I assumed it was important. I also wasn't sure how we'd get under the floorboards. Though I had remembered a flashlight this time around, I had neglected to bring along a crowbar.

"Any ideas on how we get under the floorboards?" I asked the assembled dead kids. Tabetha was still cradling her severed head in the crook of her arm.

"Leth make thure thereth thomething down there firth," Derek suggested. Why he needed to suggest it using so many

words with Ss in them, I'll never know. Had he never heard of synonyms?

Derek Running Water knelt in front of the night table and phased his face through the floor.

"Can you see anything?" I asked.

"Too dark."

He pulled his head out of the floor and pushed one ghostly arm through the floorboards.

"What about now? Can you feel anything?"

"No, my handth intanthible."

"I'm working with a bunch of geniuses," Kirby muttered while pacing the back wall.

"Wait," Derek said. "Thith might hurt."

In a heartbeat — me being the only one with a heartbeat present — he turned tangible again, but the effect caught his arm on either side of the floorboards. Resultingly, his hand was sliced off at the wrist, and Derek fell backward with his ragged arm stump in the air. His hand must have been trapped somewhere beneath the floor.

"What the — ?!"

"Derek!" Morna shouted.

"You okay?" Cyril asked, as Morna helped get Derek to his feet.

"Yeah, fine," he said, rubbing his stump like he was polishing a pool cue with chalk. "I can thill feel my hand and ith on top of thomething. Feelth like a book!"

"A book?" I shouted. "We need to get into the floor! We need to see what's in that book!"

"I would like to get my hand back," Derek added, raising his hand-free arm in remembrance.

"How do we get down there?" I asked.

"Why d'ya think I wear these boots?" Tabetha asked.

Tabetha Scott placed her head on top of the nightstand and began to stomp down in the middle of a floorboard, driving her heel into the beam's weakest point. The beam began to warp like a paper clip that's been bent back and forth too many times. The other kids joined in, save for Kirby, who thought his shoes were too nice for this sort of activity, and in a minute they had splintered through the wood. As with many things that happened that evening, my first thought was: Alyosha

Diamandas is not going to be happy about this. Training my flashlight on the small crevice in the floor, I could make out the silhouette of a severed hand (which I really hoped was Derek's) lying atop a book.

"My hand!" Derek exclaimed, reaching into the hole with his left appendange to retrieve his right, which he then stuffed into his back jean pocket. Once the severed hand was out of the way, I pulled out the book and turned open its pages.

"So, what is it?" Tabetha asked, still panting a bit from kicking the floor to death.

"Looks like Roxy Wotherspoon's diary."

☠

Total Sam-
demonium

That's right, readers, October and her well-meaning but quite destructive friends discovered the diary of Roxy Wotherspoon, proto-feminist and Sticksville's only suffragette. Nearly as soon as they uncovered the journal hidden beneath the floorboards, the dead kids and October returned to the Sticksville Cemetery. The dead kids had been content to stay in the Crooked Arms as long as possible, but October — knowing the propensity of realtor Alyosha Diamandas to appear at any second, like some sort of absent-minded time traveller, and realizing the damage they'd done to the building — figured the Wotherspoon diary was best analyzed far from the boarding house's vicinity.

October led the charge back to the graveyard, attempting to read the diary by flashlight as she did and often losing track of where they were headed.

"Let me thake over," Derek said. "I know the way back to the themetery." But all the other dead kids remembered Derek Running Water's "knack for direction," and thought October should remain in the navigational seat.

By the time October and the dead kids filed back through the wrought-iron gates of the cemetery, she'd found the entries dated near the end of 1914, when Morna MacIsaac had died. Cyril re-opened their usual tomb-cum-meeting-place and they sat in a wide circle, with October and Roxy Wotherspoon's diary as its centre.

"I don't understan'," Tabetha admitted. "I mean, didn't we figger out it was the Chinese guy, Sam, that killed Morna? The one covered in blood? How come we're lookin' at this lady's diary then?"

Concentrating on anything Tabetha said proved difficult for October. After all, Tabetha was still currently speaking through her severed head, which was resting in the lap of her headless body. Still, her question was a fair one. Morna had a vivid memory of the Chinese launderer, Sam Cheng, covered in blood, and hadn't mentioned Roxanne Wotherspoon, her upstairs neighbour at the Crooked Arms, at all. Roxanne, or Roxy to most, was Sticksville's resident suffragette, in addition to being one of the town's only schoolteachers — a deadly combination in the eyes of many of 1914 Sticksville's more, say, *traditional* residents. Wotherspoon was the head of the Sticksville Suffrage Squad (S.S.S.). Tragically, she was the sole member of the S.S.S. Despite her best efforts to involve her students' mothers and fellow teachers, the suffrage movement in Sticksville remained a solo endeavour. But while her political leanings may have made her seem dangerous to some in Sticksville at the time, October and the dead kids didn't think her capable of harming a child. Sam Cheng, who had been arrested for sabotage, still seemed the best bet.

"I do what the phone tells me to do," October explained, flipping through the pages of the diary to a relevant date. "The voice hasn't steered me wrong yet."

"But what about Sam?" Morna asked, leaning forward on her palms.

"He's still the prime suspect," October said. "But we don't have his diary. Just Roxanne Wotherspoon's, and I'm thinking we might find a clue in her entries from the time around Sam's arrest and your death. Do you remember anything about this lady, Morna?"

Of course Morna remembered Roxy Wotherspoon. Morna MacIsaac idolized Roxy Wotherspoon: she lived on her own and had gorgeous brown hair to her shoulders and long leather gloves and dresses that were probably made in Paris or London or a *city*, at least. Her name had an X and a Y in it, for goodness sake!

She was everything her own mother was not. Roxy frequently travelled to Toronto, the big city, on weekends, while Morna accompanied her mother as she scrubbed toilets and dusted the corners of the Coopers' near-mansion. You can understand why Roxy Wotherspoon seemed like Beyoncé to Morna MacIsaac, even if they lived in the same crummy boarding house.

"Yeh," Morna admitted. "I liked Miss Wotherspoon. She was always nice t'me. She had such pretty dresses."

"Okay, well, let's see what she had to say in the month that you died." A grim declaration if ever there was one. October took a deep breath before starting to read aloud Roxy's century-old words.

☠

And so, through several diary entries, October revealed to the dead kids a story about Sam Cheng and why Morna saw him covered in blood. I'm sure October Schwartz (using Roxy Wotherspoon's words) did a perfectly serviceable version of this tale of urban unrest and woe, but you, accustomed to the subtleties, vivid detail, and range of emotion in my narration, would find something lacking in this rather pedestrian record. As such, I'll take on the task of recounting the diary entry dated December 13, 1914.

According to Roxy Wotherspoon, a silent snow fell on Sticksville that night. All snow is silent, really, but there was no wind, so even the sound of wind, which people might normally associate with snow, was absent. (Aren't you glad you're not hearing this from October?)

Roxy Wotherspoon was busy in her room. With the oil lamp on, she used some of the art supplies she'd collected in the past few weeks to make a sign for an upcoming rally at the provincial legislature in Toronto. Dipping her paintbrush into a half-filled jar of India ink, she wrote one of the suffragettes' slogans, *Women Bring All Voters into the World*, on a bright white placard. While finishing the final swoop of the D, a piercing cry, like that of an alley cat, startled her. Dropping the damp brush into a glass of water she'd set out for just such a situation, she looked to the window, assuming someone had left it open — the noise was that loud — but the window was closed. Given the frigid temperature outside, the closed window was not surprising. The yowling persisted, becoming something like a low mewling. Every now and then, a sharp cry would pop up, like the audio equivalent of toasted bread.

The most obvious explanation was that the sound was coming from a cat, but Roxy's own cat was safe and warm inside, nestled at the foot of her bed.

It was true: Roxanne Wotherspoon, living on the third floor, was a cliché before her time. Her blue-grey cat, Athena, was more often found rooting through the garbage cans behind the boarding house or prowling the back door of the local pub, the Bishop and Castle, than in Roxy's room. The yowling from outside *did* sound a lot like a lonely cat. Perhaps another neighbourhood cat had been locked out in the snow.

Roxy opened the door to her room to see if she could hear the sound any better, or perhaps see if anyone else in the Crooked Arms had taken note of the awful sound. Across the hall, Dr. Alfred Pain, *Titanic* survivor, had his own door open. Still seated at his desk, he leaned back so Roxy could only see his head and upper torso, along with the book he held in his hands.

"Do you hear that, Dr. Pain?" she asked. "Sounds like an animal in considerable pain."

The doctor smiled. "I'm sure it's just a cat feeling the cold, looking for food."

"Shouldn't someone do something?" she asked.

"If you're really concerned, why don't you go outside and retrieve it?" Pain said. "I'm sure you could keep the cat in your apartment overnight. You do like cats, don't you?"

Wotherspoon grumbled as she scampered down the stairs to the front lobby, wrestling with her winter coat as she descended. She passed the landlord's longcase clock, showing a time of eleven, and noticed the front door had been left open. Immediately outside, on the front porch, was the young daughter of the Scottish family (that's Morna MacIsaac, FYI), shivering and staring into the darkened street.

"What are you doing out here, Morna?" Roxy asked.

"I was going t'find that cat," Morna said. "M'brother Boyd an' I thought it might have been yers."

"It's not. Athena is upstairs."

"Now I think I might be too scared t'go out there."

"Why don't we go together?" Roxy suggested and took our Morna MacIsaac by the hand, which was always tangible back then.

The meowing was louder outside; Roxy and Morna could hear it emanating from just yards beyond the Crooked Arms. Darkness surrounded the lit boarding house in every direction and despite some bravado, Roxy later confessed in her diary she was hesitant to venture too far. See, there weren't as many streetlights in 1914 as there are now, so when I say it was dark out, I mean place-a-garbage-bag-over-your-head dark. Just as the two were screwing up the courage to investigate the sound, the sound came to them.

The yowling was not, unfortunately, coming from a lost cat, but instead coming from a man. From the women's neighbour in fact: Sam Cheng. Sam was crawling toward them in his rumpled navy work clothes. He was bleeding from his head and the blood had stained an amorphous shape down his chest. He did not appear able to stand on his own. It looked like Sam Cheng had been placed inside a rock tumbler but because he was a man and not a rock, instead of being polished to a fine smoothness, he was quite severely injured. All this is a very florid way of saying Sam Cheng had been beat up something fierce.

Morna raced over to Sam just as he collapsed to the dirt road and howled in pain. Roxy didn't know what to do! As Morna tried to wedge herself under Mr. Cheng's arm while he again attempted to hoist himself off the ground, Roxy raced through the light snow to help them. Mr. Cheng had about a hundred pounds on Morna MacIsaac, and not much fewer on Roxy, so they'd need to work together. Lifting him was no easy task. Somehow, the two of them managed to get him upright, and they very slowly, very painfully (for Sam) limped toward the Crooked Arms.

"Who did this t'ye, Mr. Cheng?" Morna asked. It was obvious to even a child like Morna that these wounds weren't the result of some unfortunate accident.

"Your father's friends," he huffed.

Roxy could see Sam Cheng's blood seeping onto Morna's dress.

"Yesterday, they come to my laundry. Threaten me," he said with some effort. "They not like my laundry. Say it hurt their wives' laundry business."

Roxy had heard the phrase "cough up a lung" before, but before this moment she never really figured she'd have to witness it live.

"Tonight, the men come by laundry as I close," he said, terror still fresh in his eyes. "They come with bats and bricks."

Roxy was too afraid to ask Mr. Cheng if Morna's father, William MacIsaac, had been among the mob that had beaten him. Mrs. MacIsaac didn't even have a laundry business, but Roxy also knew what kind of person Mr. MacIsaac was, having confronted him a few times over women's suffrage, and knew how sharply his personality could transform after a night with his so-called friends at the Bishop and Castle.

"Try not to speak, Mr. Cheng," Roxy panted, lifting her neighbour up the wooden stairs. "Morna, think we can get him to his room? I'll get Dr. Pain to look at him."

"I should get Mr. Rasmussen," Morna said. She reasoned her Swedish landlord would have more luck hoisting the beaten tenant up the stairs.

"He's out," Roxy coughed. "Hasn't been in all night. You'll have to help me."

"All right," Morna gulped, looking to the flight of stairs before them. "Ready whenever ye are."

Roxy left Mr. Cheng with Morna on the second floor to retrieve Dr. Pain. She only hoped, pounding on the doctor's door, that he was the kind of doctor who could fix up her neighbour; that he wasn't secretly a dentist or something useless like that.

Less than a minute afterward, Dr. Alfred Pain ran down the steps following Roxy to where she'd left the MacIsaac girl and Mr. Cheng. The doctor groaned at the sight of his downstairs neighbour. Sam Cheng's assailants had certainly provided him, as a physician, with a challenge.

The three of them walked Mr. Cheng into his room. The interior was about the saddest thing Roxy had ever seen, and she lived in a pretty sad apartment herself. They lay him down on his mattress on the floor, no frame or bed to speak of, and the doctor asked Morna to fetch a bowl of water.

The girl went over to the washbasin and filled it with some water from the jug beside it. The walls had no decoration, no adornment. The only thing in the room Roxy could see that could not be considered bare-bones furniture was a tiny framed photograph of a Chinese woman. When Morna returned to the doctor with the water, she asked, "Who d'ye think tha' woman in the picture is?"

"My wife," Sam groaned.

"Try not to talk, Sam," Dr. Pain suggested, dabbing the blood from his forehead with a cloth.

"Yer wife?"

It had never occurred to Roxy (or Morna, apparently) that Mr. Cheng might have a wife, that she might live thousands of miles away in China, that the head tax prevented him from bringing her to Sticksville to live with him until he could save $500, and that his laundry business was his plan to save that $500. Roxy realized she barely knew anything about the others in the Crooked Arms, that she was sharing a floor and one wall with a near-complete stranger. This realization, combined with Mr. Cheng looking like he went three rounds in the ring with a grizzly bear, made her feel just awful.

"Do you think the abrasions are serious, doctor?" Roxy asked him.

"Abrasions? What now?"

"You know, his cuts?"

"Oh, we'll see," the doctor said. "I can take it from here. You two did a good thing tonight."

And while it troubled Roxy to no end that this doctor didn't seem to know what an abrasion was, she left him to his work, hoping his medical expertise was greater than his vocabulary.

☠

"An' that's it?" Tabetha asked, disappointed.

"Guess so," October replied, closing the journal. "Roxy was concerned the doctor didn't know what abrasions were, but apparently Sam Cheng was patched up enough to commit sabotage. Morna," she said, turning to the Scottish girl whose face had turned even whiter than normal. "Does any of this ring a bell?"

"Ring a bell?" Cyril repeated, extremely confused.

"Do you remember any of it," October clarified.

"Oh my goodness," Morna gasped, staring into space. "I remember all a' that. That's why Sam was covered in blood. He was beaten up at the laundry."

As delighted as October was that Morna was beginning to remember things, she was also disheartened that their Chinese saboteur no longer seemed like a plausible killer. Why would Sam Cheng murder the poor girl who brought him to the doctor after he'd been savagely attacked? Just seemed like bad manners.

"What doeth ith thay about Tham Chenth's arretht?" Derek, whose front teeth everyone hoped would grow back very soon, asked.

"Nothing," October said, flipping forward several pages. "It's not mentioned by Roxy at all."

"Is it missing pages?" Kirby asked.

"What does it say about my death?" Morna asked, her eyes rimmed with red. "Can ye see? Does Miss Wotherspoon talk about my death?"

October slowly thumbed through the pages of the Wotherspoon diary. Of course, it mentioned Morna MacIsaac's death. Though she seemed pretty willy-nilly about including important things like front-page-worthy stories of saboteur arrests in her diary, Roxy must have felt a connection with Morna because there was an entry in which the suffragette seemed like she was trying to understand what happened that night and how it tied to Morna's body being found in the snow outside the Bishop and Castle early that December morning (if it did at all).

What Roxy did remember was an unbelievable commotion the night before Morna's death. From her room on the third floor, she heard what sounded like a game of dodgeball being played on the floor below. The diary didn't use those exact words (dodgeball hadn't been popularized yet); basically, she heard a ruckus. When she took the stairs to investigate, she found the MacIsaacs' door wide open and no one inside, save the youngest boy, Boyd. Boyd was ill and only eight, and it was very unlike the MacIsaacs to leave him home alone. If Mrs. MacIsaac had to work late, cleaning up the Cooper House, she'd either leave the eldest boy, Rory (who was now enlisted in the war effort and training at nearby Fort Hannover), or more likely Morna with him.

Morna couldn't be found that night, and when Roxy approached the little red-nosed, red-haired boy to ask where his parents, where anyone in his family had gone, he couldn't say. His watery eyes were stretched wide with shock; at first he couldn't speak, even when Roxy (maybe against her better judgment) shook him by the shoulders. And after the vigorous shaking, Boyd kept saying "735, 735," over and over again. This was the Crooked Arms' phone number, but Roxy could make no sense of why the

boy was repeating it, and why he seemed to have no idea where his sister or mother were. The police, evidently, could make no sense of the numbers either. The following day, when they found Morna's body, they interviewed everyone in the boarding house. Roxy informed them of what she knew, but Morna MacIsaac's death remained forever unsolved.

"Ho-lee thmoke," Derek marvelled. He was clutching his severed hand up against his right stump.

October, too, was astounded. Those three numbers were also how she communicated with the voice on the telephone. They'd been scrawled on the walls of the Crooked Arms. What did they mean? Was October talking to the ghost of Roxy Wotherspoon through the lobby telephone? Or to Boyd MacIsaac?

"Morna, are you okay?" October asked.

Morna, sitting in front of the tomb's central coffin, looked like she'd fallen backward onto a bed of nails. To hear someone else's account of your own untimely end is something no person should have to experience.

"I think," she gasped, "I need some time ta' meself."

☠

Maintaining Radio Silence

As you might have guessed would happen at some point, my dad caught me sneaking back into the house at three in the morning. Of course, this was just days after he'd forbidden cemetery visits, forbidden travel from the house without adult accompaniment altogether. I didn't notice Dad was waiting in his pyjamas and slippers, straight out of a sitcom from the 1950s (he might as well have been smoking a pipe, too), until *after* I had gingerly slid open the door and placed one wet sneaker onto the linoleum kitchen floor.

"Have a good night out?" he yawned, crossing his arms across his chest.

"Dad!" I was surprised to see him. Not, like, you have a long-lost identical twin surprised, but I was startled. "Hey . . . I was just . . . trying to break up a fight between some noisy raccoons."

I must have snuck out of my house at night at least three dozen times by this point, but I still hadn't constructed one mildly plausible excuse. I added it to my mental to-do list.

"October." Dad's exasperation was at an all-time high. "I didn't even like you spending time in that cemetery at night before I knew what this town is like. Now we know there are psychotic history teachers and violent phone-booth tippers to worry about. I think the past couple months have *proven* it's not safe for you to be out there this late."

"I know, I know," I said. "I shouldn't be out there, but I'm just working on my book."

Dad grunted while I prayed to whoever was making all these dead people come to life that Dad didn't call my bluff. Skyler McGriff still had my composition book. He rubbed his face up and down with his long fingers. "I suppose I should be glad you're not out there smoking."

"I swear, Dad, I'm not doing anything wrong out there. And it's perfectly safe."

"October," he said, leaning on the kitchen counter. "Can you try to see things from my perspective? Just for once? My daughter was attacked in a phone booth and the people responsible haven't been caught. I can't spend my nights patrolling the hallway just to make sure you don't sneak out of your bedroom."

"You don't have to," I whined. Not a proud moment.

"I can't," he said. "October, you know I love you. I just don't want to see anything worse happen to you than has already happened to your face and hand."

"I know, Dad." My dad was good guy, and not even particularly harsh as a parent — at least, not when compared to Yumi's dad — so I felt bad about putting him through all this worry. But I figured that it was also part of the territory when you're running a secret detective agency.

"Also, keep in mind if I see you sneak in again like this, you're not allowed to go into the cemetery until you're eighteen. Understand?"

"Yes."

"Unless, y'know, I *die* or something . . . then you can visit," he grimly relented. "To see my grave."

"Fair enough. Now, can I go to sleep?"

Dad had made his ultimatum: if I made any more evening graveyard visits, I would never be allowed there, day or night, until I left home. Given I had five dead kids' deaths still to solve, combined with my less than perfect track record with sneaking in and out undetected, I had a feeling that was an ultimatum that would be put to the test.

Moments after I took my seat in resident Twi-hard Mr. Santuzzi's math class, Skyler McGriff laid the *Two Knives, One Thousand Demons* composition book on my desk.

"I think you'll find I've returned it in one piece," he said,
smiling his terrible grin that probably made Yumi's heart melt
or soar or something else hearts don't really do.

"Thanks."

Having *Two Knives, One Thousand Demons* back in my pos-
session was more of a relief than I'd expected. Before I had
handed it him, I'd completely forgotten the book didn't just
contain the ongoing adventures of Olivia de Kellerman, but
also a pile of notes from October (the month, not me — ha!)
when I was researching Mr. O'Shea's death. If Skyler McGriff
had read it with any degree of scrutiny, he'd probably call the
cops to send me to psycho-jail.

"You're very talented," he said. "Perhaps not so much at
math, but that story was epic. I can't wait to see what happens
at the swimming pool."

Crack about my math skills aside — I may not have been
top of the class, but I wasn't some mathematical knuckle-
dragger — I couldn't help appreciate the flattery. And just like
that, I began to see what Yumi saw in Skyler McGriff. I felt
terrible for judging him so harshly earlier by his clothes and
hairstyle.

"Your descriptions of demon evisceration? Perfection," he
declared. This guy was all right. A big improvement over his
younger brother. The McGriff parents should have quit while
they were ahead. I was concerned: if Skyler *had* read *Two Knives,
One Thousand Demons* thoroughly, as his reference to swimming
pools suggested, then he'd have seen all my notes about the Mr.
O'Shea case. But if he hadn't really read the whole book, he
was just lying to make me feel good. So I tried something out —
they don't call me a detective for nothing.

"How did you feel about the climactic battle inside the
doughnut factory?" I asked.

"Oh, that worked really well," he said. "I love how the bitterness of the fight and blood shed by the demons, uh . . . was juxtaposed against the sweetness of the . . . um, surrounding doughnuts."

What a liar! There was no doughnut factory scene. He hadn't read the book at all, which was a relief. I much preferred his empty flattery than having him think I was some paranoid delusional taking notes on all my teachers. The school therapist already thought that. I didn't need to give him any disciples.

"Thanks!" I said, smiling probably more than I should have. Sometimes I forget I'm goth.

"No, thank *you*," he said and gave me the double-guns, which made me upchuck a little. "By the way, how is your little friend Yumi doing? She's not going to be leaving town or anything? I hope an incident so horrible like that doesn't, you know, turn her family off the whole neighbourhood."

Yumi wasn't going to like being called my little friend, but her brain would surely liquefy if I told her Skyler McGriff was expressing concern for her actual well-being.

"Oh, Yumi's pretty resilient," I said, hoping I was making her sound totally fierce, instead of like an overcooked steak. "I'm sure something like a monstrous hate crime won't scare her."

"Glad to hear."

Then, just when I thought the torture of Mr. Santuzzi's class was about to begin, it was interrupted by something far worse: the Sticksville Central Student Council. There was a boy hovering at the front of the class wearing his baseball cap backward (which is apparently still a thing). He stood there with the girl I'd been calling Goose Neck since my first day of school. She was a member of Ashlie Salmons's entourage, so I didn't think I had any moral obligation to learn her name. The two of them were there to tell us about candy cane grams.

Our student council seemed dead set on ruining every single holiday with some form of terrible organized fun. First it was the apple bobbing on Hallowe'en and now, the candy cane grams had arrived like a nuclear warhead of humbug. I'm sure some public shaming ritual was lined up for Valentine's Day.

"Candy cane grams," the Student Council leader, who was named Zogon (I think), explained, "are the perfect way to tell your secret crush you like him or her as a holiday treat — for both of you!"

To me, a girl with more dead friends than living ones, this pointless announcement seemed like just another way for the popular kids to feel even more popular, and the loner ones to feel even worse. But that was the general purpose of a student council, as far as I could tell.

"Remember, you have until Tuesday to order your candy cane grams," Goose Neck, who I'm sure must have introduced herself with her real name, reminded us, as though this weren't the first all of us (save Zogon) were hearing about these things. Maybe they had mentioned it earlier and I hadn't paid any attention. "They're just three dollars per candy cane gram!"

First of all, three dollars seemed pretty steep when an anonymous note dropped in a locker was totally free. Second of all, "per candy cane gram"? Hold up, player. Who's planning to send out multiple messages?

As Goose Neck and Zogon walked the aisles and passed out copies of the order form, I immediately categorized the paper slip as something I would shove in my bag and try hard to forget. Then I had an idea: these candy cane grams could be useful. If, by Tuesday, I had a few suspects for the phone booth incident, perhaps I could draw the real culprit out with these anonymous messages . . . somehow. That was something a detective might do, wasn't it? I almost raised my hand to ask if the candy cane grams could be sent to teachers, until I realized that would earn me years of ostracization and even more appointments with Dr. Lagostina, the school therapist.

I'd have to save my lunch money, just in case.

☠

It was Hanukkah, a timely fact I learned from Yumi's radio show at lunch, her first since their notorious Mr. Santuzzi special. In retrospect, it seemed a little crass for Dad to get angry with me on the first night of Hanukkah, the annual Jewish celebration of familial unity (as far as I understood it; I think the menorah candles represented family members?), but seeing as how Dad was the most non-religious of non-religious Jews and we'd celebrated Christmas (possibly in memory of my Unitarian and Christmas-loving mother) ever since I could remember, I couldn't blame him for not observing the occasion.

DJ Yu-sless and Stacey Kasem were back at the microphone, and to most people it was something of a letdown. Gone was the merciless needling of teachers. Some students had even taken informal wagers on which teacher would be next for parody: maybe the flighty Mrs. Tischmann, or Mr. Humboldt, the comically elderly social studies teacher who wore kilts more than was warranted. (Since we didn't live in Scotland, in my mind, it was *never* warranted.) Still, I enjoyed their toned-down show, even though it meant another solo lunch in the cafeteria. Yumi was much more entertaining on the air than she had been on their first show, though Stacey spoke even less than usual, probably due to the numerous cuts on his face.

"We've got a very exciting announcement today, Sticksville Central," Yumi boomed over the P.A. "And, no, it's not that we're trading Ashlie Salmons to New Hammersmith for four soiled gym mats."

Some of the loser kids like me cracked up at that, but even at a distance, I could feel the withering stare from Ashlie and her friends.

"Shh, Yumi!" Stacey whispered (over the mic), reminding her of Ms. Fenstermacher's warning.

"Yes, anyway, the one, the only, the best Orthodox Jewish punk band of all time — The Plotzdam Conference — will be playing our stupid little holiday pageant on December 20, giving it the Hanukkah representation it most sorely lacked."

Yumi, impressed with the addition of an actual, real band to the holiday pageant, immediately blasted The Plotzdam Conference's "Keepin' Kosher" into the cafeteria. For my part, I remembered that their clarinet player was Mrs. Tischmann's son, so convincing one of Yumi's favourite bands to play our school holiday pageant probably wasn't quite as difficult as Yumi imagined. Still, I was happy.

Ashlie Salmons dropped by my cafeteria table with the full Phantom Moustache lineup, just as the song moved into the clarinet solo. She *would* visit me while I was eating lunch all alone.

"Zombie Tramp," she called, then flicked her perfectly smooth auburn hair toward the closest loudspeaker. "Think you can convince your ugly friends to turn this crap music off?"

"I don't know, Ashlie." I swallowed a lump of peanut butter sandwich. "I would, but I fear they'd just start talking about trading you for school supplies again."

Boston Davis snickered at the back of the group.

"Devin," Ashlie shouted, clearly outraged. "Are you going to let this fat vampire talk to me like that?"

"Uh . . . this seems like a chick fight kind of thing."

"That should be *you* in the radio booth right now, and we should be listening to *your* band. Not this music for freaks."

"Oh, yeah," Devin said, realizing he should dislike me a lot more than he was currently managing. "You're the Chinese girl's friend."

"Japanese," I said. "And not even, really. Canadian."

"Whatever," he said, displeased to have been corrected. "Just tell her to watch out. I hear she won't have a radio show for long, and guess who's next on the waiting list?"

I didn't have to guess; obviously it was Devin McGriff, which made me almost certain he was behind the phone-booth tipping. He certainly wasn't fond of Yumi or Stacey, and he *had* just made the mistake of calling Yumi Chinese. Maybe the whole Phantom Moustache band was in on it, though it didn't really make sense that they'd ask Stacey to replace their drummer. Were they keeping their enemies close? If so, that was some serious next-level Sun Tzu stuff going on.

As if in answer to Devin McGriff's vaguely menacing question, Yumi cut The Plotzdam Conference's song short and took to the microphone again. "Sorry to interrupt, listeners, but Ms. Fenstermacher is here with a special announcement."

"Thank you, Yumi," Ms. Fenstermacher's voice crackled through the P.A. I couldn't imagine how Stacey was holding it together in such close quarters with his dream-date teacher. "Unfortunately, I don't have good news. Effective immediately, Radio Sticksville will be going off the air. The radio program will be on indefinite hiatus until further notice, as decided by the school administration. That is all."

Bombshell: dropped. The cafeteria groaned with such force, I felt like everyone had been simultaneously kicked in the stomach (but that was probably impossible). I couldn't believe Ms. Fenstermacher announced it mid-radio-show. The school administration must have sent her to do their dirty work, knowing she was one of the more liked teachers at the school. I smelled Mr. Santuzzi behind this. That is to say, I smelled aftershave.

Ashlie and the Phantom Moustache gang were still assembled around my table, which put me in a very dangerous position. As Boston Davis put it:

"Your stupid friend Yumi ruined everything!"

"You know this is because of her Santuzzi show," Devin concluded.

They then turned from me and began to talk amongst themselves. I wasn't invited to this portion of the conversation; they were probably too angry even to look in my direction. This was a troubling development. Seemed unfair that Yumi was squarely getting the blame, as Stacey was certainly involved, and Mr. Santuzzi seemed most directly responsible for the radio show's cancellation.

Moments later, one of the last DJs of Sticksville Central, Stacey, walked through the cafeteria double doors, looking for yours truly. In some ways, this was like having a live grenade dropped in my lap. Stacey strode through the cafeteria, oblivious to the waves of frustration rising like cartoon stink lines from all his new fellow band members, and took a seat beside me. The dream of playing their favourite music for all to hear was dead. I could tell they wanted to rip Yumi and Stacey apart for bringing an end to the radio program, but at the same time, Stacey and I were recent victims of a terrible crime, so they didn't have strong words for him.

"Did you hear about The Plotzdam Conference? Awesome, eh?"

His comment cut some of the tension around the cafeteria table, mainly because people seemed to generally like Stacey better than me (unfairly), just because he's a boy.

"Yeah, that's great, Stacey." I was wondering if there was a way I could subtly convince him to walk me out of the cafeteria like a secret service agent, away from Ashlie and her clique.

"Apparently they heard about the phone booth, and about how we got all cut up, and the racist message, and they want to play the pageant in, like, solidarity. They said they were with us in our 'fight against racism.'"

"How do you know all that?" Boston Davis asked.

"I'm on their email list."

"Hey," I said, finally having an idea. Surrounded by Devin and Ashlie and their friends, I felt a bit like a half-eaten wildebeest next door to a lioness's bachelorette party. "Why don't we visit Yumi *right now?*"

I stood up from the table, gathered my belongings, and deposited my garbage where it belonged.

"Sure," Stacey agreed, clueless as always. The blowtorch stare of Devin McGriff followed us with every step.

We were just a few paces from the cafeteria doors, almost free of Devin McGriff and Ashlie Salmons for another day when Preston Sinclair jogged up to us in his loafers.

"Wait up, Stacey," he called.

We (I, reluctantly) turned to face him.

"Sunday night, Boston is having a birthday party. We're going skating on Trundleduck Pond. You should join us; it would give you a chance to hang out with the band."

I was so confused and upset. Shouldn't Preston hate Stacey

just as much as Yumi? Stacey was really getting an unfair pass.

"Okay," he said. "I'll see if October and Yumi want to come, too."

"That's probably not the best idea," Preston winced as he said it, tried not to look in my direction at all.

"You think maybe they don't have skates?"

Stacey was even more clueless than I thought. Did he not realize Devin and Ashlie Salmons would *most certainly* be at Boston Davis's party, and that they were most likely to greet Yumi and me with a skate to the face, especially after this stupid radio stuff?

"No," Preston laughed and coughed at the same time. "You're cool, but I think Devin and Ashlie will probably want to sharpen their skates on your friends' faces."

That was a better line than the one I'd thought up. I was a little disappointed that Preston Sinclair — a *bassist* — had a quicker wit than mine.

"Yeah," Stacey said. "But Yumi and October are my friends. And I'm also the only drummer in our grade who can play a kit. So if you want me to come to your weird Archie's Pals 'n' Gals ice-skating party, I'm bringing them."

Preston Sinclair just stood there adjusting his glasses to make sure, I guess, their temporary drummer wasn't, in fact, some strange, vaguely insulting mirage. I accompanied Stacey to Yumi's locker and was reminded why, while really strange, he could sometimes — very occasionally — be my hero.

☠

Fittingly enough, given Ashlie Salmons and the members of Phantom Moustache had made me feel like garbage over lunch, I spent that night with the dead kids picking through garbage in the dumpsters behind my high school. Derek, Tabetha, and I were in the recycling dumpster to the right, largely filled with paper. Cyril and Morna clawed their way through the other dumpster, which had more . . . "garbage juice," let's call it.

Waist deep in cold trash, my hands freezing though double-mitted in regular and work gloves, I barely remembered how we reasoned this project was the best use of our time. "Remind me again," I said, tossing aside some file folders. "Why are we doing this? Wouldn't it be better if I called that number on the phone again?"

"Speak up!" Cyril shouted. "These metal bins are very echoey!"

I repeated my question.

"Oh, I don't think I like that phone," Morna said, wiping some wet garbage from her forehead.

"I think Morna's mystery could use a night off," Cyril said, pantaloons obscured by the trash in the second dumpster. "I think we were all spooked a little by Miss Wotherspoon's diary; perhaps a night off will help calm all our nerves. Especially those of young Morna."

"Thank ye, Cyril."

"Tank ye, Cy-ril," Tabetha mocked, clasping her hands and fluttering her eyelids.

"Besides, you can call the telephone at any time," Kirby, clean and garbage-free, shouted from the pavement outside.

"We're trying to make the best use of our dead talents. That's why we're searching your school garbage receptacles for some kind of evidence of your phone booth assault."

"Why aren't *you* digging?" I asked.

"Because I'm wearing nice clothes," Kirby answered.

"You're *dead!*" I shouted, fashioning a little megaphone with my cupped work gloves.

"Shh," Cyril said. "You don't want to alert anyone that we are in their refuse."

"Can't one of you just, like, fade through all this garbage and see if there's any yellow paint here?" I asked. Seemed like a reasonable question to me. "Wouldn't *that* be the best use of your talents? Also, I'm starting to smell like vomit or something. That's going to be a hard smell to get out."

"Good idea," Derek said. Thankfully, his teeth had fully grown back, as had his hand. It must have been depressing, having your hand reattached and the first thing you do with it is dig through someone else's trash. Derek, Tabetha, Morna, and Cyril disappeared into the massive pile of junk. Kirby supervised (I guess) from the pavement outside.

A transparent brown hand emerged from between a pile of incorrectly photocopied tests and a crumpled banker's box, holding a used can of Krylon yellow spray paint. Tabetha crawled from the trash, holding the can aloft like some kind of dead, garbage-strewn Statue of Liberty.

"This it?" Tabetha asked.

I took the can in my gloves, the dripping yellow excess crusted to the sides of the aluminum cylinder. "Looks like it."

"Now we can dust it for fingerprints," Derek cheerfully announced, still waist deep in garbage.

"Yay!" Morna shouted.

"Dust it for fingerprints? I don't know how to do that," I said. "Do you?"

Given that most of them lived before using fingerprints to identify criminals was a thing, I knew the answer was going to be no. Also, it would be weird for a fourteen-year-old to have fingerprinted someone, no matter when the process had been invented.

"Can't you just look it up on a computer or something?" Derek asked, exasperated.

"No."

"Then what will you do with it?" Cyril asked.

"I was just planning to go around to hardware stores to see if anyone remembered selling it."

Okay. So I wasn't Sherlock Holmes, but it was an idea. The dead kids sullenly extricated themselves from the garbage and we all trudged back to the cemetery.

☠

11

Listen All, Y'all, It's Sabotage

Despite October Schwartz's very astute assertion that she was not, as if there were some confusion, the world's greatest detective (who, for the record, is Batman, not Sherlock Holmes, I recognize), she did have some tricks left up her sleeve. That Saturday morning, she awoke with a full day ahead of her, already planned out. Like some kind of fork used mainly to spear fries, her plan had two prongs: to bring Roxy Wotherspoon's diary to the Sticksville Museum in the hope that Ms. Fenstermacher could provide some information about the fate of Sam Cheng in return, and to search local hardware stores until she figured out who recently purchased yellow spray paint and if that person was someone she knew. (She was hoping either Devin McGriff, Ashlie Salmons, or possibly some other random member of Phantom Moustache had recently run up a bill on yellow spray paint and camouflaged tarps. Though now that she thought of it, the camo-print tarp really did scream Santuzzi.)

The pressing concerns of the late volleyball season meant that Mr. Schwartz was occupied for most of the afternoon with a Saturday practice. The thought of spending the Saturday at school made October Schwartz's head swim. Even if the Saturday had been as hijink-filled and revealing of the human condition as that Saturday in *The Breakfast Club*, she couldn't have imagined it would be worth it. Besides, if the film was to be believed, someone like October would end up getting a makeover and kissing Emilio Estevez, so it's just as well she wasn't on the volleyball team.

October's first stop was the Sticksville Museum, which she no longer had trouble finding. With confidence, she strode through the door and turned to her left, expecting to find Ms. Fenstermacher. Instead, a much older woman with a hairdo that resembled an elaborate cupcake topping sat at the front desk. Her glasses, remarkably, were nearly identical to Ms. Fenstermacher's. (I suppose the possibility she was a future version of Ms. F who time-travelled to the past was out of the question.)

"May I help you, young lady?" the woman behind the desk inquired. October was only ever called young lady when she'd accidentally lit something on fire.

"I was looking for Ms. Fenstermacher?" October said, not entirely sure herself. "Is she in today?"

"Oh, yes," she said. "You must be one of her students. Look at you, all made up like a skeleton. Let me call her down."

The older woman pressed a few buttons on the phone on her desk while October sulked.

"Your name?"

"October."

"You must be unhappy eleven months of the year, ha!" The woman laughed at her own joke before informing Ms. Fenstermacher, via the phone, that an October was here to see her. October could only raise her eyebrow. She should have told that woman that her October hadn't been particularly swift either, what with the teacher death and abduction.

Taking a bit longer than either the museum docent or October would have liked, Ms. Fenstermacher eventually came down the stairs, dressed in a festive sweater and jeans. Jokingly, she raised her fingers in a cross, as if warding off some evil spirit. She probably wouldn't have done that if she'd known how much October was teased for being, alternately, a fat vampire or Zombie Tramp.

"If you're here about the Sticksville radio program," she warned, "I'm sorry, but my hands are tied. I really can't help your friends. Mr. Santuzzi was adamant that the radio station was becoming a forum for disrespect and bullying — targeting both him and some of the other students — and Principal Hamilton agreed."

"Oh, I'm not here about that," October said.

134

"Phew," Ms. Fenstermacher said, dropping her hands. "So, I won't have to check if you've put sugar in my gas tank?"

"I don't think so."

(Seriously readers, never do that to anyone unless they really, really deserve it.)

"What brings you to the Sticksville Museum then?"

October saw no reason to delay the big reveal, so she pulled her backpack around her chest and dug out Roxy Wotherspoon's long-lost (one can imagine) diary. "I found this."

One must be careful not to overstate the historic importance of this diary. It's not as if October had uncovered the first written draft of Abraham Lincoln's Gettysburg Address. She had found a relatively obscure suffragette's diary. But to a local historian like Ms. Fenstermacher, for October to say she'd just "found" this document was akin to saying she'd just stumbled across the equation for cold fusion.

Ms. Fenstermacher lowered her glasses. "Do you know what this is?"

October, wisely, chose to play dumb. She often made this

decision and at times secretly wondered if everyone thought she really was unintelligent, given how often she pretended she was.

"October, this is the personal diary of Roxy Wotherspoon, Sticksville's most famous suffragette!" Fenstermacher chirped. "She's right over there on the wall of famous Sticksvillians. And this is *her diary*! This is amazing!"

"Yeah, my friends and I were just hanging out in the Crooked Arms and we —"

"That decrepit old boarding house?"

"Um, yeah."

"What were you doing there?" Ms. Fenstermacher was concerned, clearly, that her students were frequenting the biggest wooden death trap in town, but she couldn't hide the delight on her face. "Never mind. I don't want to know. Do you think this is real? I'll have to contact the Sticksville Historic Society."

"Okay," October said. For someone who worked at a museum, the woman at the front desk certainly seemed unfazed by this major Sticksville historical watershed moment happening just inches from her face.

"Don't worry," the history teacher said, tucking the diary under her arm. "I'll give you credit for the discovery. One hundred percent. I can't believe this is happening! And I was just looking into the history of the Crooked Arms, too."

"Yeah," October said, interrupting her teacher's unbridled glee. One half-expected Ms. Fenstermacher to throw on Puff Daddy's "It's All About the Benjamins," tear out the pages of Roxy Wotherspoon's diary one by one and make it rain. "Actually, I was wondering if you found out anything about that Chinese saboteur, Sam Cheng."

"Follow me," Ms. Fenstermacher said, and she took October by her free arm as they ascended the stairs to the second floor of the Cooper House.

☠

Ms. Fenstermacher led October through a few rooms on the museum's second floor until they'd reached one that was distinctly not decorated to reflect any particular period of Sticksville history, unless one counted the present moment as a historical era. The room served as the museum's office, with three desks at right angles to one another, topped with computer terminals from about ten years ago. Across one desk, a panoply of photocopies was scattered like puzzle pieces.

"I did some further investigation into that Sam Cheng's sabotage case," Ms. Fenstermacher said, tucking Roxy Wotherspoon's diary into the top drawer of her desk and locking it. "It has everything to do with Fort Hannover — now New Hammersmith. In World War I, the fort served as a training ground for soldiers before they went overseas."

Fort Hannover was, in 1914, the closest military base to Sticksville, just about a twenty-minute trip by train. In the midst of the war, Fort Hannover changed its "German-sounding" name to Fort Hammersmith. Despite the numerous German immigrants who lived around Fort Hannover (eventually Hammersmith), they decided to keep a low profile as anti-German sentiment grew as the Great War progressed (or failed to progress). They worried about finding themselves in toppled phone booths spray-painted with "Go back to Deutschland," if you catch my drift. So, Fort Hannover begat Fort Hammersmith begat New Hammersmith (when the wars were over and the town consisted of more civilians than soldiers). But I digress.

"Apparently, in December 1914, some kind of break-in happened at the fort. A bunch of supplies were taken from the armoury — dangerous stuff," Ms. Fenstermacher explained. "Gunpowder, grapeshot. Actual things used in weapons."

"And that Chinese guy was the one who stole it?" October asked. While the old newspaper had reported that Sam Cheng had been arrested as a saboteur, the sad story October had read in the Wotherspoon diary certainly didn't make him seem like a criminal mastermind.

"Well, that's the thing. Around the time the supplies were taken, the fort was receiving prank telephone calls. The phone would ring, no one would speak from the other end. Just breathing. That kind of thing. The phone company eventually determined the calls were being made from the Crooked Arms. Sticksville-735. In the middle of the night. Can you believe it?"

Considering October's history with the phone number Sticksville-735, she could just about believe anything.

"But the Crooked Arms had a whole bunch of residents," October protested. "What about the inventor? He'd know how to make a bomb, right? Or the suffragette? She was, like, a political activist. Don't you think it's unfair they blamed the immigrant from China? Just because they were at war or whatever?"

"They weren't at war, October. I thought we went over this in class. China and Canada weren't on opposing sides during World War I. But I really don't think we can blame Roxy Wotherspoon," Ms. Fenstermacher scoffed. "But I suppose her diary will tell us all we need to know on that front. The inventor could assemble a bomb, I suppose, depending on his training."

October felt momentarily vindicated. It's not that she wasn't willing to believe Sam Cheng was a murderer, but given the story in Roxy's diary and recent events at school, she was more ready to chalk up his arrest to old-fashioned racism.

"Right?" October said.

"But racism alone didn't lead to the arrest," Ms. Fenstermacher continued. "They found the gunpowder in his water jug when they searched the Crooked Arms, and hauled him off to jail that night."

December 1914 was not a great month to be Sam Cheng. Still, as October realized, while this proved Morna's across-the-hall neighbour to be dangerous, it didn't really point to him as a murderer. He'd have been imprisoned when Morna's body was found.

"So, Sam Cheng really was just a saboteur out to weaken the Canadian military?" October asked, utterly disappointed.

"Not necessarily," Ms. Fenstermacher revealed, moving one photocopy to the top of the pile. "See here, a *Sticksville Loon* story three years later. Sam Cheng was released due to lack of evidence. He moved back into the Crooked Arms and lived the rest of his life free of any run-ins with the law."

The mystery of Morna MacIsaac's death was like some endless corridor, with each step revealing more doors opening to reveal more rooms inside. And rooms within each of those rooms.

Basically, it was the hardest mystery anyone had ever tried to solve, and a thirteen-year-old with some dead friends may not have been up to the task. Still, Sam Cheng's exoneration didn't have to be a dead end.

"Did Sam Cheng have any children?" October asked. Deep down inside, she hoped the Chengs stretched on for generations in Sticksville. Maybe there was a Cheng in another grade at Sticksville Central whom she could befriend, become a confidante, and learn the uncanny family secret of the Chengs, which would unravel the mystery of Morna MacIsaac's death once and for all. Sadly, this was not meant to be.

"I'm sorry, October. No such luck," Ms. Fenstermacher said, moving Sam Cheng's 1933 obituary into view. "He died childless, survived by a wife who still lived in China. She died eight years later during the Second World War. There are no more Chengs from that family."

October left the Sticksville Museum glad she could cross one item off her list, but also feeling like someone had removed her organs, slathered them with Vicks VapoRub and haphazardly shoved them back into her body. Poor Sam Cheng never raised the money to bring his wife to Canada, probably because bigots destroyed his business and framed him for sabotage, and both Chengs died alone, thousands of miles apart. Her case had suddenly become the most tragic thing this side of Russian literature (or *Forrest Gump*).

☠

The overhead bell jangled as October entered Beaver Hardware, which, according to *It's a Wonderful Life*, meant an angel received its wings. But all the dead people October had seen thus far made her extremely skeptical of the existence of angels. The empty can of yellow spray paint rested in her bag, but she wasn't sure how to find out who purchased it. Hardware stores were not yet fingerprinting customers with every sale. October shrewdly supposed if she pretended the paint had been used to deface her home or parents' business, maybe the store staff would be more forthcoming with information.

She walked up to the boldly bearded man at the front cash and placed the spray paint on the counter.

"Sir," October said. "I was wondering if you could help me with something."

That's when, out of the corner of her eye, October saw someone we shall henceforth refer to as Goth Hardware Clerk. He was dressed in the green golf shirt and black pants that was the uniform of all the staff at Beaver Hardware, but that's where the similarities between him and his mortal co-workers ended. Goth Hardware Clerk had long black hair that had been buzzed near to nothing on the left side, Doc Martens for footwear, and a fresh coat of eyeliner. Even more remarkable, he was wearing fishnet gloves. He was stocking energy-saver light bulbs and electrical outlet covers onto metal shelving while wearing *his fishnet gloves*. Clearly, October was speaking with the wrong person.

"Oh, I just saw where these are kept," October said before the bearded man even had the chance to offer his help. "Thanks!"

She made a beeline for Goth Hardware Clerk, his face down in a shopping cart of SKUs (that's what those in the retail biz call products), and stood there in front of him. Waiting for him to look up.

"Hey," he said.

"Hey," October answered, rocking back and forth on her sneakers. "Nice gloves."

"Oh, thanks," he said. "Did you . . . need help looking for something?"

"Yeah, can you tell me if you've sold any of *these* lately?"

October displayed the spray paint can in front of her, like she were a model on *The Price Is Right*. "I'm trying to find who put graffiti all over my . . . dad's car," she decided.

"Whoa, Jessica Fletcher!" he exclaimed.

"Jessica Fletcher bought this recently?"

"No," he said, narrowing his heavily lined eyes into paper-thin slits. The fluorescent lights were probably too bright for Goth Hardware Clerk. "You're just like Jessica Fletcher. Y'know, the character played by Angela Lansbury? From *Murder She Wrote?*"

Somehow October felt like this was similar to how Mr. O'Shea's mystery had pivoted around someone named Phoebe Cates. Must all crimes in Sticksville have some sort of 1980s pop-culture connection?

"Nevermind," he said. "Probably before your time. You're asking about that colour in particular? Is that the actual can they used?"

October nodded as he continued to fill the shelf with boxes of light bulbs.

"There was a guy who's been here twice in the past week — both times he bought cans of yellow paint," he said. "He was, like, a teenager. I'm not really supposed to sell the spray paint to teenagers, but I'm also trying to not be, like, a total jerk."

"What did he look like?" October asked. Improbable as it was, Goth Hardware Clerk was proving to be an extremely valuable snitch. He must have trusted the information with one of his own.

"I don't know . . . normal. Kind of sporty."

If only Goth Hardware Clerk's powers of observation or ability to describe salient details had been more vivid. Though that description could match Devin McGriff, it could have also matched 200 other kids at October's school.

"Tell you what," he said. "If you leave a number, I'll call you if he comes in for more yellow spray paint. I'll try to get a name, too."

The phone number posed a dilemma for October: giving her

phone number to Goth Hardware Clerk could prove that Devin McGriff or some other teenager was buying all this spray paint and committing all these hate crimes, but at the same time, she couldn't pretend the clerk wasn't a *little* bit creepy. He *was* wearing fishnet gloves in a hardware store, and was definitely quite a bit older than her. Plus, October would have to give out her home phone number, which posed a whole multitude of problems if her father ever picked up if and when he called. Grounded forever problems. October devised an easy solution: she gave him Yumi's cell number.

Sk8 or Die
(or Do Both)

Later that night, the dead kids and I caught up in the tomb. I told them all about Sam Cheng, and Morna now vaguely remembered him being arrested. However, I also had to tell them that Sam Cheng had no descendents, and I currently had no new clues for either of our mysteries. Solving two mysteries at once was hard! Mysterious bad guys: 1, October Schwartz: 0. I herded the dead kids toward the tomb's door, which I then shoved shut after we'd all landed back in the very cold cemetery. I buttoned up the black peacoat that (apparently) looked like my mom's.

"Good work, Dead Squad. We're onto something," I said and raised my fists in mock triumph. It was hard to get excited when so many evidence wells had run drier than my dad's mashed potatoes. The dead kids seemed to be settling in for the night. Well, morning, technically. "So, we'll meet back in the cemetery on Monday night?"

"Wait, what's happening tomorrow night?" Derek asked.

"Yes," Cyril added. "I, too, am curious."

"I've been invited to a party," I answered, starting to turn.

"Well, la-di-da," Tabetha responded with a little curtsy.

"October," Derek moaned, tapping at his Swatch, which I'd never noticed before. Was he wearing it over his recently cut wrist? Wait? Derek's mom buried him with a Swatch on? Derek's mom buried him in a T-shirt, so I guess anything was

143

possible. "The clock's ticking between full moons, and with no leads, we really need all the time we have to solve Morna's case!"

"An' what about yer Chinese friend?" Tabetha added. "She's still in danger. No offence, Morna. You've got a fine mystery, too."

"It's okay," Morna said.

"I know! I know!" I shouted. "And Yumi's Japanese-Canadian. But I can't be digging through garbage and raising the dead *every* night of the week. I have to have some fun! Besides, one suspect I like for the phone booth tipping will be there, so I kind of *have* to go . . . to protect Yumi."

Why wasn't the debate team knocking my door down, I ask you?

"Then we should be there, too," Cyril decreed. "If your friend needs protection, who better than us to provide it?"

October assumed this was a rhetorical question.

"Where is this party?"

"Sounds miserable," Kirby said, pre-emptively.

"The party," I huffed, "is at Trundleduck Pond. Do you know it? We'll be ice skating."

"Yay! Ice skating!" Morna exploded into holiday cheer.

"No. No 'yay.'" I had to put my foot down. "There's going to be, like, a hundred people from my grade at this party, so the five of you grim spectres of death have to remain out of sight at all times."

"Heck, no," Tabetha asserted. "We're goin' skating!"

"No, you're not."

We went back and forth on this issue several times, but in the end we compromised that they would go skating. I was, despite the glaring difficulties, somewhat pleased because Morna seemed so keen on skating. I wanted to get back on her good side because (a) I had been bombing on her case, and (b) I'd never seen her so despondent as when we'd read that diary entry. That said, bringing a bunch of ghosts (essentially) to go skating at a birthday party came with a unique set of problems.

"*If* I allow you to come skating," I said, eyebrows already raised in suspicion, "how can we be sure people won't see you?

Yumi can see you. I'm sure a couple other kids will be able to, as well."

"We bundle up," Derek explained. "Then everyone can see us, sort of. Only our clothes! We all put on coats and snowpants and gloves and hats. Ski masks for our faces. We'll be so tightly wrapped, no one will realize there are ghosts underneath."

"Wait, that would work? And how are you going to get all this clothing?"

"Same way we got everything before you came around," Tabetha said. "Steal it."

Condoning clothing theft to solve a murder was one thing, but I wasn't sure how I felt about stealing just so my dead friends could go skating.

"Won't you get hot in all that winter clothing?" I asked. "I mean it's cold out but not . . ."

Kirby just returned a stony face.

"Well then, what about your voices?"

"What about 'em?" Tabetha replied.

"If people can see and hear ghosts, that's great, but if they can't, you won't be able to answer any of their questions. Questions might come up, such as: *Who are you? Why are you at my party?*"

This one stumped them for quite a while.

"I got it!" Morna cried. "We can pretend we're from a foreign country! We don't speak English."

"You barely do," Kirby said.

"Kirby, shut your mouth," Cyril warned. "That's a fine idea, Morna."

"I've always wanted t'be from Finland," she said wistfully.

"Fine," I relented. "You've got it all figured out, I guess. You can come to the party. But I don't know this weird bunch of Finns who show up and they don't know me, okay? Now can I go home and at least get a couple hours' sleep?"

"Yes, go," Derek said. "And we'll go rob a thrift store while it's still dark out. Just one more thing, October."

"Mm-hmm."

"Do you know how to get to the closest thrift store?"

Reluctantly, I took my composition book from my bag and began to draw a map.

☠

With two weeks left until Christmas, Dad was in full holiday mode. On Sunday morning he had the radio locked to some weird station that only played carols and holiday classix (with an X, I'm assuming) from December 1st onward.

The station was providing the soundtrack as I rummaged through the front hall closet, trying to find Dad's old skates. The Christmas music worried me slightly — the holidays were never a good time for my clinically depressed father. I feared he was setting himself up for big disappointment this year, with the volleyball streak and the extra scoop of Christmas cheer. That said, he had been almost chipper lately, though I had no idea why. Maybe the school had given him a raise for being one of the few Sticksville teachers who hadn't committed a major felony.

In little time, my dad realized I was doing a full cavity search of the closet and began to ask questions.

"October," he said. "What are you doing?"

"Looking for your skates," I said, elbow deep in a box of scarves. Why did the two of us have so many scarves? "You don't mind if I borrow them, do you?"

"No, but are you planning to go skating right now?"

"Tonight, actually. There's a party."

I regretted the words as soon as their syllables crossed my teeth. Tied up in my double-mystery stuff, I'd completely forgotten I technically wasn't supposed to be leaving the house unaccompanied for any reason. I was doubtful Dad would be supportive of my going-to-parties-at-frozen-ponds-at-night initiative.

"Oh, sorry, Dad," I backpedalled. "I should have asked earlier. I know I'm not supposed to —"

"Will you be going with Yumi and Stacey?" he asked.

"Yes. And almost the entire grade. Stacey's dad is driving!"

I'm not sure why this would make any difference, but I was shooting for the moon.

"Go with my blessing," he said, taking a sip from his quantum-physics-themed coffee mug. "And my skates are hanging above your head."

His old hockey skates were indeed dangling above me, their laces tied through the white wire shelving above. But I didn't understand why Dad was acting so strangely. Since when did I have a free licence to skate on strange ponds on a Sunday night?

"Dad, did you take too many pills or something? The words you're speaking are strange and unfamiliar."

"Ha ha," he groaned. "Maybe I'm just in a good mood."

"Just days ago you gave me a whole speech on safety and never leaving this house until I'm, like, forty basically. What changed?"

"Nothing changed," he said, almost smiling as he drank more coffee. "I still don't like you walking alone or spending time in that cemetery. But it's nice that you're making friends."

"Don't Yumi and Stacey qualify? Are you paying them or something?" I wouldn't have been surprised; part of me had suspected it the whole time.

"Oh, you know they don't really count," he said, which was kind of super offensive. "This is a big class party with skating. Whose party is it?"

"This guy in a band at school. Boston Davis."

"Boston is a name now?"

"Really, Dad? From you?" *Très* hypocritical. I untied the skates so they became two separate things.

"You know how to use those?"

"It's been a while," I said, "but it's just like riding a bike." Which had also been a while.

"Be careful on the ice," Dad added, suddenly allowing his normal incredible fear of everything to overwhelm his concern with my popularity. "It's still early in the season. Make sure it's thick enough."

"I'll let some of the other kids test it out first," I said. "If they fall through to their deaths, I won't go skating."

"That's the kind of attitude that will get you invited to fewer parties."

☠

After Stacey's dad dropped us off in the parking lot by Trundle-duck Pond, we stood in the snow, just at the edge of the frozen pond, for a good ten minutes. Not venturing forward, not saying anything — just watching our breath turn to vapour in the air. Nearly everyone in our grade was there already. A lot of them were skating by the far end near the forest, and a bunch of the others were standing on the edge of that forest, smoking cigarettes or just talking. The girls, without fail, were all wearing nice white figure skates. Only *I* was dumb enough to wear my dad's taped-up hockey skates. Yumi had white skates, too, but she'd drawn the anarchy symbol on the sides with a Sharpie. The little girl with the big laugh — one of Ashlie Salmons' besties — did, like, a triple Axel directly in front of us, proving to be some sort of champion figure skater.

"Ughhh," Yumi bellowed.

"Just because they invited us," said Stacey, "or me, doesn't mean we have to go. My dad gave me thermoses of hot chocolate. We could just sit here and drink them," he said, unzipping his backpack and producing the evidence.

"Is your dad Mr. Rogers?" Yumi asked.

"No, he's Mr. —"

"Shut up a second," Yumi stopped him. "Check out the psychopaths."

The psychopaths were, as you may have guessed, my five dead friends. Blending in, as usual. This was sure to be the most public of my many humiliations since first raising them from the dead. Today, the dead kids had all worn puffy white winter clothing from head to toe, like five marshmallow people.

White hats, white jackets, white gloves. They even managed to find five white ski masks. I had a sneaking suspicion they broke into more than one thrift shop last night. They had obscured the little area where your typical balaclava might reveal skin with ski goggles that flashed in the moonlight.

Distressingly, the dead kids were really talented skaters. Maybe not as talented as Little Girl, Big Laugh, but light-years ahead of me.

"Who are those people?" Yumi asked, unable to stop herself from laughing. "What are they doing here?"

"I heard they were from Finland," I muttered, playing my part in this really weird scam. "Like, exchange students or something."

Whatever it was — the mention of Finland, the sight of the dead kids in their ridiculous snowman suits, the realization that we'd been standing there for twenty minutes — the three of us started skating and gradually moved closer to the actual party. I was kind of amazed Yumi could stay upright with one arm in a sling, but she managed better than I did with no excuse save a cut-up hand. I can wholeheartedly say the skate party wasn't the worst thing in the world. We even talked with some nice people, like Tricia MacKenzie, who we used to curl with. Even Preston Sinclair wasn't *so* bad. Mostly, everyone was gawking at the five people in matching white outfits who'd crashed the party but hadn't really associated with anyone. To do damage control, I skated in and out of conversations saying things like *I hear they're from Finland* or *No, I don't think they even understand English!*

Oh, and did I say skate? Because I should have said, jerked myself forward as if by an invisible chain all over the pond. To my credit, I only fell three times, and one time, my butt didn't hit the ground, so it didn't even really count.

Everything was about as pleasant as could have been hoped: Devin McGriff and Ashlie Salmons staying to one side, the dead kids skating clear of everyone, and Yumi, Stacey, and me somewhere in the middle. The trouble only started when a bunch of the guys decided they wanted to play hockey.

"I'll be a captain!" Devin McGriff shouted, though his skates hadn't yet touched the ice that night.

I automatically assumed Yumi and I and even Stacey would be disqualified from team play, due to our general lack of athleticism and likelihood of bumming the team out. So I was surprised when they asked Stacey to play (not on Devin McGriff's team, though, obvs). Don't get me wrong. The guy's tall, but about as useful on the ice as a croquet wicket. (That was my one and only sports joke.)

Unfortunately, Devin McGriff got the bright idea that Finns know how to play hockey, and that while one of the weirdos in white was tubby and two were clearly girls (unacceptable as hockey players in Devin's mind), the other two looked kind of sporty. So Devin skated over to the group of white Finns to extend the olive branch of Canada's most dangerous sport. Both, to my eternal horror, nodded their heads in agreement to whatever Devin McGriff asked them and soon they were joining his team's starting lineup. Cyril, given the time period he came from, probably knew as much about hockey as he did about the internet. Disaster was written all over this game.

To add insult to injury (just wait — the injury is coming), Devin, after securing his two undead all-stars, drifted over to where Yumi and I were standing to ask if I'd be goalie.

"I know you don't know much about hockey," he sneered, lighting a cigarette like a true champion athlete, "but you'd make a pretty decent goalie — purely based on surface area." Then he spat something off to his left, which was extra gross, as we were on the ice and that *stuff* didn't get absorbed. "You'd nearly block the whole net."

"That's wicked, McGriff," Yumi said, jumping to my rescue. "Why don't you tell us more about it on your radio show — oh, wait . . ."

"Just wait, Gothra," Devin said, now waving his cigarette in Yumi's face. "As soon as everyone stops feeling sad for you because of your busted arm, I'm going make your life miserable."

"Just try it," Yumi said, pawing at the ice with her left skate like a horse (a horse that was standing on ice).

Devin blew smoke in her face, then returned to centre ice.

A Subaru's trunk opened and hockey sticks were handed out to all the players. Pylons were set down as goalposts and anchored with nearby stones. Yumi and I were two of many spectators lined up like fenceposts at the edge of the woods. By the time the hockey game started properly, Devin's brother, Skyler, showed up with two of his friends from university. His arrival undoubtedly reduced Yumi's focus, but not so much that she didn't heckle the players mercilessly at every turn. Morna, Tabetha, and Kirby, in their large, white disguises, joined us to observe from time to time, but also spent a lot of time playing crack the whip by themselves.

I won't bore you with the details of the match — seriously, if you want to know about hockey, you're looking at the wrong person — but one notable feature was how truly terrible Cyril was at it. A St. Bernard with a hockey stick lashed to its muzzle probably stood a better chance of scoring a goal. Luckily, Derek was surprisingly talented for a dead guy and was generous with his skill, sticking close by Cyril and feeding him the puck. Another notable feature of the game was just how creative and effective Yumi's taunts were. She was backing whatever side was playing against Devin McGriff, which, coincidentally, was the team Stacey was playing for. She catcalled, "You stickhandle worse than you play guitar," and "My grandma's got better hustle, and she's in an iron lung!"

Stacey skated off the ice and hopped up onto the snow where Yumi and I were waiting while Tricia MacKenzie skated on to take his place.

"I'm not very good," he exhaled heavily and the cloud of condensation obscured his reddened face, still covered in partially healed cuts.

"No," I said. "You were doing well." He wasn't really — he looked like one of those windsock balloon people you see at used car lots — but he could use the encouragement, I figured.

Yumi, meanwhile, brought her good hand, in a black-and-white striped glove, to her face to amplify her voice, and screamed, "Devin, you're moving so slow, you're collecting dust! A life-drawing class is using you as a model!" She was far from finished with her magician's-never-ending-handkerchief of insults.

"Oh, October," Stacey Mc-No-Name said, "I meant to show this to you earlier. In the car."

He dug into his back pocket and pulled out a creased photocopy of a snapshot. The photograph, extremely old, was of a boy around my age. Stacey just grinned like we'd won the lottery.

"What's that?" I was really confused.

"Do you still have that picture from your history class?"

I was beginning to follow, and as I followed, I was beginning to lose my freaking mind.

"Yeah, follow me." We had to trudge back in our skates a bit to my bag, where the picture from the old *Sticksville Loon* was probably mashed under a half-dozen textbooks. On our short journey, we passed by Morna, Tabetha, and Kirby, skating around in circles like a three-part length of chain.

Digging through my bag, I found the crumpled paper and unfolded it, pressed it flat on a rock, and tried not to get it

damp from the snow. Stacey's photocopy still in my hand, I held it beside the other one and compared. He looked a bit older, a bit thinner — like he'd grown into his face (I was so excited for when that might to happen to me!) — but the boy in Stacey's picture was unmistakably Morna's little brother, Boyd.

"I knew I recognized that photograph from somewhere," Stacey exclaimed. "I took a look through my parents' old photo albums and I found this. It's not the same, but *he* is, and I'm pretty sure that's the same building behind him."

"Stacey," I asked, suddenly feeling extremely stupid that I didn't know the answer already, "what's your last name?"

"MacIsaac."

"And the kid in this photo," I continued.

"My great-great-grandfather."

"Stacey!" I shouted and leapt up in the spot on my skates. "Holy smokes! You're related to these people!" Unable to restrain myself, I gave my lanky friend a big shove which, unfortunately, knocked him onto the ice, where his legs slid out behind him, causing him to career backward on his stomach.

As it happened the three dead kids who weren't in the hockey game were skating by. One of the dead kids — Morna, I thought, though it was hard to tell when they were all bundled up in white winter clothing — nearly skated over Stacey's prone body but leapt at the last second. This also sent her tumbling face-first onto the ice.

Stacey scrambled to his feet — not an easy task, given how poor he was on skates — and lifted Morna to her feet.

"Sorry. I'm so sorry!" he said. "My friend pushed me and ..."

The girl in all white just stared at him through blank ski goggles.

"Oh, I forgot. You must only speak Finnish," he said.

Stacey gazed skyward then blinked rapidly. He dropped to

his knees on the ice, and in the dusting of snowflakes carpeting the pond, he drew a pictogram with his finger.

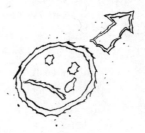

I would normally suggest it's impossible to see someone smile when she's entirely bundled in a massive white snowsuit, but it was as if Morna's whole body smiled at the sight of that crude drawing. She responded with a picture in return.

I'd just discovered Morna and Stacey were, in effect, relatives. I really hoped Morna wasn't falling in love. In nearly the same moment, out of the corner of my eye, I spotted an altercation of sorts over by the hockey game — one involving, as always seemed to be the case these days, Yumi. The international communication had to be disrupted.

"Stacey!" I shouted and pulled him with me as I awkwardly skated over to Yumi as fast as my non-technique would allow, leaving Morna with Kirby and Tabetha to continue cracking the whip.

The scuffle was already beyond the point of no return. Apparently, Yumi had crossed that sensitive heckling line when she said something unkind about Devin's mother, and now Devin had forcibly dragged Yumi onto the ice and was shouting in her face like it was an unresponsive microphone.

"Devin!" his older brother shouted. "Leave her alone. She's just messin' with you." But Skyler McGriff seemed to be the only voice of reason in attendance at the ice skating party. Everyone else was shouting and jeering like they were at their first dog race.

"Let her go!" I yelled from the snowy ground, but no one was listening to me. No one seemed concerned that Devin was dragging around a girl with a broken arm. The volume of the random shouts from fellow partygoers was such that I couldn't hear anything Yumi and Devin were saying to each other while they circled on the ice, Devin grasping her hood. Worst ice dance partner *ever*.

What was Devin thinking? Would he actually punch Yumi, this adorable girl, barely five feet tall, with nearly his entire class and older brother watching? Stacey hobbled over the ice, hoping to reach them before it happened. Mercifully, I didn't get the chance to find out, because Morna and Tabetha speed-skated over to the fracas, at which point they cracked the whip. Again. But this time, Morna and Tabetha released Kirby, whose sizeable mass landed in the small of Devin McGriff's back like a cannonball.

The gathered crowd gasped in collective horror — or sympathetic back pain — as Devin crumpled to the ice. To them, some weird Finnish stumblebum had just ended Sticksville Central's favourite lead guitarist's future career. Kirby lay slowly turning on the ice, like a beached starfish on a Lazy Susan. Yumi, in the sudden commotion, scrambled back onto the snow and ran for the forest. Devin McGriff, not as much a future paraplegic as we'd all assumed, got to his feet — no easy task on ice when your back feels like it's broken — and reached for the coasting white starfish and lifted him from the ground. My heart stopped for, like, a full four seconds at this very troubling and unexpected confrontation between living and dead. Was Devin going to punch Kirby? And would Kirby think quickly enough to turn intangible if he did? And would that be better or worse than if he simply took a punch like an actual live person? Life just doesn't prepare you for these situations.

"You Finnish puffballs have been annoying me all night!" Devin announced, a fresh crosshatching of cuts across his chin. "I'm going to tear your head off!" And he ripped the ski mask from Kirby's face.

I can't say what Devin McGriff saw then, nor the rest of the gathered crowd: either nothing at all — a hat set upon a complete void — or the slightly translucent, bluish-white face of a long-dead quintuplet. Whatever they saw, they all screamed like the ice had suddenly lit on fire. The dead kids scattered in the panic, while my classmates gathered backpacks and skates, jumped over each other to get to a hiding spot or the closest street or far, far away from the ghosts. Preston Sinclair had taken off a skate and was wielding it like a dagger, slashing wildly around him. Stacey and I followed where Yumi had disappeared into the woods a minute earlier. Boston Davis's fifteenth birthday party was memorable, to say the least.

☠

Brotherly Love from Another Mother

Stacey and Morna being branches on the same long-lived family tree sort of changed everything in October's equation. And not in an entirely productive way. It changed everything in that she was now even more unsure of what to do with the two mysteries. Should she attempt to introduce Morna and her fifth cousin or whatever Stacey might be to her? Should she consider making Stacey MacIsaac an official member of the Dead Kid Detective Agency, as official as that collective ever was? October had no way of knowing if Stacey could see dead people. More likely than not, she'd introduce him to an empty chair and look like a total nutcase, and October already had a bit of a reputation with everyone at school.

Mostly, October wished she could share the secret of the dead kids with Stacey and Yumi; they'd proven trustworthy and sharing the secret might bring them closer together. Another part of her, more concerned about this plan's potential for utter chaos, wanted to keep the dead kids all to herself. But one thing was certain: if Morna was, indeed, harbouring some sort of weird cross-generational crush on Stacey, October was going to have to tell Morna the identity of this gentlemanly but clumsy skater sooner rather than later.

☠

Monday morning, talk of the mysterious Finn ghost children was more subdued than one would expect, especially since no Finn exchange students could be found at Sticksville Central. October half-assumed kids would arrive on Monday morning with *I Survived the Ice Skating Party of the Dead* T-shirts and related merchandise. Make no mistake, the halls reverberated with chatter about Devin McGriff and Yumi's fight and the weird Finn kids and Devin *claiming* to see a ghost. But since Devin McGriff and perhaps a few other rubberneckers near the action were the only ones who'd had a direct view of Kirby when he was unmasked, school skepticism of the true supernatural nature of the event reigned supreme. Even Devin's brother, Skyler, didn't believe Devin's claim of a real ghostly encounter.

"Devin?" he scoffed when October asked him during mathematics how his brother was doing. "I think that fat Finn kid hit him pretty hard. He claims the kid was a ghost or invisible man or something."

"Like Kevin Bacon?"

"Like Kevin Bacon," he nodded, admiring October's reference to one of the worst movies featuring invisible men of all time, before continuing to pass out quiz results.

The feud with Devin McGriff was also taking a toll on Yumi, something that became readily apparent when she arrived with the now fully named Stacey MacIsaac (oh, how his last name melted October's little black heart!) in the cafeteria. Yumi, Stacey, and October had hidden in the woods by Trundleduck Pond for a full twenty minutes after the Finn ghost hockey disaster before Yumi used her phone to call Stacey's dad to evacuate them. Mr. MacIsaac then took the three to Stacey's, where they spent the

remainder of the night ingesting hot chocolate and watching episodes of *Dark Shadows*. So, all in all, not a bad birthday celebration for Boston Davis.

"Answer me two questions," Yumi commanded as she seated herself on the cafeteria bench.

She had gone extra heavy on the eyeliner today and was wearing her favourite Smiths shirt (only partially obscured by her black sling) with a blue plaid kilt. "How can Devin McGriff be such a bottom-shelf toiletface, and his brother be such an adorable, mature babe? And *will* this affect my chances for lifelong bliss with said non-toiletface?"

"Got me," Stacey said, already deep into his traditional tuna sandwich. Presumably that was his answer to both questions.

"Skyler's not that great," October said, though he had impressed her with his knowledge of *Hollow Man*. "I have a question for *you*, though."

"Shoot," Yumi said.

"So what happened with Radio Sticksville? Was it all Mr. Santuzzi? Will you ever get your radio show back?"

Technically, that was three questions, but Yumi was prepared to let that slide because she and October were close.

"Oh, didn't you hear?" Yumi asked. "Freedom of speech is dead." And with that she crushed a Chips Ahoy! from her lunch dramatically with her good fist.

"Mr. Santuzzi wanted the school to shut down the radio program. When Yumi insulted Ashlie, he had the ammo he needed," Stacey said with less hyperbole, then added, "I would have eaten that cookie."

"I guess my harmless Ashlie Salmons remark was all it took. But because Santuzzi is, like, a wizard or master of puppets or something, he convinced the principal to cancel the radio station altogether."

"Sucks," Stacey added. "Also, have either of you seen my Guitar Wolf T-shirt? Yumi, did I bring it to the radio booth for our last show?"

"I don't think so. We didn't even play any songs by them."

Suddenly, a tiny little organ started playing. It was like the world's tiniest carnival was somewhere on Yumi's person and was open for business. She dug into her bag and flipped open her phone.

"Ugh," she grunted.

"Was that your ring tone?" Stacey asked through his tuna.

"Yes."

"What was it?" October asked.

"'Gypsys, Tramps and Thieves,'" she machine-gunned.

"The Cher song?" Stacey asked, incredulous.

"What? It's a good song."

Stacey raised his hands in surrender, then stuck in his Walkman earphones to avoid further conflict.

"Who's calling you?" October asked. "Stacey and I are both right here." There was no way Goth Hardware Clerk had solved the case of the yellow spray paint for October already, was there?

"Nobody. It's a text."

October folded her arms and gave her impression of what someone else might term a penetrating stare. Though that kind of makes it sound like something out of Advanced Dungeons & Dragons, which it certainly was not.

"What?" she shouted. "Okay, some guy has been calling me and hanging up, and sending me threatening texts ever since I got the phone."

"Threatening texts?" October was concerned for her friend, but also knew a clue when she heard one. Always on the job, this girl. "Let me see!"

Yumi turned the open phone to her friend.

U R GOING DOWN, CHINATOWN.

How weird is it that this anonymous threatener used U for you, but opted to include a comma? He must be mercurial in his grammar.

"How many of these have you been sent?"

"About six."

"Do you mind if I . . ." But October had already started to scroll through Yumi's saved messages.

"Go hog-wild."

All the text messages October found had a similar vaguely menacing and racist tone, and all were from the same phone number. A number with a 519 area code. (Thank goodness it wasn't from number 735. That would have been ridiculous.)

"What area code is that?"

Yumi shrugged and crammed a Fuzzy Peach between her teeth.

Their friend, Stacey, was in another world, listening to whatever music he normally listened to. October wasn't really sure what fell within his musical tastes, other than The Plotzdam Conference and (now) Guitar Wolf. Not Cher, one would guess. October snapped her fingers in front of Stacey's face to get his attention.

"Stacey, what's the 519 area code?" October had a hunch that Stacey "Secret Old Man" MacIsaac would know his area codes.

"Guelph, I think." Earphones temporarily out, he named a town about an hour's drive from Sticksville.

"Yumi," October said, "you can't just let this happen. We have to find who's doing this."

"Whatever," Yumi said. "It's probably just Devin McGriff or one of his friends, angry about the radio shows being cancelled. They think I ruined it for everyone."

October and Yumi glanced over at Devin, seated with Ashlie and the rest of Phantom Moustache. When he noticed them looking his way, he *did* slowly drag his index finger across his throat, pirate-style, so perhaps Yumi had a point.

"Come on," Yumi said, reclaiming her cell phone. "You done?"

"Yeah," October sighed. "I have to get to another therapy session with Dr. Lagostina."

"Wake up, Stacey."

☠

"So, we meet again," Dr. Lagostina announced, settling back into his wheeled desk chair and holding his pen in front of him like a ceremonial wafer. October had had sessions with him in the month she was named after, back when she and Ashlie were brawling.

"Does that make me a repeat offender?" October asked, attempting to disappear into the burgundy armchair seated opposite Dr. Lagostina and his pen.

"You haven't committed any offence," Dr. Lagostina insisted, taking October a bit more seriously than she'd intended.

"I just meant . . . never mind." October didn't bother. "What should we talk about?"

"Tell me how you feel about what happened to you in the phone booth," he said.

October hadn't been thinking about the phone booth. In her mind, she was seven chambers beyond the phone booth already. If October was forced to do a series of sessions with the school therapist, Dr. Lagostina, she figured it couldn't hurt to bring up the campaign of harassment against her friend.

"Yumi has been getting threatening text messages," October said.

Immediately, she felt like a tattletale. She didn't know why; telling someone about the threats Yumi was weathering was certainly important. Still, her stomach flipped inside out, all the acid spraying her insides.

"That's very serious," Dr. Lagostina said, no longer holding the pen aloft like a religious icon. Instead, it had become useful tool, and he was scribbling notes in his ledger. "So this is since the phone booth attack? Yumi has been receiving threats via text message?"

"Yeah," October said.

"And do we know who these threats are from?"

"No," October said. "We couldn't figure out the number. Confusingly, it seems like a long-distance number."

"I'm glad you told me this, October," Dr. Lagostina said, folding his hands into his lap again. "Unfortunately, I can't take further action until Yumi herself mentions it to me, but I'll certainly bring it up in her session. Now is there anything you wanted to tell me about yourself?"

October could think of a billion things: how she probably shouldn't have given Dr. Lagostina that information, how she was probably spending too much time with the dead, how she worried about immersing herself in murder and depravity during all her free time, how she constantly felt guilt and fear for her dad and his depression. But she didn't mention a single one of them.

☠

Several hours after the school day concluded, October came across the dead kids playing Connect Four in the cemetery. If there was ever any doubt they were dead, seeing them lying belly-down on the snow-covered ground without so much as a jacket would have convinced October. Notably absent was Morna MacIsaac, the dead kid October was most hoping to speak to.

"Where's Morna?" October asked.

"Nice ta' see you, too," Tabetha said, plunking a black disc into the Connect Four frame. "What about the rest of us?"

"Yeah," Derek added.

"I'm sorry; I was just hoping to tell her something about the Crooked Arms and her younger brother," October said. "She went somewhere?"

"She said she had something to do," Cyril said.

"Like what?" Really, aside from helping October solve mysteries and play board games, there was very little the dead kids had to occupy their evenings. And they almost never worked solo. A terrible thought crossed October's mind, but it was too twisted to speak aloud. "Oh no . . . she wouldn't."

She had a nagging sensation she knew exactly where to find Morna MacIsaac, and she knew she should get there sooner rather than later. She gathered the four remaining dead kids and they took to the streets.

October and the dead kids walked along the darkened sidewalks of Sticksville. Based on her suggestion, the four lifeless friends stayed farther from the road and all kept their eyes out for passing vehicles and late-night dog-walkers. October didn't worry much about the drivers, but it would be hard to explain why she seemed to be having a heart-to-heart with herself to anyone travelling on foot. After about fifteen minutes, October led the group onto the street to their left. The streetlights were even more infrequent here, and their path was largely lit by the moonlight reflecting off three-day-old snow.

At one gingerbread-like house, October held out her arm like the barrier outside a pay parking lot and pointed toward the wooden gate that led to the house's backyard. The dead kids easily ghosted through it completely, while October moved her hands up and down to find the latch like a safecracker and eased her way into the backyard. She gestured toward two rows of bushes situated near the rear fence. From their position, crouched behind the bushes, they could see a lit window on the second floor of the narrow house before them.

"Hate to bring this up," Kirby said, "but what exactly are we doing here?"

October held one finger up, but whether she wanted him to wait or look up, it was unclear. "We wait," she clarified.

Staked out in the backyard, as if Carlos the Jackal or some international crime lord were about to emerge from the door and empty his recyclables, the dead kids were finally amazed to witness Morna MacIsaac, clutching a black T-shirt to her gingham dress, stroll through the house's rear wall.

"Morna?" Cyril whispered.

October simply nodded and reached out with her hand as the Scottish ghost passed by the bushes. Morna's mind must have been elsewhere, because she was still tangible and completely startled when October's fingers encircled her bony ankle.

"Wha'?!" she exclaimed, dropping the shirt. "October? Cyril, everyone? What're ye doing here?"

"I think the better question is what *you're* doing here," Kirby replied.

"Ah . . . I'm . . . I'm sorry," Morna said with downcast eyes. "I met yer friend yesterday when we were pretendin' t'be Finns an' he seemed so nice. I followed him home."

Derek lifted the black shirt from the ground, displaying a gaudy Guitar Wolf logo across the breast. "What's this?"

"Oh, you stole his T-shirt." October felt like she was about to cry.

"Oh no." Tabetha nudged Morna in the ribs. "Morna's got a crush. I knew it."

Morna looked up to the scene framed by dusty brown shutters. Stacey MacIsaac — just some tall teenage boy to her for the moment — was sitting on his bed, practicing on his drum pad. On the desk in front of him, clearly visible, was Cher's *Greatest Hits*.

"That's yer friend, isn't it?" Morna asked.

October nodded and added. "That's Stacey. Stacey MacIsaac."

"MacIsaac?"

"I did the math and I think he's your great-great-grand-nephew."

Morna's eyes opened up like she had suddenly caught on to an entirely new dimension. Kirby, in the meantime, made intense gagging sounds.

"So, it would be really handy if you didn't have a crush on him," October continued. "Because you're kind of related."

"Oh, gross," Tabetha spat into the lawn. "Y'all are sick!"

Unfazed by the fake vomiting and insults, Morna continued,

"Why does he have a girl's name?"

"I haven't figured that part out."

Morna just stood there, as if mesmerized. "What's he doin'?"

"He's practising drums," October said. "He's a drummer in our school band."

Morna clasped her bony white hands together. For an instant, it looked like she might scream. "My great-great-grand-nephew knows how t'play drums?"

"Well, he plays them," October answered, but immediately regretted her cheap joke. A sad, lonely Scottish girl was seeing her crush turn into her descendant, and realizing he was her one living connection to the present, and October did nothing but make disparaging remarks about his drumming. Additionally, based on the printout he was studying, Stacey appeared to be practising Cher's "Gypsys, Tramps & Thieves," but for what reason? Had he discovered it was, in fact, a great song? Was he learning it just because Yumi liked the song? Soon, October felt sad and entranced, too, watching this weird boy learn the drum part to a song he mocked earlier today, without the use of a drum set. The snow on the ground, the clear black sky — it all became overwhelming for a few seconds.

"Morna?" October finally asked.

"Yes."

"I'm glad you could meet Stacey," she continued, "but I think you should give back his T-shirt."

With that, Derek took the Guitar Wolf T-shirt, walked through the house's walls, and returned it. Cyril put his arm around Morna's shoulders and the dead kids walked with October back to the cemetery in eerie wordlessness.

☠

14

The Unsinkable Alfred Pain

"Dad," I called. "Why is the door locked?"

Tuesday morning, as I was about to leave for school, I noticed my dad's bedroom door was closed. And upon further inspection, not just closed but fully locked. This was a bad sign. Was it possible that my dad, who'd been doing so well this holiday season, riding so high off a championship volleyball season that his depression seemed to be an afterthought, was now in an official funk?

"Dad?"

No answer. I hadn't really been worrying about my dad, but I also knew that with depression, you should always take any warning signs very seriously.

"Dad, are you in there?" I pounded on the door.

"Yes," his voice peeped from the other side of the door. "I'm here."

"And you're not going to do anything stupid?"

"No," he said, sounding offended. Seconds later, the lock unlatched and his face appeared at the door jamb. Surprisingly, he was clean-shaven, smiling, seemingly happy and bright. "What do you mean?"

"Just . . . you don't normally lock the door." Was I unreasonable in expecting the worst?

"Oh, sorry about that. But I'm fine."

"You guys didn't lose a big volleyball match or anything like that?" Times like these — when I was acutely aware of his difficulties — I felt pretty ashamed I didn't follow Dad's volleyball coaching career as closely as he'd probably have liked.

"No, October. We're headed to the regionals in the new year, thanks to the dynamic duo of Ashlie Salmons and Wanda Pang."

I was also acutely aware that my dad would probably never refer to me as "dynamic," whether in duo or other form.

"I'm actually really looking forward to today," he said, face breaking into an unfamiliar smile once again. "And it's the last day for candy cane grams. You going to send any?"

Was there some kind of school-wide conspiracy to make people send these ill-advised confessions of love to one another during the holidays? Wasn't the season depressing enough? I *was* planning to make use of the school's candy cane gram system, though not in the way it was intended to be used. I'd be making a mockery of it. Still, it wasn't a total lie when I answered, "Could be."

☠

The first thing I was greeted with as I walked through Sticksville Central's double doors was, unfortunately, Ashlie Salmons. She was in the festive spirit, wearing a red plaid dress with a green belt.

"Zombie Tramp," she called. "What's up? Stay in any good tombs lately?"

The most disturbing thing was that I had an actual answer to that.

"So where's Kung Fu Zombie Tramp?" Ashlie asked, making me suspect her for the harassment campaign all over again. She could certainly afford a spare phone with a long-distance number, couldn't she? "I thought you two were, like, girlfriends or something. She sending you a candy cane gram?"

It was like people at my school were being paid by the word to mention these stupid things.

"No," I rasped, afraid to tell Ashlie of Yumi's love for her boyfriend's older brother. "Where's Devin?"

"*That* loser?" she pffted. "I ditched him for good. The Ashlie-Devin dynasty is most extremely and officially over. We are no longer an item and if he sends me a candy cane gram, I will ram it in his stupid gap-toothed mouth."

"He seemed to keep you on a pretty short leash," I said, looking around for someone I knew to enter the atrium so I could escape this horrible conversation. Man, I wished I knew more people!

"You noticed that, huh?" she said. "He also was starting to get pretty heavy with the mean comments about Asian people, which was really not okay. I mean, I realized it was because he hated Yumi and I completely sympathize, but you can't just make jokes and insults about people based on their backgrounds. Any anti-Asian sentiment is also directed squarely at my volleyball co-captain-slash-champion and, like, blood sister Wanda Pang, and *no one* laughs at Wanda Pang in my presence. Especially not since we're both taking this stupid school to the regionals."

That was, I thought, a remarkably mature way to handle her terrible boyfriend. For a second, I worried I was going to start to like Ashlie Salmons, and she was my arch-enemy. Thankfully, Yumi and Stacey arrived at the front doors, loaded up in coats and scarves.

"Sounds like you made the right choice," I said, sort of coasting over to them and out of my chat with Ashlie. "I really have to go now."

"Whatever," she said. "Call me when you learn how to do your makeup."

While it had been difficult speaking with Ashlie Salmons, alone, with no friends of any kind to back the either of us up, I did learn that Devin's flirtations with racism led to his and Ashlie's breakup, which meant Devin McGriff was looking better and better as a suspect while Ashlie was not. Maybe there was a way to draw him out and admit it.

"Stacey, lend me a dollar," I said.

"What for?"

"I need to buy a candy cane gram," I said, digging into my bag to find the form. "And I don't have enough cash."

"Oh," Yumi said, patting her heart with her one free hand. "Schwartz has the hots for someone! Call the papers. It'd better not be Skyler McGriff, because that stud is all mine."

"Do I have to call the police?" I asked. "He's, like, in university." We stopped at my locker and I flattened the order form against its surface. "Besides, this isn't a romantic gesture. If it works, we'll be able to prove who broke your arm."

I scribbled Devin McGriff's name on the form while Yumi sighed.

☠

Being less than two weeks away from winter break, many teachers had abandoned lessons altogether, moving straight into *Jeopardy!*-like review exercises and movie viewings. In other words, it was the best time to be at school. Ms. Fenstermacher brought in a DVD (from the library, I assume) of James Cameron's *Titanic* that she forced us to watch, though she fast-forwarded (as fast as she could) through those brief scenes featuring nudity. However, we weren't just allowed to watch the movie — that would be too much like fun. Instead, about every three minutes, Ms. Fenstermacher paused the DVD and randomly quizzed one of us about some history tidbit or date or famous historical item that was featured in the clip we'd just seen. It was the worst! The whole experience made me rethink the hypothesis that Ms. Fenstermacher was cool. *Titanic* wasn't even that cool a movie, and she was turning it into a pants-wetting oral exam. I found it strange that she didn't seem to get along with Mr. Santuzzi, as she seemed to be adopting some of his more devastating techniques. (Santuzzi, for his class, refused to resort to fun or videos or anything along those lines; he was determined to follow the lesson plan as if it were a direct order from a four-star general.)

So, while history class didn't really inform me of new factoids or increase my appreciation for *Titanic*, it did remind me that the ship, the *Titanic*, actually existed and that one of the survivors had lived in Sticksville with Morna's family, according to Ms. Fenstermacher. She'd mentioned it earlier at the museum and it came up a few times during the film screening. I felt stupid for not thinking of it earlier, but perhaps Dr. Alfred Pain's family was still around and perhaps they knew something about the unusual death of a Scottish girl who once lived in the same boarding house as their ancestor.

☠

Since we don't have a home computer with an internet connection, my venue choices to research Dr. Pain's family were the school library, the public library, or the Sticksville Museum. I chose the town's public library, since it seemed the least likely place I'd run into any other classmates or teachers.

Those wooden catalogue drawers at the public library? Apparently they are still used, and some of them are filled with the town archives' birth, death, and marriage notices, dating back to 1861. The nice librarian at the information desk tried to convince me to use those to search for Dr. Alfred Pain, but I was all about the information super-highway (or, more plainly, the internet). I took a seat at a free computer terminal and began searching the *Sticksville Loon*'s archives: the births, deaths, and marriages data had all been turned into an online database a few years ago. But, typing away at the keyboard, I found no sign of "Dr. Alfred Pain" or even just "Alfred Pain" in the births, deaths, *or* marriages. Then I searched for just "Pain," and still nothing, though the *Loon* database suggested there were a few "Paines" to consider.

So, Dr. Alfred Pain was not born, not married, and didn't die in Sticksville. Conceivable enough, though in my experience, I'd found it very hard to escape the place.

"Hello there," said a chipper voice to my right. At the terminal beside me appeared my history teacher, Ms. Fenstermacher, who must have been sleeping at the library, since the two whole times I'd been there in the past month, so had she. "What brings you to the public library?" she asked. She was probably going on *Battlestar Galactica* online forums or finding more history DVDs to ruin in class.

"Oh," I said. "After we watched *Titanic* in class, I couldn't stop thinking about that local survivor. So cool. If I'd lived through the *Titanic*, I'd never stop talking about it. At parties, I'd be like, *Would you like a glass of water? You know what contained a lot of water . . . eventually? The* Titanic. *In fact, it was sunk by a chunk of frozen water.* So, anyway, I wanted to look him up, but I can't find him listed in the births, deaths, and marriages database."

"Who, Alfred Pain?" she asked, pushing a stick of cinnamon gum into her mouth.

"Yeah, Dr. Pain."

"Such an unfortunate name," she said. "Well, why don't you just do a general internet search for Dr. Alfred Pain? The *Titanic* is one of the most well-documented disasters in history. Researchers have found information on even the poorest passengers on the ship."

Cinnamon gum notwithstanding, Ms. Fenstermacher was

full of good ideas as usual. I typed Alfred Pain's full name (and profession) into the search engine and the first page listed was something, I kid you not, called *Encyclopedia Titanica*. When I clicked through, the information was all there: born in 1888, occupation: doctor, second-class passenger. It all checked out with what the museum and Ms. Fenstermacher and Roxy Wotherspoon's diary said, save one minor detail. *Encyclopedia Titanica* said Dr. Pain sank with the ship and died in 1912.

I checked Alfred Pain's name on a few other sites, all of which claimed the man died in 1912, two years before Morna did. I could feel my hands getting clammy and sweat beading on my forehead, but I hid it from Ms. Fenstermacher as best I could. Still, there was no escaping the fact: either Morna and Roxy Wotherspoon and the Sticksville Historic Society were mistaken about the man's name, or Dr. Alfred Pain was an impostor!

☠

Blame It
On Cane

You probably never would have guessed it, but candy cane grams turned out to be the worst. I had expected they would be after my first introduction to the concept last week, but the most I'd expected was the beloved students getting a little more beloved (and via a holiday theme). I was not expecting the magnitude of awfulness that arrived with the candy cane grams in Mr. Santuzzi's math class.

Mr. Santuzzi was in the middle of tearing the clearly suicidal Mike DeCaprezi a new parabola (math joke) for talking during class, when the two student council representatives started rapping at the door. My math teacher looked like a dog who'd had his chew toy taken away when they interrupted. Zogon and Goose Neck heaved a large canvas bag filled to the brim with red-and-green candy canes on top of Mr. Santuzzi's desk. Zogon unfurled a list of candy cane gram recipients and started calling out names, making the whole undertaking extra embarrassing. I could have told you beforehand which people in my math class would and wouldn't be receiving these stupid rip-off gifts; I was on the wouldn't list. But then Zogon shouted "October Schwartz!"

I raised my hand hesitantly; I was certain this was a prank — that I was going to receive a pie in the face or atomic wedgie instead of a candy cane gram. Colour me surprised when Goose Neck sighed heavily and tossed an already shattered candy cane and its accompanying note onto my desk. Way more confused than excited — there was no way my combination of goth chic, no sleep, and less-than-inviting attitude had won me any secret admirers — I carefully unfolded the "gram" portion of the candy cane gram.

I should have known it would be a death threat. Printed in a plain computer typeface, it read: *Keep playing girl detective, and you'll end up a girl corpse.*

I smiled and tried to look pleased, as if it had been some sweet little nothing from some well-meaning clean-cut boy. At the same time, my eyes were working overtime scanning the room in case the sender of said death-o-gram was in the classroom with me. Mr. Santuzzi was standing right there, but he seemed to be more ticked off by the class interruption than, say, meaningfully burning a hole in my forehead with his steely eyes.

At lunch, my paranoia moved into overdrive. Any diner (if you can call anything happening in the cafeteria dining) was my potential Secret Santa of Doom. When someone looked at me for more than two seconds, I tried to remember who they were and why they might festively threaten me. Devin McGriff was still Suspect Number One, and since I had sent him a similarly cryptic candy cane, I suppose it was only fair. (To my credit, my candy cane gram wasn't a death threat.) But I couldn't rule out anyone.

I took a seat with Yumi and Stacey, assuming I could trust them, at least, if no one else.

"This candy cane gram thing is sort of draining my holiday spirit," Yumi lamented, pushing her macaroni and cheese around with a fork.

"And after it had just been heightened by the cancellation of the radio program," I said.

"What about you, Schwartz?" Yumi inquired. "You the proud recipient of a candy cane gram?"

"Ha, no," I scoffed. Maybe I trusted the two of them, but I didn't want to worry them with the whole death threat thing. Yumi was, after all, receiving threats of her very own.

"What about you, Yumi? Did you send one to Skyler McGriff?"

"No. That's stupid," she said, slowly turning red.

"We've got bad news for you," Stacey warned, disengaging his ear buds. "Guess who *did* get one. Your *dad.*"

"That is . . ." I tried to think of a good synonym for something that made me want to stick a soldering iron in my eye socket. ". . . problematic."

An impending candy cane gram, if he knew to expect one, would explain why Dad had been so smiley recently. Was he dating someone? I'd never seen him even notice anyone, save Crown Attorney Salmons, and I don't think I could handle my dad seeing an older version of Ashlie.

"Think it's Ashlie's mom?" Yumi said, smiling wide. "You two going to be stepsisters?"

"Boom," I said, blowing my brains out with a finger gun. "I'm not going to let that happen. I'd *Parent Trap* that situation before it got out of hand. Stacey, did you see if Devin McGriff got a candy cane gram?"

More important than my dad's love life was the news that (a) I'd sent Devin a candy cane gram designed to call him out on his attacks on Yumi and the entire Asian-Canadian community, and (b) that I knew one of his bandmates really well.

"He did," Stacey said, "which was weird, because I heard he and Ashlie broke up. But I guess she reserved it before they split? It would explain why he flipped out."

"He got angry?"

"Yeah, he lost it. Ripped up the note and stomped on the candy cane gram. He was sent to the principal's office for scaring the other students."

Things couldn't have been more perfect. If Devin was so frustrated by my note, essentially an "I know what you did last summer" thing, it meant I was on the right track. But what was the next step? I'd have to catch Devin in the act of terrorizing Yumi, and I had no way of knowing when he'd strike next. My best guess was that he'd try something at the holiday pageant next week. That meant I could devote my weekend to Morna's mystery and find out who Dr. Pain really was.

Then, with the jingle-jangle of "Gypsys, Tramps & Thieves" from Yumi's handbag, things *did* get more perfect.

With her one good hand, Yumi dug into her skull-emblazoned bag and fished out her phone. She flipped it open and made a little explosion sound with her cheeks.

"Another threatening text from Guelph?" Stacey asked.

"Yes, but this one's not for me." Yumi swivelled the phone around so I could read the message: TELL UR FRIEND OCTOBER 2 BACK OFF OR SHE'S NEXXT.

Double Xs aside, this seemed like a near-identical message to my candy cane gram. I glared over to the Phantom Moustache table, but Devin McGriff didn't seem to be fiddling with his phone. That's when a genius idea struck me.

"Stacey," I said. "Can you do me a *big* favour and call Devin over to the table?"

"Why?"

"Just do it, please? Pretend you need to know when the next band practice is."

"Whatever," Stacey said, then twisted his body half around to shout "Devin! Devin, over here!"

Devin didn't look too pleased to be yelled at by his new drummer across the cafeteria. As he reluctantly extracted himself from his cafeteria bench, I started typing my response on Yumi's phone: THANXX 4 THE WARNING.

I waited until Devin had reached our table and mashed my thumb down on the Send button.

"What do you want?"

"Oh," Stacey, who had resumed eating his sandwich already, said. "When's the next band practice?"

"Tomorrow night," Devin spat, throwing his hands in the air. "How many times do we have to tell you that?"

Devin exhaled in extreme disappointment and retuned to the table. He must have been upset he crossed the cafeteria aisle just for that. He wasn't the only disappointed one.

"What was all that about?" Yumi asked, taking back her phone and dropping it into her purse like a quarter into a wishing well.

"Sorry, I thought that would work," I said. "I replied to that threat and figured if it was Devin, we'd hear his phone go off."

"Unless he has it turned off," Stacey suggested.

"Stacey, what are we, at the opera?" Yumi elbowed him in the shoulder. "Of course he has his phone on. It's okay. Thanks for trying, I guess. I'm sure the text messages will stop eventually."

To know Yumi had these threats hanging over her head until the dead kids and I or someone else (*unlikely*) did something about it was terrible. She cast her eyes downward and picked at the fabric of her sling with her free hand. Unsure of what to say, I finished the remaining few bites of my sandwich.

"So, October." Yumi's face lit up once again. "You have exciting plans for the weekend? Stacey and I were going to watch Christmas horror movies — there are four *Silent Night, Deadly Nights* we haven't seen. Want to join us?"

"Maybe, guys," I said. "But I have a lot of history homework I need to tackle."

☠

A lot of history homework may have been a bit of an understatement. In both of my investigations, I had hit dead ends, which seemed impossible. I felt like I was standing in the centre of a busy train station, suspects and facts swarming all around me, and all the directional signs were in a foreign language. No, worse than that — the signs had no words at all. Just unmarked arrows leading every which way.

Yumi's tormentor had to be Devin McGriff, but his phone hadn't reacted when I'd texted the number. The number had a 519 area code, so it hadn't made much sense for it to be Devin's phone, but if it wasn't him, then who was it? One of the other Phantom Moustache band members? They could conceivably have had a communal out-of-town telephone to make death threats with, but I doubted any of them were that clever. I had to catch Devin McGriff (or whoever the mystery attacker was) in the act or taking a look at his cell, and, unfortunately, it seemed like that might have to wait until the holiday pageant on Tuesday. The pageant would be the only real shot I'd have at getting Devin alone and (I hoped) sneaking a look at his phone history.

Morna's murderer was another giant question mark. Sam Cheng, who had seemed like such an ideal murder suspect (if such a thing existed), now appeared to be a really unfortunate red herring. Dr. Alfred Pain, since he'd faked his identity, now seemed a likely culprit, but I had no clue how to investigate him. The problem with impostors is that they could be almost anyone.

Though it tore at me to admit, I had to return to the telephone in the Crooked Arms. As a problem-solver, I worried I was using this mystical limbo-phone as a crutch. How was I going to solve mysteries once the Crooked Arms was demolished and gone? What would I do without my trusty raspy-voiced sidekick? These were questions for later, because I had to swallow my pride and whatever amount of dust hung in the air of that boarding house's lobby and call 735 again. My dead-kid time was running low. By my calendar — everyone's calendar, really; mine wasn't anything special — I had just two weeks left before the dead kids disappeared.

☠

A considerable amount of shame accompanied my visit to the dead kids that night. They had no interest in returning to the

Crooked Arms, and I could tell they sensed whatever detective skills I once had were atrophying. They probably figured, in no time, they wouldn't need me to help solve their mysteries anymore, just that magic telephone. (The joke was on them, though, because the phone voice only spoke to me. So there.)

Again, the six of us found ourselves in the lobby of the Crooked Arms, untouched since we'd been there last. Even the glass door of the grandfather clock was still lying diagonally along the wooden floor.

"Can we get this over with?" Kirby asked, rubbing his half-closed eyelids. "I don't understand why we're even here. You can talk to that phone by yourself."

"We could be playin' board games," Tabetha agreed. "Or writin' love letters ta' our great-grandchildren."

"Ha ha," Morna deadpanned, then stuck out her tongue. "Very funny."

"We're a team, you guys," I reminded them as I knelt down beside the telephone on the lobby desk. "Whatever this voice on the phone tells me, I want you all to hear it so we can figure out what it means. Morna, especially."

"Can't you just ask the voice on the phone who killed Morna so we can end this?" Derek asked.

"I have asked, twice, and it didn't tell me. If you'd been paying any attention, you might have noticed the answers the phone gives me are pretty cryptic."

"So, you need us to solve the puzzle," Kirby said, still unimpressed.

"Basically." I lifted the phone and recited the numbers written on the wall again. I waited for the telltale hiss. "Uh, hello . . . how are you?"

Okay, so that was probably a stupid way to start my phone conversation with the mysterious voice, but how often do you think someone asked the voice how it was doing?

"Are you there?"

"Yes," she answered.

"I need your help . . . again."

"Yes."

"Can you tell me who killed my friend, Morna MacIsaac? She lived here. She's really great and I'd like to help, y'know, solve her murder," I explained.

"Look at the inventor," it answered, then promptly hung up.

"Look at the inventor?" I repeated, though more as a question. I dropped the mouthpiece into the phone hook. "Morna, what about the inventor? An inventor lived here in the boarding house, right? My history teacher mentioned him to me. Gideon someone?"

"Mr. Sundbäck," Morna said.

"Yeah, Gideon Sundbäck," I agreed. "Do you remember anything about him?"

Morna sat down suddenly, scratching slowly at the wooden floor with her right hand. "He was . . . Swedish, I think. Had a moustache."

While *I* was willing to consider a moustache evidence of criminal activity, most people were not.

"It's okay," Cyril said, kneeling at Morna's side. "Take your time."

"Did he hurt you, Morna?" I asked.

"I . . . I don't know."

"What was he inventing? Do you know that?"

"I saw the invention one day," she continued, seeming to grasp at memories as best she could. "It was hidin' in the clock." Morna's eyes were darting back and forth, like a wasp was hovering before her face.

"What was it?" I asked. Following a long shot, I retrieved my composition book from my backpack and opened it to a fresh page. I pressed a Bic pen into her free hand. "Try drawing it!"

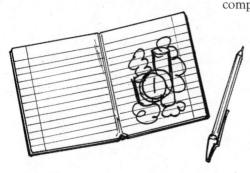

While the dead kids' faces were pinched in disbelief at

my admittedly unorthodox line of questioning, when Morna started scribbling on a blank page of *Two Knives, One Thousand Demons*, they were convinced by the results. She illustrated two cylinders, one wider and shorter than the other, and a series of dark black wires to connect them, then finished with a wide circle in the middle. I took the book back from Morna and turned it so I could better see.

"Are you sure this is what you saw in the clock, Morna?" I asked.

"Yeh, I'm sure," Morna confirmed. "Why?"

"I don't want to alarm you, but this invention you saw . . . it looks like a time bomb."

☠

Fasten Nation

And boom went the proverbial dynamite. Fasten your seatbelts, readers, these mysteries just started getting fast and furious, and soon we'll be Tokyo Drifting toward the climax. As October realized, though the suspect trail for Yumi Takeshi's mystery had run momentarily cold, Morna MacIsaac's mystery had suddenly become white-hot with the power of a million suns. The Swedish inventor downstairs built a time bomb and hid it inside the boarding house's grandfather clock, while the Chinese laundryman upstairs was framed for sabotage? Can you say, "Hello, motive?" Why, if Morna MacIsaac had discovered that hidden bomb (and it certainly sounded like she did), and if the inventor Sundbäck discovered she discovered that hidden bomb, that could lead to a very dead Scottish girl, depending on the inventor's temperament. And considering he was building secret time bombs, let's assume he wasn't the most level-headed person in Sticksville.

October Schwartz, for what felt like the first time in recent weeks, was certain of her next step. Again, she had to form an uneasy alliance with Ms. Fenstermacher and find out, from her Sticksville Museum archives or whatever resources she had, everything she knew about Gideon Sundbäck: where he went after living at the Crooked Arms, if he was ever apprehended for his crimes, and whether he had any living descendents. Tragically, she had to sit through three other classes and lunch before history class, and she felt like the waiting just might kill her.

The classes that day were especially interminable, and October was hard-pressed not to just leap to her feet in the middle of class, sprint down to the history department, and demand Ms. Fenstermacher reveal every detail she knew about the inventor Gideon Sundbäck and his (presumably) nefarious plot against the Canadian military. Instead, October was keeping it cool, sitting in Mrs. Tischmann's music class, rehearsing for the upcoming holiday pageant. She was seated between Dan, the other trombonist, and a miniature girl named Meg — even shorter than Yumi — who played the tuba. Mrs. Tischmann began with a few scales to warm up the class, then proceeded to "Hark, the Herald Angels Sing."

"The drama class that will precede us at the holiday pageant," Mrs. Tischmann explained, "is doing some revised version of *A Christmas Carol*. Something with computers, I hear." She stuck out her tongue like she'd accidentally put cat food in her sandwich, which was not something out of the realm of possibility. "We're going to have to raise the audience's spirits after that."

Sixteen bars into "Hark, the Herald Angels Sing," Mrs. Tischmann brought the music class to a sudden halt. Apparently, the percussion section (of which Stacey MacIsaac was a member) was not anchoring the rest of the group the way they were supposed to. Tischmann needed to focus on the one student, Hans, who was playing the tubular bells, because he seemed to be having the most trouble. October Schwartz, still torqued up from the revelations about the inventor, took the opportunity to jump-start things on her second mystery. Throwing her head into the jaws of the lion, she poked Ashlie Salmons, seated a row ahead of her with her fellow clarinet players, between her small shoulderblades.

Ashlie turned her head around — not, as one would expect, *Exorcist*-style, without moving her body — to face her poker. The look on her face was not one of amusement.

"Did you just poke me, Zombie Tramp?" she rasped, as if her next action would be tearing October's larynx clear from her throat.

"Uh, yes," October whispered. "Sorry?"

Ashlie's eyes narrowed to black rectangles. "What do you want?"

"Okay, you're, like, done with Devin McGriff, right?" October asked, unsure whether her wording was sufficient.

"Oh, yes." Ashlie savoured the word, as if enjoying a really good piece of Belgian chocolate.

"So, can you please tell me? Was he the one who tipped the phone booth? Is he sending Yumi those texts?" October kept her eyes partially on Mrs. Tischmann and the tubular bellman, knowing as soon as his little private lesson ended, so did her opportunity for a heart-to-heart with Ashlie Salmons.

"What?" Ashlie asked. "No. I mean, I don't think so." She thought further about it. "I mean, he can be disgusting and insensitive, to say the least, but I don't think he's capable of something like that. To be honest, I had my suspicions it was Boston."

"Boston?" October was surprised.

"Mm," Ashlie said, indicating with her narrow eyebrows that Mrs. Tischmann was nearly done. "Boston hated Yumi the most. He's probably planning to turn Stacey against her using the band."

"Boston Davis? But isn't he too dumb for that?" October had real difficulty imagining Boston Davis as the mastermind of anything. If he'd attacked the phone booth, he'd probably have used a clear tarp and crushed himself under the booth's weight.

"Okay, conversations over," Mrs. Tischmann announced, taking her place back at the music stand at the centre of the room and tapping at it with her baton. From behind her cat-like glasses, she scanned the various rows of musicians. "Let's take it from the top."

Several run-throughs of "Hark, the Herald Angels Sing" and "Ukrainian Bell Carol" later, followed by one meagre practice of "Jingle Bell Rock," music class ended and October was left with her confused thoughts regarding the intelligence and disposition of Phantom Moustache's lead singer, Boston Davis.

☠

With relief, she took her seat in Ms. Fenstermacher's class, because she knew she could ask her about Gideon Sundbäck, and, potentially, have Morna's whole murder mystery wrapped up by the end of the weekend. Then it would be time to move onto buying a few presents for her dad (only eight shopping days left!). But time always seemed to move much slower than October would like.

After sitting through the final third of *Titanic*, or, more accurately, *Titanic: The Endless Quiz*, October rushed to the front of class, eager to mine Ms. Fenstermacher for her historic knowledge of Sticksville. As Ms. Fenstermacher stacked her books one atop another, October fidgeted at the corner of the desk, looking all the world like she had drank seven straight tureens of coffee.

"Yes, October?" Ms. Fenstermacher said.

"Do you know who Gideon Sundbäck is?"

"He's an inventor, right?" Ms. Fenstermacher said. Bingo. "He's on the wall of famous Sticksvillians. I'm pretty sure we have his journal at the museum." Fenstermacher slung her bag over her shoulder and exited the classroom, but soon noticed October was following about eight inches behind her like some goth shadow. "Yes, October?"

"Can I see the journal?" she asked. "Can we go there now?"

"I can't wait to see this family tree you've been working on. Must be exhaustive." Ms. Fenstermacher exhaled with gusto. "Come by the museum tomorrow morning. I'm working then. I'll let you read Sundbäck's journal."

"Not tonight?"

"Tomorrow."

"Okay, thanks." October knew she was trying her history teacher's patience.

"And one of these days, you're going to have to tell me why you're so obsessed with the Crooked Arms."

It's probably safe to say Ms. Fenstermacher harboured her suspicions. Were I to guess, I'd say the leading theories Ms. F held were that October had been left outside the Crooked Arms as a baby or one of her ancestors left a fortune of silver dollars with one of the residents. But it's more likely she didn't even care and was just glad a student was interested in history.

☠

Not typically an early weekend riser, October arrived at the Sticksville Museum within minutes of its opening. She was hot on a hundred-year-old murderer's trail and she wasn't about to waste any time. The older woman behind the front desk didn't even ask when she saw the familiar harshly made-up teenager walk through the entrance; she dialled Ms. Fenstermacher's extension immediately. October's history teacher beckoned her up the stairs to the office once again and, donning white velvet gloves, showed her the journal of inventor Gideon Sundbäck.

Ms. Fenstermacher opened the book to a random page, and October could see how different his journal was from Roxy Wotherspoon's diary. For one, the handwritten text was printed in squarish, block letters, instead of the suffragette's Tilt-a-Whirl script. The journal also contained the occasional technical diagram, which was probably typical of an inventor's journal. What wasn't clear was why a historic *man's* personal thoughts were included in a *journal*, while historic *women* exclusively wrote in *diaries*. Pretty sexist, no? Such historical bias aside, October was awestruck to see the inventor's journal.

"May I read it?" she asked, puppy eyes turned toward her history teacher.

"Yes, it's okay," Ms. Fenstermacher said. "But you have to wear these," she continued, placing the journal carefully on her desk and removing the white gloves, "and I'm going to sit over here the whole time. Okay?"

"Yes, understood," October nodded, pulling on the protective mitts as fast as humanly possible.

"That's an important historic text," Ms. Fenstermacher said, seating herself behind her computer monitor. "It's right up there with that amazing diary you found." Or journal. Whatever.

October wasted no time and zipped through the dates, which Sundbäck had consistently placed in the upper outside corner of the pages, until she found entries from December 1914. Stopping there and taking a seat at the free desk across from Ms. F's, she began to read, soaking in every single word as if it might unravel the mystery.

☠

Once again, readers, we travel into the past with the help of the writings of someone who was really there: the chronicles of inventor Gideon Sundbäck. Though what follows aren't his exact words, I think I've conveyed the essence of what he recorded and what October read and absorbed like a sponge.

A blizzard was just building momentum one December day when Morna MacIsaac knocked at Gideon Sundbäck's door. She seemed startled to find him inside when he opened the door.

"Gosh, Mr. Sundbäck!" she shouted. "Ye scared me!"

We should stop here to note that Gideon Sundbäck was not what one would describe as a scary man. If he hadn't been so mysterious and so rarely seen around the boarding house, his appearance could even be described as comical. About five-foot-six, he was a squat man, not much taller than Morna herself, with a moustache that resembled the end of a push broom and a shock of hair that seemed to suggest he'd played with electricity a few times too many. That night, he answered the door in his work outfit, with a bow tie around his neck and a grey work apron over his clothes.

"Yes? Who are you?" he asked. For Sundbäck, the problem was questions always rushed to his brain faster than his memory did. So he asked who the girl was just seconds before recognizing her as one of the children from upstairs, the MacIsaacs. "Oh, of course, the MacIsaac girl."

"Sorry, Mr. Sundbäck," Morna said. "See, I'm takin' some of Mr. Cheng's clothes t'the fort, but his clothes are missin' some buttons. D'ye have any buttons I could use?"

Sundbäck didn't at first know who this Cheng without buttons was, but, as earlier, his memory caught up with his inquisitive mind and he remembered Mr. Cheng was the Chinese man who had been arrested earlier in the day. But Gideon Sundbäck had no buttons. Far from it. He had no need for buttons ever again.

"So, d'ye not have any buttons . . . ?" the Scottish girl asked again.

"Follow me," he said, then retreated into his room.

Gideon Sundbäck led Morna into the interior of his room, filled with dozens of gadgets and apparatuses, and not much arranged for living in at all. It more closely resembled a workshop that happened to have a bed in it. Mr. Sundbäck did much of his inventing here at a massive workbench, which had a large magnifying glass and lamp hanging over the surface and numerous metal tools littering the area. If there had been a reclining chair in sight, it could have passed as an old-timey (read: terrifying) dentistry office. Instead a lone swivel stool stood behind the workbench.

Mr. Sundbäck was thrilled to show off his new invention. "I would like to show you something," he said. For her part, Morna was just praying it wasn't a knife or leather strap or something like that.

"This is where you work?"

"Most of the time," he said. There was also a factory in St. Catharines, a town between Sticksville and the American border where he often travelled to work. "Now take a look."

Mr. Sundbäck proudly held out his palm. Draped across its surface was a skinny little thing that looked like two strips of fabric linked in the middle by a railroad track of metal teeth.

"You may hold it," he said.

"What is it?"

Gideon Sundbäck called it the "Separable Fastener," and if all went according to his plan, soon people would be using it instead of buttons. He said as much to Morna.

"This?" Morna was really confused as to how this flattened sardine-looking thing would ever work like a button.

"Is it confusing?" Mr. Sundbäck said. "Maybe if I were to show it in action. Wait here!"

He returned with a single leather boot. A small metal tab was at the top of the boot, and Sundbäck slid the tab up and down a track of metal teeth that ran along one side; it separated and connected as he did, opening the boot, then fastening it closed. What Sundbäck had invented, readers, is a common machine we all know as the zipper, though that term wouldn't be used for years to come.

"I am hoping this will revolutionize the way we fasten clothes," he announced, encouraging Morna to try out the separable fastener on the boot. "Separable fasteners everywhere instead of buttons! No more running around, losing buttons and so on!"

Gideon Sundbäck was trained as an electrical engineer in Sweden. But he fell in love with a woman named Elvira, and she was the daughter of the plant manager at the American Universal Fastener Company, so he moved to the United States and soon became a head designer at the company. But by the time Morna visited, Gideon's wife, Elvira, had been dead for three years. She had died in childbirth, along with their baby. Afterward, he left his adoptive home of New Jersey for southern Ontario and focused all his efforts on perfecting the separable fastener.

"Since Elvira's death," he admitted, "I have become very

single-minded. Almost like a hermit. I don't suppose you've seen much of me here at the boarding house."

"Wait, so ye've only been workin' on this . . . separable fastener?" Morna asked.

"Well, yes," he stammered. "I realize I am no Thomas Edison, but the separable fastener is a quite complicated and intricate device to design."

Sorry to interrupt the saddest inventor story ever, but here's the thing: the separable fastener looked pretty much like a zipper, and nothing at all like the invention Morna had found in the longcase clock. Could there have been more than one inventor in the Crooked Arms? Or was Mr. Sundbäck just hiding the truly amazing thing he'd created?

"But I found one of yer inventions in the clock in the hallway."

"You found a separable fastener in the longcase clock?" he said, astonished. He didn't remember leaving one of his inventions in the hallway clock. He barely remembered touching it. Unless he was, unbeknownst to him, a sleepwalker, this seemed impossible.

"No," Morna said. "The other invention — with the pipes and wires."

"Can you show me this invention?" he asked. "Please?"

Morna obeyed, leading the Swedish inventor to the lobby of the Crooked Arms. She slid her little fingers behind the front face of the clock and pulled it open. In the clock's base: nothing.

"Are you sure you saw an invention in here?" he asked.

"I swear," she said. "It was here jus' the other day. I told Dr. Pain an' he figured it was yers."

At that point, Mr. Sundbäck, like October did nearly a century later, retrieved some craft paper and a piece of chalk and asked the young Scottish girl to draw what she'd found within the clock. Morna did as best as her memory and iffy artistic talents would allow. When finished, she dropped the stick of chalk back into Gideon Sundbäck's hand and passed him the paper. And that's when he realized that Morna had seen a time bomb.

☠

"Wait a second," October said out loud, putting down the journal. "This guy invented the zipper?"

"I thought you knew that," Ms. Fenstermacher said from the corner.

October just gave her history teacher a bug-eyed stare of disbelief and read on, just in case there was anything at all useful in the book. Clearly, Gideon Sundbäck wasn't the mad bomber she'd hoped him to be — at least, not according to his journal. In retrospect, October should have known if Gideon Sundbäck confessed to making time bombs in his journal, some historian would have uncovered that news long before she did. Still, it was possible Sundbäck wrote something about the night Morna died, so she flipped a couple pages ahead.

Unfortunately, October found little of any use. Gideon Sundbäck alerted the local police about Morna's story, and they determined that the bomb she'd seen was Sam Cheng's. Where it had gone, however, they couldn't determine, since the military had found nothing but the gunpowder itself in Sam Cheng's room. According to the journal, the missing time bomb worried Sundbäck to no end.

Of slightly more interest to October were Sundbäck's writings about the night of Morna's death. Unlike Roxy Wotherspoon, he wasn't in the building the night Morna died. He'd been at the police station to discuss this bomb. But like the suffragette, he also reported the strange speech impediment of the youngest MacIsaac boy, who could say nothing but "735" for a day afterward. As for Morna's death itself, Sundbäck only wrote that when he learned of her demise, he was greatly saddened and wished, after having shown her his workshop that one day, that he'd known her a little better.

☠

Beat the Clock!

Gideon Sundbäck invented the zipper?! I couldn't believe it. The telephone voice had steered me completely wrong, and I was now having some serious telephone trust issues. I really thought I was on to something with the time bomb and the mysterious inventor downstairs, but apparently everyone in the world but me knew this guy with the impossible name had just invented the zipper. I would have said I was at square one again, but there was the recurrence of the number 735, which I was seeing so often I felt like I should get it tattooed across my bicep. What could it mean? I felt like taking another trip to the Crooked Arms with the dead kids, but this time, I was going to avoid the telephone. Clearly, it needed a timeout.

There was still the mystery of Yumi's harassment to deal with: for one, the candy cane gram and Yumi's recent texts proved that someone at my school knew that I was investigating the recent phone booth incident or Morna MacIsaac's death (or both) and wasn't happy about it. That same person (most likely) used yellow paint from Beaver Hardware to make their offensive message on the tarp. But only Stacey, Yumi, her parents, and I knew her phone number, or so I thought. It couldn't have been Stacey, could it? But who else had found out Yumi's number? I had (maybe) hastily given it to Goth Hardware Clerk, but he didn't even know anyone at our school.

These were problems that would have to wait until the

school week began. Right now, I was on the cusp of something historic, I was almost certain, and returning to the Crooked Arms was my only halfway decent idea. Morna was counting on me and we were so close to uncovering the truth, I could taste the sweet justice at the back of my throat. Also, a hair. Gross.

That night, I loaded two flashlights into my backpack and did up my black coat. The great thing about my personal style was that in most situations, I was already perfectly dressed for utmost secrecy. The dead kids were invisible to most people, I was all in black, and Sticksville was deader than my friends, it being a Saturday night and, well, Sticksville. Making my way through a minor snow incident, I met up with them in the cemetery, then the six of us quietly trudged our way through the snow until we reached the very end of Turnbull Lane. Nobody did much shovelling on Turnbull Lane.

The Crooked Arms that night looked as if someone had converted despair into, like, architecture. Its porch was like a challenge in the snow, its crumbling face an indication of the danger inside, and the fence and sign marking it for demolition acted like a cruel laugh in the face of my efforts. The sign reminded me that if I didn't figure out Morna's story before the dead kids disappeared again, there'd probably be no more spooky boarding house to search through, let alone a mystical telephone to avoid picking up.

"Guess we should get started," Derek announced.

"Here, take a flashlight." I pulled one of the heavy metallic torches from my bag and passed it to Cyril, figuring there'd be no one inside the Crooked Arms, and thus, no one to get spooked by the demonic

flashlight floating by itself.

Cyril, Tabetha, Morna, Kirby, Derek, and I ascended the wet, termite-ridden steps to the front porch. With no one around to maintain the property, the snow from the first few storms had accumulated on the porch, so I couldn't really see how high the steps went. With black gloves on, I tried the door, but it was locked shut. That was strange. All the times we'd visited before, Alyosha Diamandas (I imagined) had left it wide open. Maybe he'd locked it due to the little snowstorm.

"Okay, dead kids," I said. "Do your thing."

Cyril left the extra flashlight with me and the dead kids leapt through the heavy oak front door as easily as I might have walked through a heavy fog. Within instants, Tabetha was opening the large window to the left of the door. I rolled over its ledge and into the building and passed her the spare flashlight.

"Thanks. Now I'm going to close the window. I know you can't feel it, but it's freezing."

"What are we looking for?" Morna asked. In the dark, I couldn't find her, so I shone the flashlight in the direction of her voice. A disc of light illuminated her pale, freckled face and I panned the light across her to the front desk, that phantom telephone, and the 735 on the rear wall.

"I don't know," I admitted, "but I think it has something to do with that number. It keeps coming up."

"Well, it was the phone number here," Morna said. "And the number you keep saying into the phone."

"Seven-three-five . . . ," I said, mostly to myself. "Now what does that mean, Morna? Why did your brother keep repeating it after you died? Why is it splashed up on the walls?"

"Right alongside this," Tabetha said, angling her flashlight toward the deep crimson words, *Asphodel Meadows*, whatever the heck that meant. "Don't forget this. It might mean somethin', too."

"October," Morna tugged at my sleeve. "How is Stacey?"

"Not again . . ." sighed Tabetha.

"It's not like tha'!" Morna protested. "Ye're wrong. He's

like me cousin. I just . . . worry about him."

"Don't worry," I insisted, starting to worry our intervention hadn't helped much. "Stacey's fine. He's totally fine. His face is healing great."

"735 could be an address," Cyril suggested

"How many 735s are there in Sticksville?" Tabetha groaned. "Not ta' mention other cities! That's a horrible clue!"

"I didn't make up the clues," Cyril said. "Besides, there would be fewer 735s in 1914."

"What about 735 Asphodel Meadows?" Derek asked. "Is that a street name?"

"I don't think so," I said.

"Morna, why'd ya' leave us such a stupid clue?!" Tabetha demanded.

"It's not her fault she doesn't remember why her brother kept saying it."

"Maybe it's a phone number," Derek said.

"Yeah," Kirby mocked. "Hers."

"But . . . it could be someone else's, too . . ."

It really couldn't.

"Maybe it's some sort of code," I suggested. "Like if you replace each number with the letter it corresponds to in the alphabet, what does that spell? Or if you held the numbers up to the mirror, what does it spell? 'Zef'?"

"*Genius*," Kirby chided. "Morna can't read or write. How is she going to devise a code based on the alphabet? And that number-mirror trick was the solution last time, with your dead French teacher. There's no way that would work twice."

"I didn't think Morna left the code, Kirby," I answered. "Alyosha Diamandas said the numbers are new."

"It's not a code," Morna confirmed, remembering that much, at least. "I can't remember what it is, but it's not that. The numbers are numbers."

"We'd better hope it's not something about this boarding house," I said. "Demolition starts first thing in January, so if we need to find something in this house, the clock is ticking."

"The clock!" Morna exclaimed.

"Is ticking, yes," Kirby said. "We all heard October."

"No, the clock is the 735!"

I threw the light from my electric torch over to the clock face and the dead kids ran over to take a closer look at the antique. Sure enough, right on the clock face, under the 7 was a smaller 35. The seventh hour and thirty-fifth minute fell in the same position of the clock, and this particular type of clock listed both the hour and minute at every interval.

"There's a '735' here, but what does it mean?" Derek asked.

"Only one way ta' find out," Tabetha announced and elbowed her way to the open face of the clock. She shone her flashlight at the 7 and noticed something metal shoved under the bottom of the clock face itself.

"D'ya see that?" she asked. "Cyril, somebody. Pull that outta there."

Cyril tugged at the little metal bit and yanked it out. As he did, a jet of decades-old dust spurted out and a little yellow paper fluttered to the wooden floor. He passed the metal object to me while Derek retrieved the crumbly paper. Cyril asked,

"Do you know what it is?"

I didn't. The object was heavy and looked like an extremely wide crucifix. The top of the crucifix was decorated with a crown; in the middle there was a capital W, and at its base, a date: 1905.

"It looks like a military medal," I said. "Like for service in the army or something. But I don't recognize it or know anything about the army. Anyone else?" I offered up the medal and the dead kids passed it around.

Derek handed me the tattered old paper.

"This fell out of the little cubby hole with the medal."

I unfolded it carefully, so it didn't, like, disintegrate in my hands. There was a date stamped at the top (also 1905), but all the typewritten text was in German. As I scanned the page for any German words I knew — no signs of *blitzkrieg* or *ubermensch* anywhere in sight — a chunk of paper in the lower right corner flaked off.

"It's in German," I said, and handed it to Kirby.

"What?" he said. "I don't know German. Isn't knowing *both* official languages enough for you people?"

"Fine," I said, taking back the paper and carefully pressing it between the pages of my *Two Knives, One Thousand Demons* book. I couldn't let it get more damaged than it already was. "Let's see if we can find anything in Morna's room. Morna, can you direct us to your room?"

She nodded. "It's on the second floor."

"Wait," Derek said. "Do you think this is such a good idea?"

"Ha ha," I said. "Are you going to roll down your severed head, too?"

"No," he said. "This place just seems different. Why was it locked?"

Apparently, the Crooked Arms wasn't only spooking me,

but the dead kids as well. And while I'd normally have liked nothing more than to leave that creaky old boarding house, I couldn't resist the possibility that more clues and evidence were waiting upstairs, in either Morna MacIsaac's old room, or perhaps the room of the not-really Alfred Pain.

"Derek, I'm with five dead kids," I said. "It's not going to get any safer than this. Let's go upstairs."

We continued up to the next level of the Crooked Arms, with myself and Cyril carrying the flashlights.

"Do you hear something?" Kirby asked the group.

There was some rustling, and the occasional sound of pebbles or grit hitting the floor, but nothing so loud as to be a person. Possibly mice or bats. Both options were creepy enough, but there would have to be something more imposing than mice around to stop me from searching Morna's room.

"I hear somethin'," Tabetha called from the back. "Just mice prob'ly."

"No, I definitely hear something," Kirby said.

"What about the red writing on the wall," Derek reminded. "What if that's the name of a street gang?"

"Street gang?" I whispered. "In Sticksville? Just keep going up the stairs."

"Why are you whispering if there's no one here but mice?" he demanded.

I didn't really have any answer to that one. He had a point.

"Morna, which one's yours?" I asked when we reached the second-floor landing.

"That one," she said, pointing to our left.

I brought the flashlight to the door handle and slowly opened it with a prolonged creak. Kirby started into the room just before me and it was only his impromptu action that saved my life. A baseball bat smashed into Kirby's face so hard, his head tore clean off his neck and, with a scream, bounced back down the stairs. Like déjà vu all over again. If his head hadn't been between mine and that bat, my face and brains would have been smashed to a pulp.

The dead kids all gasped to see Kirby's head so forcibly

removed from his body, but I only began to scream when I saw who was responsible. Three guys, dressed all in black save their brightly coloured face masks, each of them wielding a baseball bat, emerged from Morna's room.

"What the — ?" the one in front exclaimed. He shook out his arms. "It was like something stopped my bat before it connected."

I recognized them — they were the same people who'd attacked us at the phone booth with the quarters.

"Girl," another baseball fan growled. "You showed up at the wrong old house on the wrong night. It's batting practice."

With that, he drew back and took another swing.

☠

Take Me
Out to the
Ball Game

Oh, the suspense! The bat smashed through the wall just inches from poor October's face, sending splinters of wood off in every direction. Her attackers, it would seem, were determined to demolish the Crooked Arms themselves by hand, and a couple weeks ahead of schedule. In some ways, despite the shoddy construction and traumatic memories associated with the boarding house, it would be sad to see the historic site razed to the ground. But given that two other batsmen were presently rushing toward October, now was probably not the best time to wax nostalgic about building preservation.

The dead kids and October dashed across the darkened hallway with their three attackers in hot pursuit — one in a red mask, one in a green one, the final in blue. October ran into the room opposite the hall from Morna's and slammed the door shut. Some of the dead kids had beaten her to the room; the stragglers ghosted through the closed door. All save Kirby were in attendance. His body had clambered down the stairs in search of its forcefully detached skull. Given the masked assailants' cries of "Get her!" and "Stop her!," it was clear they couldn't see the dead kids, so at least October didn't have to worry about that.

"Maybe we can get out that window," October whispered, pointing to the far window frame coated in cobwebs. "We're only two storeys up. If all of you jump first, maybe you can form a cushion of bodies that I can safely land on."

"Cushion a' bodies?!" Tabetha said, incredulous.

"Flashlights off!" October whispered and extinguished hers. Tabetha did the same. The five hid in a darkened corner of that room and waited for the goons with the baseball bats to arrive, which was taking a very long time considering they *had* been just steps behind them.

"I know you're not allowed to intentionally harm anyone because of the ghost rules," October whispered to Cyril. "But what if you made some accidents happen to those guys with bats? I'm going to need all your help if I'm getting out of this house with my face intact. And I'm sure those guys can't see ghosts."

"Shh!" Derek said. "I hear someone coming. We'll wait for you by the door."

The dead kids divided and took positions in various spots within the room — Derek and Tabetha waited by the room's entrance, while Cyril and Morna continued to lurk somewhere further beyond the door. The very same door clicked and yawned

open, the green-masked thug stepping quietly inside. As soon as he crossed the threshold, Derek and Tabetha began to jimmy one of the floorboards at the entrance loose, while October tried to use her natural camouflage to blend into the shadows.

"C'mon, girl," he barked, moving his bat back and forth like a Jedi's lightsabre. "We know you're hiding in here!"

A square of moonlight stood out on the darkened floor about a foot from October's shoes. She made a quick promise to herself: as soon as Green Mask stepped into that square, she was going to kick him in the shins and make a run for it. His black boot pressed down on the moonlight square and October jammed her heel into the man's lower leg as hard as she could, then sprang for the door. He howled and pursued, but October had a distinct advantage — two legs that hadn't recently been kicked. As she passed Derek and Tabetha, holding a floorboard by the open door, they called out.

"Run!" Tabetha shouted.

"And whatever you do, *duck* once you pass through the door," Derek insisted. "*Duck!*"

October sprinted through the door and lowered her body by about a foot, a surprisingly athletic feat for our heroine. Another intruder, the one in the blue mask, swung wildly, clearly hoping to split open October's head but aiming much higher than where her head actually was. October easily dove under the arc of his swing while behind her, the green-masked one stepped into a large gap in the floor where Derek and Tabetha had ripped away the floorboard. In what looked like an extremely painful maneuver, he fell about crotch-deep with one leg fully through the floor before his weight caused him to tear a hole and drop through to the room below with a crash.

The man in the blue mask recovered from his wild swing quickly, so there was no time for October to relish the dead kids' clever ploy. She rounded the corner to find the staircase that led to the front lobby. Cyril and Morna were waiting, shouting words of encouragement like those people who hold out cups of water to runners during a marathon.

"Keep goin'!" Morna said.

"We'll take care of your pursuer!" Cyril said.

October galloped down the stairs and as soon as she'd passed the two dead kids, Morna rolled her flashlight onto the top step. The blue-masked attacker, in chase, hopped onto the stairs and stepped right onto the metallic cylinder. His body shot forward and hung suspended in mid-air for a second before he landed squarely on his face and tumbled halfway down the steps.

Two guys in masks had been incapacitated by the dead kids, and October was only steps from the front door and freedom (of a sort). Unfortunately, she found the third and final assailant, his identity hidden by a red mask, blocked the exit. He tested the bat out in his open palm over and over again, not saying a word. October knew if she didn't act soon, the other two would come to, but on the other hand, she didn't see any way of escaping the Crooked Arms but through that door. Sweat stains began to develop in her general armpit region. October considered making a break for either room on the first floor, in the hopes one had a window she could jump through, but she was sure the man in the red mask moved much faster than she did. Also, she had no way of knowing for certain that either room even had a window. And broken glass is very sharp.

The man in the red mask began to lurch toward October when her salvation came from a very unlikely place. Just as Red Mask lined up his swing, the front lock clicked and the heavy oak door was thrown open. The edge of the door caught him on the back of his head, and October's enemy dropped to the dusty wooden floor like a potato sack. Holding that door open was October's least favourite Sticksville realtor, Alyosha Diamandas.

"What is happening?" he said, alarmed to find a masked man with a baseball bat prone on the floor and a teenager in front of him. "I know you. You're back? I thought I told you to never return."

"Mr. Diamandas?!" October said, never before so relieved to see the unusual little man.

The guy in the red mask wasn't as unconscious as October had hoped and dreamed, and he took the moment of confusion to scramble to his feet and escape to one of the adjacent rooms.

"What are you doing here again?" Diamandas asked, but

October's answer was drowned out by the sound of shattering glass. Both October and the real estate agent ran to the front door to see the three masked men sprinting up Turnbull Lane as fast as their injured legs could carry them. Two witnesses must have been two too many for them, or perhaps Alyosha Diamandas was a more intimidating figure than he looked. Running into a vaguely Eastern European version of John Waters in a darkened boarding house *would* be extremely scary.

"Who were they?" Alyosha asked, noticing the men's baseball bats. "Did they hurt you?"

"No, I'm fine," October panted between staggered breaths.

"What did you all do to the house?" He switched on his own flashlight and searched the front hallway. "Last time it was the clock; now look at the windows and floors!"

"Mr. Diamandas," October said. "Sorry. But this wasn't me. Those guys were ripping this house apart . . . I don't know what they were after."

"They better not have taken anything," he called out the front door, as if they could hear him from several blocks away.

"Sorry, Mr. Diamandas," October said again. She sincerely hoped the dead kids didn't choose this moment to check on her.

"There is no sorry. This does not appear to be your fault," he said, wiping his upper lip and thin moustache as he spoke. "I had come with my Yaris to pick up more of the antiques. But then I start hearing yelling and crashing so I came to investigate. But you're okay?"

Alyosha Diamandas's rescue made October feel conflicted about the dead kids' perennial amusement in pestering and annoying him. At least the dead kids were smart enough not to show their faces while she was talking with him. Earlier encounters at Mr. O'Shea's house had proven he could see the dead kids, and was not a fan of them, given how much grief they'd given him over his years of realty.

"Come on," he said. "I'll give you a ride home."

"No!" October blurted.

Alyosha Diamandas driving October home to the Schwartz residence would be problematic in several ways. Namely, Mr.

Schwartz didn't know October was out in a bad part of town at one o'clock in the morning, and she desperately wanted to keep it that way.

"Thanks, Mr. Diamandas," October said. "I'm fine. I'll just walk home."

"But —"

"No, it's totally okay. Thanks again!"

October ran out of the house and down Turnbull Lane as fast as the considerable drag of her black peacoat would allow her, but she was careful not to travel so fast as to catch up with the area's most aggressive baseball team. Luckily, she caught up with the dead kids before she did anyone wearing a mask.

"Psst, living girl!" Tabetha hissed from behind a mailbox. "Over here!"

October scurried behind the mailbox and found all five dead kids, lying in wait. Even Kirby, who was holding his head in his hands, had rejoined the group.

"Is it safe?" Morna asked.

"Is Alyosha Diamandas gone?" Derek asked.

"Yes and yes," October responded. "Now let's get back to the cemetery before those guys with baseball bats return. Once I find someone who can translate German, we'll get to the bottom of that medal and Morna's death."

Morna looked up at October and gave her a lopsided smile. But before either could say anything, the bright halogen lights of an early model Yaris illuminated the side of October's face. Alyosha Diamandas pulled his car, aged like a fine wine, up to the curb just beside the post box, and opened the front door. Accordingly, the dead kids vanished into the nearby woods.

"Really," he insisted. "I should make sure you get home safe."

☠

Sprechen Sie Deutsch?

To my horror, Alyosha Diamandas didn't just drop me off around the corner this time. Instead, he pulled into my driveway at about two in the morning. Already, I could imagine the conversation between my dad and Alyosha. I'd never be let out of the house again, especially once Alyosha told Dad about the dudes with baseball bats. I found myself seriously wondering about whether nuns were allowed to wear eyeliner, as I was half-convinced my dad would force me to enter a convent after hearing where and how Alyosha Diamandas had found me.

Unfortunately, Mr. Diamandas was in no mood for leniency. He nearly sprinted for my front door as soon as he'd removed the key from the ignition, leaving me to scramble up the wet, snowy driveway behind. I arrived at the front step well after Alyosha Diamndas had pushed the doorbell, so we stood there freezing and wiping the thick snowflakes from our faces, for a full five minutes. He rang the doorbell again. Normally, I'd chalk up the delay to the fact that it was two in the morning and my dad would have had to wake up, maybe put on shoes, that kind of thing. But after the third and fourth attempt, I knew Dad wasn't home.

"It's okay. I'll just use my key," I said.

"I feel like your father should know where you have been spending your time," Diamandas said, undaunted. He brushed a few snowflakes from his thin, dark hair. "You know where he is?"

"M-m-m-maybe he's out?" I chattered.

"Possibly," Alyosha agreed. "He may be out looking for you."

That was, of course, my next thought and my worst-case-scenario nightmare. If my dad woke up and found me missing, he'd either be roving the streets, shouting and throwing garbage cans from his path like a madman, or he'd have contacted the police and have six squad cars patrolling the alleyways and avenues by now. This was not the first time I had gone missing, after all. The only silver lining of this pitch-black rain cloud was that Alyosha — after entering the front hallway and yelling up the stairs — finally decided to leave me safely inside the house alone. As the headlamps from his Yaris receded down the street, past the cemetery, I half-expected my dad to jump out from behind the kitchen doorframe.

However, it was no joke. The house was completely dark, and a quick search upstairs revealed his room was empty. I sat on my bed and wondered what I'd do after I was pulled from Sticksville Central and home-schooled. Just as I was deciding how I'd tell Yumi and Stacey, I heard my father enter through the front door downstairs. In fact, the whole block probably heard my father coming home. If I made half the racket he did when sneaking in late at night, I'd have been caught every single time.

I pulled off my shoes and threw on some pyjamas as fast as I could then descended the stairs to find my dad flipping his thin hair back and forth, smiling, making facial expressions in the closet mirror.

"Where were *you*?" I asked, because filing a police report for his missing daughter was definitely not the answer.

"Out," he smiled.

"Out?" In all my worst-case scenarios, I hadn't imagined this. "Wait, you mean, like, *out*? With a woman? Does this have something to do with a candy cane gram?"

"Perhaps," he said, finally taking a break from posing and hanging up his jacket. "But I'd rather not say."

"Holy smokes," I said, completely grossed out by what might have happened prior to my arrival home. "You went out on a date! Who is it?"

"Listen," Dad explained. "We didn't want to say anything until we'd been out on a number of dates and knew it was somewhat serious . . ."

"*Dad!*"

"You know her daughter," he said. "It's Ashlie Salmons' mother."

The convent was looking really good, all of a sudden.

☠

Monday morning, I awoke thinking about the holiday break. My dad's stomach-churning need for companionship reminded me the holidays were coming up fast and I'd done nothing to prepare, save practice a few Christmas songs on my trombone. Originally, I'd planned to do my gift shopping after I solved Morna's mystery, but as it was now December 19, that plan was looking naively optimistic, at best. What should I get my dad? And did I have to buy his new girlfriend (yuck), Ashlie's mom, something, too? Should I buy Yumi and Stacey something? I was going to find out who'd been tormenting Yumi and bring him (or her) to justice, which, if you thought about it, was kind of the greatest gift of all.

I put on one final layer of eyeliner, pulled on my torn-up peacoat, then my gloves, and headed off to school. Normally, first order of business would have been to find Yumi and Stacey at school and talk about the weekend, but since my weekend involved nearly being beaten to death by masked assailants while investigating my dead friend's murder then discovering my dad and my arch-enemy's mom were dating, I decided that it would probably be best if I didn't even see them.

First order of business, instead, was to find out just how German Ms. Fenstermacher was and see if she could translate the old note and the medal I'd swiped from the clock. I mean, her last name was German. But my last name was German, too. I hoped her family was more in touch with the old country than ours.

French class wrapped up a bit early, so I took the opportunity to go full stalker on Ms. Fenstermacher and tracked her down to her first-period classroom. Her morning class filed out and I lingered by the doorway. I unsheathed my *Two Knives, One Thousand Demons* book from my bag and crept up to the front of the room where Ms. Fenstermacher was tidying her desk.

"Mrs. Fenstermacher, can I ask you a question?"

"October?" She was probably surprised to see me so early in the day, but the earlier I asked her to do me this huge favour — *please translate this pivotal piece of evidence* — the better. "Sure, shoot. Though I don't know what you'd have a question about. You're running circles around the rest of your class. It's like watching Starbuck fly loop-the-loop around the Cylons."

That must have been a *Battlestar Galactica* thing again. Seriously, lady. You're allowed to have more than one hobby.

"It's not about history; it's about German," I said.

"German? What about it? I don't teach it, but I'm pretty sure you can start taking it as an elective in grade ten."

"Yes," I stuttered. "I was . . . uh . . . was wondering if you knew how to speak German."

"Oh." Ms. Fenstermacher seemed surprised. "Yes. I mean, my parents spoke it at home. I'm very rusty, but I think I could get by in Deutschland. Why do you ask?"

"I need someone to translate this," I said, heartened that she seemed to know the German word for *Germany*, and unfolded the crispy eggshell paper and placed it on top of her lesson book, just like you might expect someone to do in a movie. Usually, I tried to avoid that kind of super-mysterioso preamble before asking for help, since whoever was watching you often assumed you were overdramatic. But the holidays were looming, classes were ending, and the dead kids would be disappearing again to wherever they go within a week; I felt the time for stupid, overdramatic gestures was now.

"What's this?" Ms. Fenstermacher asked, holding the paper up as gingerly as if it were a baby bird that had fallen out of its nest. (Truthfully, I don't think you're supposed to pick those up or the mama bird rejects the babies or something cold like that.)

"I found it in my great-great-grandfather's old stuff, along with this." In another one of those grand gestures, I placed the medal on her desk. "Can you tell me what they say?"

I couldn't read the look on Ms. Fenstermacher's face. She was either truly amazed and impressed, or completely horrified — as if she were talking to a teenaged grave robber. Which I guess she was.

"Yes," she said. "Yes, I can help you translate this, but I have to run to my next class — and I imagine you do, too. Can we meet at lunch? Come to the library at a quarter after twelve."

I nodded before folding the paper back into the composition book and pocketing the medal. Ms. Fenstermacher, whatever she was thinking, was wise: I *did* have a class to run to, too. The only class I never wanted to be late for: Mr. Santuzzi's.

When I arrived, out of breath at the math class door, I found — surprise, surprise — the monster had locked me out! After rapping at the little window in the door for thirty seconds, chipping my black nail polish and everything, the face of the teaching assistant, Skyler McGriff, appeared on the other side. He let me in with an admonition.

"October, if there were one class for which I'd be sure to arrive on time, it'd be math," he whispered, so as not to interrupt Mr. Santuzzi's lecture on how knowing about a triangle's hypotenuse could be used in military surface-to-air attacks. "Keep showing up late, and Santuzzi is going to make you a corpse."

Having Devin's older brother in Mr. Santuzzi's class almost felt like we students had someone on our side. Unbelievable to think he was brothers with the Cro-Mag I was ninety percent sure was harassing Yumi and leaving her racist messages. I tried to slink over to my seat without attracting Mr. Santuzzi's attention, but it was no use.

"Miss Schwartz," he roared, interrupting what I'm sure was a riveting presentation on the military applications of grade nine geometry. "Have your holidays started already?"

As sure as I was that Yumi's tormentor was Devin McGriff, it never made sense to rule out Mr. Santuzzi. His sadistic streak meant he was always a potential candidate whenever human suffering was involved.

☠

At lunch, all people could talk about was tomorrow night's holiday pageant. So intense was this widespread feeling of pre-show jitters or excitement or whatever it was that when I arrived in the cafeteria, I saw something I never thought I'd see: Ashlie Salmons talking with Yumi and Stacey.

Not that Ashlie was, like, eating lunch with the two of them. Even someone with the most basic understanding of high school social strata knew that would be as unlikely as the Queen of Monaco having tea with a dirty-shirted *World of War-craft* addict. Ashlie Salmons was standing a good two feet from Yumi and Stacey's table, like it was some kind of jungle cat enclosure, but they were definitely talking — and not just insulting each other, either. They were discussing the abridged *A Christmas Carol* that was part of the pageant, and, as collegial as their talk appeared to be, I did note that Ashlie kind of snarled when I sat down across from Yumi.

"What's up, Zombie Tramp?" She flipped her perfect bangs my way. "Your friend here and I were just discussing our little Christmas play. It's too bad you're not in our class."

I could just imagine having drama class with Ashlie Salmons. One class with her and I'd make like Ophelia and drown myself in a stream. Or drown her in a stream.

"Why's that?" I said.

"You could play the Ghost of Christmas Future and you wouldn't even need any makeup. Scary enough, as is."

"Nice to see you've been overtaken by the spirit of the season," I muttered.

"Oh, there were much *worse* things I could have said," Ashlie warned, then rotated ninety degrees and returned to her usual table, already occupied by Novelty T-shirt ("No Mistletoe Required"), Goose Neck, Big Laugh, and Wanda Pang. But no Devin McGriff nor any other Phantom Moustache members were to be seen.

"Yumi," I said, taking hold of my sandwich. "What happened? Where are the bygone days of Salmons hatred?"

"She's gone soft," Stacey said.

"I have *not* gone soft," she said, punching him hard in the shoulder. "I just respect her a bit now because she broke up with her boyfriend over racist humour, you know? Besides, it was all business. We had to talk about the play."

"How is *A Christmas Carol* coming? You going to be ready by tomorrow?"

Yumi shrugged. "Have to be, I guess. Though everyone's disappointed that my arm's broken — my legs are supposed to be the problem. It's tough to use a wheelchair with a cast and sling."

"Whatever happens, we've got you covered in the music department, right, Stacey?"

Stacey, chewing his sandwich like an overtired cow with bedhead, made no rush to agree.

"Are The Plotzdam Conference really coming?" I asked.

"Yeah," Yumi said. "Apparently they're total do-gooder choir boys and were really moved by our school's struggle against anti-Asian sentiment."

"But aside from that assembly and our therapy sessions, what has the school done about it?" I asked, genuinely ignorant.

Yumi shrugged. "Not much. But I'm just happy they're letting The Plotzdam Conference play our holiday pageant. They're going to play the Dreidel song and one other Hanukkah song."

A moment of silence followed during which we tried to think of a second Hanukkah song. The silence was interrupted when Yumi's phone began to ring. No "Gypsys, Tramps & Thieves" this time.

Yumi explained, "I haven't set a ringtone for actual calls yet, just texts."

"Who's calling you?" Stacey asked. "Your dad?"

"No, it's an unknown number," she said.

"Maybe they've moved on to threatening phone calls," I suggested, probably not helping.

"No. It's a different number than before. Our area code."

"Oh," I said, the phone now well into its third ring. "Answer it! I forgot to tell you, but I gave this goth guy at the hardware store your phone number."

"What?!"

"Listen, I'm sorry, but I don't have a phone of my own and I couldn't risk my dad answering."

"October, you can't just give my number out to any hot goth you see," Yumi argued.

"It's not like that. He's *old*."

The phone rang a sixth time; Goth Hardware Clerk was going to hang up for sure. Or go to Yumi's voice mail. But during my argument with Yumi, I realized Goth Hardware Clerk had Yumi's number, as well. Could he have been making the threatening texts? Or have given the number to someone who was? Why had I been so trusting of a stranger just because he probably wore a Nine Inch Nails T-shirt under his work uniform?

"Yumi!" I yelled and yanked her phone out of her hands. I tried to maintain a somewhat calm and casual tone as I answered the phone while fleeing the cafeteria. "Yes, hello."

"Oh, hey. I was just waiting for voice mail," the voice said. "This is Percy, from the hardware store? You asked me to call if that guy came in again to buy spray paint?"

"Oh, yeah," I said. "Thanks. Did he?"

"He came in yesterday, but it was a big bucket of yellow house paint this time. He wouldn't give me his name, but I went all Jason Bourne on him and saw his name when he opened his wallet. His last name is McGriff."

"McGriff? Really?" I could barely believe my luck. The one person I had suspected the whole time was the guy actually responsible.

"Yeah, pretty sure. I mean, he opened his wallet pretty quick, but that's the name."

"Listen, thanks. I owe you one."

Percy was, I think, attempting to give me his name again as I hung up. Like I'd ever forget a name like Percy.

When I returned to the cafeteria, Yumi wasn't too pleased with me for stealing her phone.

"It was important, trust me," I said, dropping the cell phone into her unbroken hand.

"How many other people did you give my number to?" she asked.

"None, I swear."

"Keep it that way," she said, stuffing the phone back into her skull-and-crossbones bag. "And if you run into, like, a punk grocery bagger . . . try to restrain yourself."

After an uncomfortable few minutes eating, I realized it was nearly quarter after twelve and I had a German lesson scheduled in the library.

"Guys, I'm sorry for acting so weird today," I told my lunchtime companions. "But I have to go learn some German from Ms. Fenstermacher in the library."

"Since when are you learning German?" Yumi asked, her eyebrows belying her extreme suspicion.

"Wait, Ms. Fenstermacher speaks German?" Stacey said. I didn't want to imagine what that meant to him.

"Yes, now I really have to go," I said, stuffing my things into my bag and just leaving my lunch garbage on the table like a real jerk.

As I suspected, Ms. Fenstermacher was already waiting for me in the library. She was seated at one of the round sturdy tables with her arms crossed tightly across her plaid Western shirt, like it was cold in the library or something. (It was not.) She saw me as I thundered through the library door, probably looking like a complete mess. Ms. Fenstermacher always looked so put together and I usually felt like a paintbrush that had been dipped in black ink and left out to dry for several days.

"Funny to meet you in *this* library for once," she said as I took the seat beside her.

"Heh." I tried to laugh more at that. I really did.

"So, this letter is from your great-great-grandfather," she said as I unfolded the dried old paper onto the table.

"Yeah, actually." As if there were any doubt.

"And this note and medal were your great-great-grandfather's?"

"Uh, it was in his stuff. I don't know if it was *technically his*," I clarified, for the likely event I was caught in a lie. Best to make things as vague as possible, I thought.

"This medal is a very big deal," she asserted, turning the heavy crucifix over and over in her hand. "It's the Iron Cross, the most prestigious medal awarded by the German military, and it looks like this one was awarded in 1905."

1905 didn't help me. Morna died nine years after that. And the fake Dr. Pain wasn't on the *Titanic* until 1912.

"The document that goes along with it is sort of like a note of commendation — who the Iron Cross was awarded to and why, that sort of thing."

"And who was it awarded to?" I asked, crossing my fingers it was a name from the Crooked Arms — a Gideon Sundbäck or Sam Cheng, even a Dr. Pain. Something I could *use*.

"Someone named Udo Schlangegriff. *For service above and beyond the call of duty in southwestern Africa. Cameroon*, it says," Ms. Fenstermacher pointed at Udo's name in the document, which, to be fair, looked pretty much like every other German word if you weren't looking for it. "October, is there a Schlangegriff branch in your family tree?"

Here's the thing — my knowledge of my ancestry goes back to my dad, who is kind of a lone wolf, so there could have been a Schlangegriff or Vanderbilt or Stalin in my family tree and I'd be none the wiser. But I was pretty confident in saying I *wasn't* related to Udo Schlangegriff, whoever he was.

"No," I said. "But my great-great-grandfather supposedly fought with the German army in World War I. Maybe he picked this up from a fallen soldier?"

"This Iron Cross," Ms. Fenstermacher said, holding it between her thumb and forefinger, "is a huge honour, October. Udo Schlangegriff's relatives might want it."

"Oh," I said. "I didn't realize. I'll see if I can find them and get in touch."

More accurately, I was going to see if I could find any information on Udo Schlangegriff and figure out how he and his stupid Iron Cross were connected to my friend Morna's death. I thanked Ms. Fenstermacher for her time and German skills before leaving for music class.

"Any time you need some German translated," she said, "I'm your girl."

☠

During music, we rehearsed for the holiday pageant, running through our three songs over and over again. Stacey enjoyed it, as it meant plenty of time behind the drum kit. The rehearsal was handy for me, too, as it gave me ample time to think. The trombone part in nearly all holiday songs is super easy, and at this point, it was the flutes who needed the most help. So, while Mrs. Tischmann ran through the difficult sections in the "Ukrainian Bell Carol" with the woodwinds, I thought about how Udo Schlangegriff could be connected to Morna's death.

Udo Schlangegriff. I wished the name sounded familiar but all Schlangegriff sounded like to me was one of the rejected names for houses at Hogwarts. Udo Schlangegriff could very well be the real name of the fake Alfred Pain, but why would he pose as a *Titanic* survivor? He was a German war hero, back when Germany was one of the "good" countries — as good as European countries ever got, I guess (what with all their colonialism). Why a German war hero would be hiding out in a ramshackle boarding house in Sticksville, posing as a drowned doctor, baffled me, and baffle was not a verb I used lightly. The only thing that made sense was if he had something to do with the time bomb. Could he have been the real saboteur, and not Sam Cheng?

☠

Snow was falling in fat, lazy flakes as I walked (again) to the Sticksville Public Library. It seemed I was there as often as I was home. By the time I reached the library's parking lot, it was covered in a thick white carpet of snow. My All-Stars left a trail behind me, all the while providing little protection for my feet. I brought a squall of flakes and frigid air with me as I barrelled through the library's entrance.

Though I was certain I'd see Ms. Fenstermacher in the library again, she was remarkably absent. I took a seat at a free computer terminal and entered "Schlangegriff" into the births, deaths, and marriages database. Whatever I had expected to find, I couldn't say, but what I did find was unexpected.

The database listed only one entry for Schlangegriff, and that was my Udo Schlangegriff, who apparently died in 1919 right here in Sticksville. But the list of (one) Schlangegriff also included an interesting note at the end: "see also *McGriff*." When I searched "McGriff," a much longer list appeared, beginning in 1916 and continuing almost to the present day.

The earliest McGriff entry was a birth, in 1916, of one Paul McGriff, the son of Udo and Elke Schlangegriff. The

Schlangegriffs must have changed their name to sound more Canadian some time after World War I began, and their son was a McGriff! Even weirder, that McGriff started a whole line of McGriffs that led all the way down to Skyler, my teaching assistant in math, and Devin, the unpleasant guitarist of Phantom Moustache, not to mention my number one suspect! Unless my detection skills were off — and, really, I thought they'd improved in the past month or so — Devin McGriff was connected to the harassment campaign against Yumi and his ancestors had, for some reason, killed my dead friend Morna MacIsaac. What a prize this guy was. His whole family tree was poison from roots to branches!

I returned the library computer to its usual homepage, just in case Devin McGriff happened to wander into the library, but really, he was about as likely to wander into a library as he was to attend Yumi's birthday party. Still, I couldn't be too careful, especially since I was now sure I was onto something massive. The wait to tell Morna I'd made a tremendous breakthrough in her case was going to be interminable, but all I could do is watch the snow accumulate and the sky grow dark.

☠

By the time I was able to sneak out that night, there was some serious snowfall on the ground — it looked like all those wishes

really hokey people had for a white Christmas were going to come true. I, on the other hand, worried that I'd have to be extra careful sneaking back in. I wouldn't want to leave a trail of melted snow from the sliding door to my bedroom, and if it didn't keep snowing until the morning, my footprints would be very visible in the snow on our porch. Those, however, were concerns for later. First, I had to find the dead kids and tell them who had killed Morna.

The dead kids were taking advantage of the snow; they'd built a snowman in the centre of the cemetery, using rocks and branches for the eyes and arms. They'd made use of a trowel from the groundskeeping shed for the snowman's nose and placed Cyril's tricorn hat on its head. I'm not sure how that worked, given that Cyril's hat wasn't strictly part of the physical plane or whatever. Hat or not, it didn't seem to me the wisest move to build a snowman in the cemetery. What living child would conceivably do that?

"Is that a good idea?" I asked, buttoning my peacoat to the top.

"Probably not," Kirby admitted. "But sometimes it's nice to do something like this and freak out the locals."

"Morna, I have important news. I may have solved your case," I said. "Can we all go talk somewhere warmer? And less snowy?" Snow was already starting to pile up in my hair.

"Oh my gosh!" Morna shouted. "Really?"

"To the tomb!" Cyril commanded.

Once there, the entire Dead Kid Detective Agency gathered. The kids were pretty enthralled as I told them how Ms. Fenstermacher revealed the secret that was hidden in the clock and what I discovered later on in the library. But none were more amazed than Morna herself. It was like opening the last little Russian doll in the set to watch a canary fly out.

"Morna, does this make any sense at all?" I asked, watching my breath form a question mark in the cold air. "You must have found out Dr. Alfred Pain was really Udo Schlangegriff, and so you hid his medal so that one day your brother would find it. That's why he kept saying 735! He never figured it out."

"I think ye're right . . . I'm starting to remember . . ."

"I think Udo Schlangegriff killed you, Morna," I concluded. "But I don't know why. Maybe he was the real saboteur and you knew that. To find out, and also find out who's been harassing my friend, Yumi, we're all going to have to go to the school holiday pageant tomorrow."

☠

Avalanche
...of
Talent!

It was decided. All five dead kids would join me at tomorrow night's school holiday pageant, and they would stay out of sight, as best they could. After the school band played, Kirby and Derek were to meet me backstage for one special mission: to steal Devin McGriff's phone. Though Goth Hardware Clerk and all other signs pointed to Devin as the devil dog who'd been tormenting Yumi all month, I still needed definitive proof (according to, like, the Constitution or something). If the dead kids could nab his phone, I'd have proof he'd sent all those horrible texts. And once we'd forced him into confessing, maybe then Devin could tell me about his way mysterioso great-great-grandfather, Udo Schlangegriff. Shortly after Derek and Kirby had stolen Devin's phone (in theory), the idea was to reconvene in the girls' bathroom and plan our next move.

With what I considered to be a mostly logical plan mapped out, I trudged back home in the snow, which was increasing rapidly. So much so that the distant possibility of a snow day, that elusive holiday, danced in my head.

☠

My snow daydreams were completely dashed, but the actual school day just flew by because my mind was so preoccupied by what would happen at the pageant. I worried I was so distracted

I wouldn't even remember the right notes for our musical performance. On the other hand, I played trombone, so no one would even notice. It usually sounded like I was playing the wrong notes, anyway.

The pageant was scheduled to begin at seven thirty, and when I arrived back at school for the six thirty band rehearsal time in my stupid white shirt, black pants, and tie, as requested by Mrs. Tischmann, the snow had really piled up. My dad, not overly pleased to leave so early, insisted on driving me to Sticksville Central. It looked like his car was was sailing through marshmallow fluff, and the snow just kept falling. Snowplows had cleared most of the main roads, including Riverside Drive, which led to the school, but side roads and sidewalks and even the school parking lot were a winter wonderland disaster. When the house lights went down in the auditorium, the crowd was not at capacity. The auditorium was only about half full, and since the snow had begun falling faster since nightfall — almost blizzard force, though I'm not a meteorologist — I think the low attendance could be chalked up to the weather and not our parents' complete disinterest in us, their children.

My dad was there, at least. Before the pageant began, I crept into the back of the auditorium to scope things out. While on my way there, I stopped to marvel at the toy mountain. The donations for the school's toy drive for needy children were piled high under a massive tree in the atrium that nearly hit the skylight. At this point, the toys were obscuring a full half of the tree's height. I had, of course, forgotten to donate anything yet, but I was bringing Sticksville justice, which is better than any Lego set. My dad had found a seat just a few rows from the stage and was sitting next to Yumi's parents and, to my complete horror *and* humiliation, Crown Attorney Salmons! I should have suspected this would happen — she did send Dad a candy cane gram after all. How perversely weird that she'd chosen such a high-school method of asking him out, especially considering that she didn't even work at my school! Before I could witness them holding hands or the Crown Attorney doing a fake-yawn arm on the shoulder thing, I decided to leave the auditorium lest I decorate it with my festive puke.

Unfortunately, leaving the auditorium early also meant missing The Plotzdam Conference's set. I could hear it all right, though, as the walls of Sticksville Central were no match for Southern Ontario's finest Orthodox Jewish punk band's renditions of "The Dreidel Song" and "Little Drummer Boy" (possibly because there was no other Hanukkah song). Their songs and stage patter — in which they spoke about standing with Sticksville Central during its time of racial tension — could be clearly heard backstage. I wished I were in the crowd to watch. I feel they might have received a more enthusiastic reaction from me than, say, all our parents waiting for their children to appear on stage.

The Plotzdam Conference finished their set, which left just one poetic recital of "'Twas the Night Before Christmas" (ugh) before Mrs. Tischmann's music class, me included, took the stage. As the applause for the last act dwindled and I shuffled into my seat in the back row with the rest of the low brass and percussion, I couldn't help but tug at the stupid black tie around my neck. How did business people wear these every day? I felt like I was being choked by a very tired toddler or something. I waved to Stacey and made a dramatic pull at my collar, like some kind of female goth Rodney Dangerfield. Stacey merely shot back with a double thumbs-up; he must have enjoyed being forced into formal wear by Mrs. Tischmann more than I did. I could picture him in the future playing in some cheeseball airport lounge band.

At a school holiday pageant, I'm prepared to witness all kinds of strange things, but I was totally dumbstruck by what happened just before we played "God Rest Ye Merry Gentlemen."

Mr. Santuzzi, in full Santa Claus regalia — sleigh bells,

white beard, gloves, and all — took the microphone to introduce our band. Since when did Santuzzi have a sense of humour? I felt like I'd heard him mention something about class clowns being the first buried in the marine corps. (But I might have mixed him up with that guy from *The A-Team*.) Either way, my horrible math teacher was making jolly like he was the most beloved teacher in school, even dropping a "Ho ho ho" here and there. The whole thing was extremely distracting when my attention was already divided between remembering the music and keeping my eyes out for menace to society Devin McGriff. Even when Mr. Santuzzi wasn't actively tormenting me, he made things difficult.

I won't bore you with the details of our performance: we played three songs, nobody booed. Goes in the win column. True to their undead word, Kirby and Derek were hiding in a corner backstage when the band had finished. I waited until everyone else had exited the backstage area before retrieving them.

While I was gone, the drama class replaced the band kids in the music room. They were slipping on their *Christmas Carol* costumes as Kirby, Derek, and I reached the door. On the one hand, this was ideal, since Devin McGriff was in drama and we needed to steal his phone. But on the other hand, so was Yumi, who could see ghosts and would probably lose her mind if I walked in with two of the dead kids. It looked like I'd have to bring McGriff to me. I pried open the door and shoved my head through the opening.

"Devin," I said, apropos of nothing. "Could I speak to you in the hall?" Considering Devin and I had only really traded insults and deathly stares before, this was a long shot.

"Who is that?" he said, pulling a hooded Harvard sweatshirt (part of his stage costume) over his neck. "Schwartz? What do *you* want?"

Rather than come up with a good excuse, I just shut the door, hoping the mystery alone would draw him out. Surprisingly, it worked. Moments later, Devin barged through the door.

"All right, what do you want, Schwartz?" he demanded. "And why are you dressed like a waiter?"

"Shh!" I whispered. We were backstage and Devin's outrage was likely to drown out the explanation of Kwaanza happening on the other side of the wall.

"Fine," he whispered. "I'm quiet. Now what do you want?"

Kirby and Derek appeared out of the shadows behind Devin, on both his left and right like oversized visualizations of his conscience. For their phone pickpocket scheme to work, I'd need to keep Devin preoccupied with conversation.

"Um, it being the holidays and all, I wanted to apologize."

"Apologize?"

"Yeah, I mean, I'm good friends with Yumi and always took her side about the radio show. But I know having a radio show would have meant a lot to you . . ." At this point, I tried to communicate with my ever-widening eyes that *now* was the ideal time for Derek and Kirby to grab Devin's phone. They finally got the hint.

"What are you talking about?" Devin said, confused by this apology over nearly nothing. "Hey! What was that?"

Devin swung his head back and forth, sending the drawstrings of his hoodie whipping around under his weaselish face. He patted his pockets frantically.

"Someone tried to grab me!"

"Grab you?"

Kirby and Derek, empty-handed, shrugged and raised their palms to the ceiling.

"Yeah!"

"Devin, I don't see anyone here." Clearly I'd chosen the two dead kids least competent at petty theft. I'd have to assist. "*Anyone except us.*"

"What?"

"You know, Devin," I said, thankful I hadn't eaten dinner yet, lest I barf it all over his face. "Now that you and Ashlie have broken up, I had been noticing how . . . um, *cute?* . . . you look."

"Uh . . ." Devin was clearly horrified.

Behind him, my two dead friends were nearly as disturbed

by my romantic gestures. I only had seconds before Devin would dash down the hallway screaming. Panicking, I lunged for Devin McGriff wrapping my arms around him in something more bear hug than embrace.

"What are you doing?" he yelled. "Get off!"

He shoved back at my shoulder as hard as he could, a move that brought us both crashing to the floor. Devin was thrashing frantically on top of me, but I refused to let go until Kirby and Derek took his cell phone. I held onto his arms, keeping them free of his pants pocket. Derek quickly sat on Devin's back and whipped the phone out of his back pocket while he was screaming. I couldn't help think this backstage incident was having some adverse effect on the Kwaanza presentation. Cell phone secured, Derek tossed it to Kirby.

"You fat cow! Let go!" Devin, ladies' man, shouted, pushing my chin upward like a sticky garage door. "Let go of me, you *beast!*"

Kirby and Derek fled into the curtains on the far side of the backstage area, which meant it was probably safe to let go of the flopping Devin McGriff.

"Sorry, sorry, sorry!" I said, drawing my arms back, acting like I'd only committed some misguided impulsive flirtation instead of full-on jumping him.

Devin got to his feet and dusted off his costume. "What was that? Ashlie was right — you're even crazier than she said. Crazier than your father!"

That stung, but I had to remain in character — lovesick Devin McGriff devotee.

"Sorry, Devin. I don't know what I was thinking. It's just . . . it's the holidays and we were alone and under the mistletoe . . ."

"There's no mistletoe here, freak," he said, entirely accurate, as if the presence of mistletoe would have excused my assault.

"Devin, please don't tell anyone," I said. I hoped the information on his phone was worth all of my dignity. Not that I had much to begin with. The things I did for my friends. "I'm sorry, I swear."

"Whatever, Zombie Tramp. You need help."

Devin then cleared his throat and exited into the music room with a dramatic flourish. I guess he *was* an actor. Meanwhile, I counted down the seconds until the normal pale hue returned to my currently reddened face. I needed to huddle with the dead kids in the girls' room before I died of humiliation.

☠

The good news was that I survived the humiliation. The bad news was that manhandling Devin McGriff backstage and acting like a love-starved donkey was probably not worth the effort.

Under the fluorescent lights of the girls' washroom, we discovered Devin's stupid phone was devoid of any stupid evidence at all. I had no idea how that was possible. I paced back and forth by the sinks, going through his phone's inbox and outbox.

"What the heck? There's nothing about Yumi in here at all."

"Here, let me see that device," Cyril said, seated on the toilet in one of the girls' stalls.

231

"Sorry, Cyril, but not only do I doubt you'd be able to work this phone," I said, "but you also won't be able to read any of the text messages."

Cyril pouted and scratched under his hat.

"Derek, you want to give it a try?" I passed the phone over. "Real smooth pick-pocketing out there by the way."

"Hey."

"Shoulda sent me in," Tabetha said, leaning against the hand dryer.

Morna shuffled over to me as I drank some water from the sink faucet. "Does it say anything in his phone 'bout his great-great-grandpa? That German guy? Udo Whoever?"

"Sorry, Morna." I'd nearly forgotten Devin was also supposed to be my key to finding more about Morna's killer. I was hoping his phone would help incriminate Devin for the phone-booth tipping and threatening texts. Then I could interrogate him about that and his great-great-grandfather. But now it looked like he had nothing to do with those things. "Derek, did you find anything?"

He shook his head. "Is it possible to erase texts?"

I'd forgotten even Derek had probably never used a cell phone before. "Yes, and that wouldn't help us at all. Give it back."

"So, where are we now, geniuses?" Kirby asked.

"The ladies' lavatory," Cyril answered, taking Kirby's question quite literally. "I had my reservations, too, but October assured us no ladies would enter during the stage performances."

"No," Tabetha said, banging her head against the hand dryer once for dramatic effect. "Kirby means we've got nowhere ta' go. We got no proof that this kid did anything."

No one appeared more disappointed than Morna, who had been staring at her boots ever since she asked about Devin's great-great-grandfather. Her bottom lip started to quiver like a Jell-O mould in the middle of a rock concert.

"No, it's fine," I said, not believing it but realizing a rousing pep talk was called for. "Listen, we've still got nine more nights before you disappear. Once this holiday pageant is over, we take a new approach. Maybe you can scare Devin into confessing. Scare the pants right off him."

"Ugh, Devin wasn't lying. You're *desperate*."

Of course, because my life was like a tragic Shakespearean tale, that was Ashlie Salmons breezing into the washroom. Thankfully, Ashlie's vision was ghost-free, or I would have had even more explaining to do, since the dead kids were all standing around, taken completely by surprise.

"Why are you talking to yourself?" she asked, making a spot for herself at the bathroom mirror and brushing her hair. "Need to psych yourself up for putting the moves on Devin again?"

"Uh . . ." I said, because, really, Ashlie had provided the best excuse.

"I thought he was joking, in some pathetic attempt to make me jealous," she said, re-applying bright red lipstick for the stage. "He said you jumped him like a dog in heat outside the music room. Are you missing a chromosome or something, Zombie Tramp?"

"Heh, must be nerves . . . stage fright," I said, wiping my palms, which were genuinely sweaty then, on my black slacks. "But don't worry, I'm not trying to steal your old boyfriend."

And with no dignity left to spare, I departed the girls' bathroom, leaving Ashlie at the sink and the dead kids with no further instructions. I would have liked to work on some kind of new plan with my dead friends, but I wasn't about to just loaf around while Ashlie finished her grooming regimen. The dead kids could manage on their own while I watched Yumi in the weird version of A *Christmas Carol* they were presenting. In the midst of applause, I ducked into the auditorium by the back entrance. The school choir had just finished up — tragic that I'd missed that — so I entered the dark theatre completely unnoticed.

Before the production of A *Christmas Carol* began, Santatuzzi again approached the microphone. As usual, he was there as a harbinger of terrible news.

"As you may have noticed, we're in the midst of a snowstorm

here in Sticksville. I just wanted to briefly interrupt to report that at this moment we are officially snowed in. The snowplows are on their way, and we're confident the parking lot and front entrance will be cleared by the conclusion of tonight's performances. But it's possible we may have to wait until snow removal crews are able to dig us out of this blizzard. Thank you for your patience. Enjoy the show!"

Enjoy the show? Mr. Santuzzi just told us all we're snowed in and could be here all night. The audience started to grumble. A few took their coats to see if they could duck out, mid-blizzard, but when they returned to the theatre only a few lines of dialogue into the play, I realized Mr. Santuzzi was speaking the truth. No one was escaping this school until the snowplows arrived.

Once those who'd attempted to break out sat back down, the anxious theatregoers became resigned to their snowy fate. The audience sat in quiet concentration as Yumi and her drama class ran through *A Christmas Carol*. By the time the Ghost of Christmas Future had shown Scrooge his inevitable death alone or whatever, the mood was unbearably tense. Either Yumi and her classmates were better actors than I'd imagined or everyone was, again, realizing they were trapped in Sticksville Central High School. But the crowd sighed a massive breath of relief when Ebeneezer Scoorge awoke on Christmas morning with an entirely new outlook. The kid playing Scrooge ran across the stage in his pyjamas, over to what was supposed to be Bob Cratchit's apartment. Yumi was there, with cast and a wheelchair — a doubly pathetic Tiny Tim. I guess because the crowd was so quiet and attentive, it was especially embarrassing when my phone bleeped. I should have turned it off before I snuck into the theatre.

But wait. I didn't own a phone! Devin McGriff's cell was making me look like an idiot *again*. I shoved my hand into my pocket while the back row of the audience turned in my direction to glare and shake their heads in disdain. My only hope was that it was so dark, nobody would be able to identify me. Shrouding the screen with my hands, I flipped open Devin's phone to read the text message, from his older brother Skyler: BRO, U MIGHT WANT 2 MOVE NOW.

I had just enough time before the incident that was to follow to note that Skyler's number had a 519 area code, I guess because he went to university in London, Ontario. Pieces fell into place: he must have taken Yumi's phone number from my composition book! My detective work was unnecessary, however, as seconds later, my best friend totally got the Carrie treatment on stage, leaving little doubt as to who Yumi's tormentor was.

By the Carrie treatment, I refer to the climax of that most terrifying old movie of high school humiliation, *Carrie*, when bullies empty pigs' blood on the titular character from the rafters during prom night. When Yumi was Carried, she was doused in something less disgusting, but probably harder to get out of clothing: yellow latex paint. From the lighting rigging above, a full can of canary yellow paint gave in to gravity and flowed forth in a golden arc directly onto Yumi Takeshi's head. Devin McGriff, portraying a family friend of the Cratchits, stood conspicuously at the stage's rear while Yumi's other classmates were all spattered with droplets of house paint.

And with that, a McGriff's purchase of all that yellow paint from Goth Hardware Clerk made perfect sense.

The previously church-quiet crowd exploded into panic — it was pretty clear this wasn't part of *A Christmas Carol*. Most of the adults in the audience leapt to their feet but couldn't figure out what to do next. Stacey, like Kevin Costner in *The Bodyguard*, jumped on the stage as if Yumi were his Whitney Houston. (Yes, I'm talking about *The Bodyguard* again.) Sort of confident Yumi's emotional terror could be project-managed by Stacey, I bolted out the back door, able to beat the panicking crowd, and headed for the girls' bathroom, where I hoped the dead kids were still waiting. Skyler McGriff was somewhere in the school and I needed their help to find him before he escaped.

235

That is, if escape were even possible — from Mr. Santuzzi's pre-performance announcement, it sounded like we'd all be snowed in for hours.

I tore into the bathroom. The swinging door sounded like an explosion announcing my arrival as I crashed into it. The dead kids, to no one's benefit, were stuffing wads of paper towel into a toilet trying to start a flood.

"What are you doing?!" I shouted, out of breath.

"Nothing!!!" (That was all of them.)

"Well, stop it! I need your help," I demanded. "We were after the wrong McGriff."

"What if people see us?" Morna asked, dropping a crumpled ball of paper towel behind her back.

"We can't worry about that," I panted. "Just be careful."

The dead kids and I exited the bathroom with caution. A small crowd of scandalized parents and their kids had left the auditorium but lingered in the hall, unable to leave the school because of the blizzard.

"Okay, be careful," I warned. "Keep a low profile."

"What does this Skyler look like?" Cyril asked.

"I don't know. Like his brother, but taller and . . . actually, that's him there."

Skyler McGriff was leaning against the wall, chatting with Crown Attorney Salmons, which, if you think about it, is extra bold. Not only had he, moments ago, committed a hate crime, but his brother wasn't even dating Ashlie Salmons anymore, so why was Skyler talking to her mom? Besides, shouldn't he be comforting his own paremts who were likely freaking out due to the snow-in? (I know, I know. Pot Kettle. Blackness.) But it was just that kind of stupid arrogance that would make it so easy to catch him.

"Wait here," I told the dead kids. "Better if the audience doesn't see any ghosts. If he runs this way, though, do whatever you can to stop him from leaving the school."

"He won't get past us," Tabetha assured.

I started powerwalking over to Skyler McGriff and the Crown Attorney.

"Skyler!" I waved.

I'm not sure if it was the determined look in my eye or if Devin had told him I'd stolen his phone, but Skyler realized I knew something and sprinted for the front doors. I sped after him, but he was a college baseball player — there was no way I'd catch him. Especially with all the lollygaggers in the atrium turning my chase into an obstacle course. Mr. Santuzzi, still in Santa suit, was near the front door. In desperation, I called out to him.

"Mr. Santuzzi! Stop Skyler! He dropped the paint!"

At this point, the atrium erupted into a melee like the one inside the theatre a minute earlier. Santuzzi chased Skyler, who had already tried the front doors and found it impossible to open them against the snowdrifts, now a few feet high. Skyler turned back into the atrium, dodging confused parents. (I would guess they hadn't expected this level of drama when they set out for their children's holiday concert.) He nimbly ducked between them, more like a football runningback than a second baseman (and that, friends, is truly the end of my sports knowledge, I swear). But Mr. Santuzzi was like a crimson-and-white heat-seeking missile, bodychecking parents out of his way. I continued my pursuit from the other direction, but I really hoped Mr. Santuzzi got to him first.

Skyler took the steps at the end of the atrium two at a time, heading toward the big Christmas tree on the raised level, but I had no idea where he planned to go from there. Unless there was a secret trap door beneath the pile of presents, the far side of the atrium was a dead end. Not missing a beat, Skyler scaled the toy mountain at the tree's base, kicking away the presents below. When there were no more gifts, he leapt onto the tree itself and clambered up it like a red panda. Both Santuzzi and I stood, completely amazed, at the tree's base and watched as he leapt from the treetop through the skylight window and sent glass raining down, mixing with the snow blowing in from the blizzard outside.

"I'll call the police," Mr. Santuzzi declared.

And I was going to find the dead kids, but there was no way I was telling him that.

Principal Hamilton, seeing the chaos in the atrium, attracted everyone's attention.

"People, if you'll please join us in the theatre! We should stay together until the snow removal services arrive. Then we can all go home."

"What just happened?" somebody's mom yelled.

"This school is a madhouse," said one dad, who seemed prone to exaggeration.

The dead kids and I watched the crowd file back into the auditorium two by two, like animals who'd just witnessed a unicorn swim off on its own, but were reluctantly returning to the ark. Even my dad, his arm around Ashlie's mom, shuffled back to the theatre. My stomach felt like it was rotting from the inside out.

It didn't take long for the shocked and anxious parents and students to repopulate the auditorium. Only Mr. Santuzzi remained in the front office on a phone call with, I assume, the Sticksville police. With him occupied, I knew it was my chance to follow Skyler . . . somehow. I beckoned the dead kids to follow me onto the raised level beside the tree. We stood in a circle around the pine tree, staring up at the Skyler-shaped hole in the side skylight, errant snowflakes spitting through at irregular intervals.

"I guess Yumi won't be crushing on Skyler McGriff anymore," I said, trying to estimate how seriously I'd die if I fell from the top of the Christmas tree.

"You goin' up there?" Tabetha said.

"Uh, I was thinking about it."

"I'd think again," Kirby said. "Unless you became an acrobat while I wasn't looking."

"Don't be so defeatist, Kirby," Cyril said. "We can give you a boost up the tree. You'd barely need to climb the tree at all."

"And then how does she get from the top of the tree out the window? That's not an inconsiderable gap."

"We can help," Morna said

"That's right," Derek added. "If you three boost her up the tree, Morna and I can go up to the roof and help her from that end. The snow won't bother us. We can just walk out the wall and find some way of getting onto the roof."

"Really?" I said.

"Really?" Tabetha repeated.

"Totally," Derek said.

"Okay, then get up there. Skyler could be halfway to New Hammersmith by now."

I stepped into Tabetha's cupped hands, then climbed on top of Cyril's shoulders — how I hoped no one would leave the theatre and see me now, climbing on top of ghost children (or thin air). Then I had to pull my body up about six feet of pine tree, which was one of the harder things I've ever done in my life. When I reached the summit, I found Morna's cold, dead hands. She was hanging from her ankles through the skylight. Derek was holding onto her waist on the snowy rooftop.

"Don't let go, okay, Morna?" I pleaded.

"I won't."

I clutched one of her arms, held my breath, then grabbed her other.

"Pull!" I yelled to Derek.

He dragged Morna face first through the snow while I climbed up her torso. We lay in the wet slush, my black pants and white shirt soaked through to my undershirt with rooftop snow. Panting, I raised myself to the seated position.

"I thought I was going to die."

"I didn't," Morna said. "Sorry, but I didn't."

Bad jokes aside, I had a terrible person to catch.

"His footprints lead that way," Derek pointed out prints from size ten skate shoes that led to a fire escape on the far side of the building. I brushed the clumps of wet snow from my shoulders. A coat and boots would have been nice. As I'd inconveniently left my snowmobile at home, I'd have to pursue Skyler McGriff on foot, in nearly metre-high snowdrifts. I turned to Morna and Derek.

"Grab the others. We have to follow those footprints!"

☠

Morna Dies

After a harrowing climb down the icy ladder, October and her dead companions were off like ground beef after a day in the sun. And speaking of the sun, there certainly wasn't any sun to speak of. The sky was as dark as a Marilyn Manson hit single and the snow was fiercer than Tyra Banks's stare. October ran as fast as her legs might carry her, but the snow drove directly into her face and her wet clothes slowed her down. Still, like the super-trooper she was, she persevered. But she couldn't help be a bit annoyed that her dead friends were completely unaffected by the inclement weather. The cold had no effect and ice and snow passed harmlessly through them.

Mid-sprint, October turned to Morna to first confirm everything that she believed about the case was true.

"Morna," she shouted over the shrieking wind. "This guy is Udo Schlangegriff's descendent. Do you remember Udo? What happened with Dr. Pain?!"

The name of Dr. Pain began to pluck photographic flashes from Morna's brain. Her memories were returning, now that her killer had been identified.

"I remember!" Morna shouted back. "I remember now! It *was* Dr. Pain!"

☠

And so, while they ran through the near-horizontal sleet, dear readers, Morna told October and the other dead kids what she could finally remember. She told them that about a hundred years earlier (a) she had discovered a time bomb in her boarding house, the Crooked Arms, (b) that the time bomb went missing, and (c) she figured out that that time bomb belonged to the doctor upstairs, since (d) it certainly didn't belong to Gideon Sundbäck or (e) Sam Cheng, who was too imprisoned at the time to move it.

Then Morna went on, in great detail, to tell her friends (living and dead) what happened the night she died. Early on the evening of Morna's death, she was alone with her younger brother, Boyd, who had the beginnings of what seemed like the flu. Morna was concerned because his face was starting to turn red (and the MacIsaacs, by nature, were not very colourful in the face), and his coughing worsened and breathing grew more laboured. Unfortunately, her mother was still at work and her father was at the local watering hole (and I do mean hole), the Bishop and Castle. Gideon Sundbäck was at the police station, informing the local authorities that a girl in his boarding house had found what appeared to be a time bomb. Kasper Rasmussen, the landlord, had been out of town for a few days, procuring some rare books in Toronto. The only adult in attendance at the Crooked Arms was Roxy Wotherspoon, upstairs, working on her lesson plans.

Her brother's health in mind, Morna tucked Boyd into her parents' bed and climbed the stairs to Miss Wotherspoon's. But, being a teacher without any more medical expertise than Morna herself, she didn't know what to suggest.

"Maybe you should just wait for your parents to return home," she suggested. "They can't be much longer."

Morna didn't think it could wait. "He's really sick, Miss Wotherspoon. An' I don't know when they'll be home. Can't you do anything?"

Roxy Wotherspoon hesitated. She was none too keen to babysit — if she'd wanted to, she'd have a litter of her own, thank you kindly — but Morna was a good kid, and Boyd sounded like he might be really ill.

"I'll tell you what," she said. "I'll telephone your father at the Bishop and Castle and let him know how ill your brother is. How does that sound?"

Morna just nodded.

"In the meantime, check to make sure Dr. Pain isn't in," she continued, as she made her way down the stairs. "I think he's out, but if not, he's a doctor. He should know what to do."

The thing was, Dr. Pain wasn't a doctor. And what he was about to do that night certainly did not conform to a doctors' solemn oath of "do no harm."

As Roxy disappeared down the stairs, Morna crossed the third floor. At Dr. Alfred Pain's room, she first knocked to no answer. After three knocks, she tested the door with a tiny push. The door swung open, which seemed as good as an invitation to Morna. If the doctor wasn't home, maybe Morna could take some of his supplies: a medicine of some kind. Even a hot water bottle could ease her brother's discomfort. She began to look through the doctor's drawers, not even knowing what sort of medicine she hoped to find. And if she'd found a bottle with benzoyl peroxide or something like that printed on the side, would she even know if it was safe to use? The question was moot, however, because Morna couldn't read and there was no medicine to be found anywhere in Dr. Pain's room. But while searching through the bottom drawer of the doctor's desk, she found something unusual: a military medal and letter typed in German.

Morna knew it wasn't polite to pry into other people's business or root through their things, but for one, it was already a bit too late for that, and for two, she'd found a bomb in her building. So, the rules about prying had evaporated from her mind. Morna held the medal up in her hand to take a closer look. To be honest, Morna couldn't read the German, but she recognized the Iron Cross from newsreels about the Great War. Why did a doctor from Hamilton have a German medal for military service? Her mind made a leap, but in reality, it was more like the tinest of bunny-hops. Ruling out her own family, there were only three potential owners of that time bomb in the grandfather clock, and one of them kept German military memorabilia lying around in his room. Dr. Pain must have been working for the Germans as some kind of saboteur! Not only that, Morna thought, he was probably the one who'd taken the gunpowder from the fort, not Sam.

Downstairs, Morna heard the front door swing open, inviting in a squall of winter weather.

"Good evening, Dr. Pain!" Roxy announced. "The MacIsaac girl was looking for you. Her brother is ill."

Crouched in Dr. Pain's own room, Morna couldn't hear his answer, but whatever it was, she knew she was in trouble. Pressing concern: a saboteur and presumably German collaborator was home and would be heading to his room within seconds, where she currently was rummaging through his personal effects. This is what the insides of Morna's heart looked like:

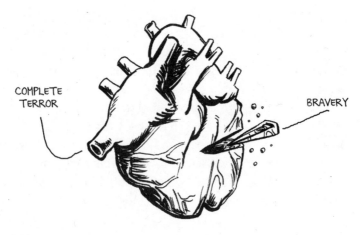

COMPLETE TERROR

BRAVERY

244

She closed all the drawers and stuffed the German medal and document down the front of her shirt. Her pounding heart was nearly the only thing she could hear. She swore she could actually hear the sweat building on the back of her neck. All of her organs seemed to amplify their sounds, for she could hear nothing else in the entire building since Roxy Wotherspoon had wished Dr. Pain a good evening. She didn't even hear his rapid footfalls up the stairs, so she was startled to run square into his chest as she snuck out his door.

"Ahh!" she yelped.

"Ah, Morna," he said. "What are you doing here?"

"Sorry, ye frightened me."

"What were you doing in my room?" Dr. Pain asked. His expression could cut glass.

"My brother is really sick. I thought I'd see if ye could help," Morna answered. "I came up t'yer room t'see if you were around."

"Oh," he said. "Sorry. I was out. But please don't enter my room without asking."

"Sorry, Doctor."

"That's fine . . . entirely fine."

Morna tried to strike a balance between running for dear life and casually hopping down the stairs. She opened her door and found Boyd twisting and turning in the large bed against the back wall. Panic struck; she had no idea what to do. She couldn't hide in her room with Boyd — Dr. Pain was sure to find his medal missing and come looking for it. Likely from the girl he'd just seen leaving his room. And she couldn't run away and leave Boyd here so sick by himself. Taking him with her in his current state was also not an option. Exposing him to the terrible weather with his flu could kill him. She could try to get help from Roxy, but her room was just across from the doctor's. What a mess she'd tangled herself in. She saw only one option: she had to hide the medal and German papers and retrieve them later.

"Boyd," she said. "Get some rest, an' whatever ye do, don't answer the door."

Morna continued on toward the first floor. As she'd done for Mr. Sundbäck earlier that afternoon, she opened the front face of

the longcase clock and wedged the documents, then the German medal, just under the clock face, directly below where the 7 was marked. The 7 had a 35 underneath. Each five-minute interval was marked on the clock. 735. Just like the telephone number at the Crooked Arms; it would be easy for her to remember and find again.

Morna left the lobby, following the wet tracks the doctor had made on the stairs, and returned to her brother. She locked their door and rested her palm on Boyd's warm forehead, trying to believe Roxy had reached her father, that he'd soon be home, but she couldn't escape her well-founded doubts. She could go retrieve her mother, but she was at work, and Morna wasn't to interrupt her at work. Besides, her mom wouldn't be able to do anything until her shift was over; the Coopers wouldn't let her leave early. She could find her dad at the Bishop and Castle, but Morna wasn't supposed to visit him there. The most natural place was the police station, where she'd probably find Gideon Sundbäck, but it was also the farthest, and in this snowstorm, she didn't relish the idea.

That's when the yelling began. Dr. Pain (or whoever he *really* was — Udo Schlangegriff, for those of you who have been paying attention to the story) began yelling, "Who's been in my room?! Who touched my things?" I wish I could report he slipped and said something in German, like *Mein Gott!* or. *Unglaublich!*, but he was too good a saboteur. No, instead he shouted angrily about privacy and that his valuables had been taken, and in time, he shouted his way down to the second floor and outside the MacIsaacs' door, since the MacIsaac girl was the last person he'd seen near his room.

He pounded on the door, frightening Boyd so much he threw up a little in the bed.

"What did you do in my room?" Dr. Pain demanded from the other side of the (thankfully) solid oak door. "You stole my things!

I know you did!" Pound, pound, pound.

Morna took Boyd by the shoulders and turned his head, dripping with vomit, toward her, looked directly into his large doe-like eyes, shimmering with fear.

"Boyd, don't worry about the doctor."

"Why is he so mad?!"

Pound, pound, pound. "Let me in!"

"Boyd, look at me. No matter what happens, ye stay here."

"But . . ."

"Stay here and remember our telephone number."

Pound, pound, pound.

"Our telephone number?"

"What's our number, Boyd?"

"Seven-three-five."

"That's right. If anything happens t'me, Boyd, ye jus' remember that number."

"Wha's goin' t'happen, Morna?"

Pound, pound, pound. "I'll break this door down, little girl!"

Following that threat's announcement — a threat that was seeming less and less empty — Morna made what you and I might consider a rash decision. However, you and I have never been trapped in a room with an outraged German saboteur pounding at the door, so perhaps we shouldn't be so quick to judge. Her rash decision was this: she unlatched the window at the far end of the room, hoisted the pane high, and rolled over the ledge onto the snowy half-gable below, all before her flu-delirious brother Boyd could protest. She toppled onto the half-gable over Gideon Sundbäck's first-floor window, leaving a distorted snow angel behind her, then crouched and leapt the twelve-foot drop into a snowdrift at the side of the building. The drift broke the fall pretty well, but she was still covered in snow, and hadn't thought ahead to wear her coat. She was just lucky she still had on her boots. In only her gingham dress, she raced off into the snowy night, in the general direction of the Bishop and Castle. She was in a hurry, and it was the closest place she could find anything resembling help or protection.

Meanwhile, in the room Morna had just fled like Julia Roberts leaving a chapel in *Runaway Bride*, Dr. Pain kicked the door in, for reals, leaving Boyd panicked and terrified. Splintered wood littered the MacIsaacs' floor, which Alfred Pain paced, overturning pillows, opening cabinets in his search for the MacIsaac girl. He interrogated Boyd — lifted him in the air and shook him until tears streamed down his fever-hot face — but the boy could only tell him she jumped out the window. He had no idea where she went.

"She jumped out the window!" he cried. "She might be hurt! I don't know where she went! She said — she said not t'worry about ye!"

"Not to worry about me?" he shouted, spittle forming at the corners of his mouth as he placed the boy back onto the floor. "Seems like she was misinformed."

Just as Roxy Wotherspoon reached the MacIsaacs' door (the cavalry, too late again), Dr. Pain jumped through the window and followed the trail Morna had left. He raced alongside her footprints, then headed toward a garage further up Turnbull Lane. He hadn't thought to put a coat on either, but it was of less concern to him than Morna, for he had an automobile stashed in that garage. He hopped behind the steering wheel and drove into the snowy dirt road. The car slid and careened through the wet snow, making Dr. Pain's travel particularly treacherous. Roxy Wotherspoon, trying to calm the little MacIsaac boy, who just kept crying "735, 735," heard the engine start and ran to the open window. Driving down Turnbull Lane was a black Ford Model T she didn't recognize.

The temperature was well below zero, but Morna could hardly feel it. The town was quiet in the evening. She felt like she was in a sensory deprivation chamber, not that those even really existed in 1914. Running in deep snow, which was really more like a series of rapid jumps, was keeping her warm. Overheated, even. But big, fat snowflakes fell steadily, blinding her eyes and soaking her old dress. Still, she was only about two minutes from the Bishop and Castle. Soon, she'd be inside, she'd explain everything to her dad and all his pub friends, and they'd protect her from the German saboteur and fix everything. Dr. Pain would be arrested and Sam Cheng could move back to the Crooked Arms. Then, she heard the engine of an automobile on the eerily silent street.

Morna turned, wiped the snowflakes from her eyes. Two hundred feet behind her, a black automobile idled. Its bright mustard headlights glared at her like the dead eyes of a shark on wheels. Without hesitation, she turned back toward the pub and sprinted as fast as she could, but the snow was thick and her damp dress was weighing her down like some cotton anchor. Dr. Pain closed up the gap between them, the front of his ebony death-mobile lapping at Morna's bootheels. With about a room-length between them, the car bucked, its pedal driven down into the floor, and accelerated to its maximum.

When Dr. Pain's car collided with Morna MacIsaac, her body slumped into the snow like a rag doll a careless child had forgotten in the blizzard. The last thing her eyes saw was the wooden sign that read *The Bishop and Castle* hanging from above the door of the pub. Inside, musicians were performing a traditional English folk song, which spilled through the closed door and into the street. She had finally made it to the Bishop and Castle.

The snow continued to fall, so that Morna's body was nearly buried when her father left the pub at one in the morning to find constables arriving at the scene of a reported automobile accident.

☠

Confrontation at the McGriff House!

"I swear it was Dr. Pain!" Morna shouted. "I don't know how ye did it, October, but I remember now. He found out I knew about the bomb and came after me! Jus' like I said."

"The devil!" Cyril shouted into the howling wind.

Given everything I'd read in Roxy Wotherspoon's and Gideon Sundbäck's journals, Morna's recollection of the past made sense. And my ghost friend's memory was a good enough confirmation as anything for me. Now that Morna had confirmed that the McGriff patriarch, Udo Schlangegriff, had killed her, we were more determined to find Skyler than ever. But what started out as deep pockets of footprints in the ever-building snow soon vanished. And beyond that, it was getting harder and harder to see farther than five feet ahead of me in the blizzard. As a reverse-bonus, the temperature was something like negative a hundred, and my stupid band performance outfit wasn't, apparently, made of Gore-Tex. I was beginning to rethink my whole aggressive attitude toward chasing Skyler McGriff.

"Can anyone see his footprints?" I asked.

"I can barely see *you*!" Kirby said.

"I think we're lost," Morna added.

"No, I know where we are." The snow started to move horizontally and sting my eyes. "I just don't know where Skyler went."

The dead kids whirled around in the swirling snow in a pretty dramatic attempt to look for some sort of clue, but it was really no use. I just stood there, getting more and more soaked, like the winner of a wet waiter's uniform contest. Or loser. I'm not sure which would be worse.

"We're *never* gonna find him in this snow," Tabetha said.

"But we can't give up now!" Derek cried.

"The problem," Kirby elaborated, "is that he could be anywhere. Who knows how long ago we lost his trail?"

"We just need to calm down a minute and think." Cyril gestured into the white void. "Where would this McGriff lad run to?"

"He could be headed home," I said.

Through mere mention, the McGriffs' house became the end destination of our search. Not that it was a great idea, but it was a good way of escaping the blizzard.

"At the very least," Kirby said, "if this Skyler isn't home, perhaps we can find something there about the Schlangegriffs and Morna's killer. The McGriffs and Schlangegriffs are the same people, right?"

"Is it close?" Morna asked.

"I don't know, I have no idea where he lives," I said. "It's not like Devin and I are great friends."

"Can we just go *somewhere*, please?" Tabetha shouted. "I feel like I'm bein' buried out in this snowstorm!"

"I feel bad fer yer da'," Morna said. "He an' all yer friends an' teachers are still trapped in that school."

Triggered by the word school, like some sleeper agent switched to assassin mode (I'd recently watched *The Manchurian Candidate*), I had an idea.

"Kirby, Derek — do you still have Devin's cell phone?"

"Yeah, why?"

"Pass it here. We're going to learn the McGriffs' address."

The hardest thing was inventing a place where Devin would conceivably lose his phone — other than at the school, where his whole family save the fugitive Skyler would be trapped by the snowstorm for most of the night.

"I'm calling," I alerted the assembled dead kids. "Be quiet! And don't make me laugh."

With one frozen thumb, I dialed the contact listed as "Mom and Dad," then pinched my nose like I was about to dive underwater.

"Hello," Mrs. McGriff answered.

"Yes, hello. Is this the parents of Devin McGriff?" With my nose pinched tight, I sounded like a duck who had been mystically granted human speech. No way was this going to work.

"Yes, who is this?"

"My name is Olivia. I work at Hi-Note Music. I think your son must have left his phone in our store." From the dead kids' incredulous looks, I felt like I might as well have been on all fours and barking.

"Oh, dear," Mrs. McGriff sighed. So far, I was convincing enough for Skyler's mom. "What is happening over there? It sounds like you're calling from a wind tunnel! Are you out in this blizzard?"

"No, ma'am. That's just one of our newer synthesizers."

I probably should have just admitted I was outside.

"Listen, Mrs. McGriff, I'm on my way home. Can I drop this phone off in your mailbox or something?"

"Actually, if you can make it through this snow, that would be a huge help. We're trapped at the high school by this blizzard."

253

"My condolences, ma'am. Okay, now I'll just need your address." I really hoped Mrs. McGriff had no desire to chat afterward. My nose was beginning to run like a faucet from the combo of pinching and freezing wind. Not to be too gross, but I could nearly write my name in the snow with the snot streaming forth from my face.

"We're at 1340 Cooper Court," she said. "Thanks! You have no idea how much I appreciate this. I'm sure Devin will, too. If we ever make it home."

"Oh, it's my pleasure," I said, then snapped the phone closed before the conversation could continue.

"Ha! I can't believe that worked!" Derek said. "That was amazing."

I dragged my white sleeve, which was nearly translucent now anyway, over my face, plastered with frozen snot.

"Do you have an address? Do you know where we're going?" Kirby asked.

"Yes, now let's get out of this blizzard!" I shouted. Trudging to the left (I'd say west or north if I were better with directions), I called out, "Follow me!"

The six of us raced deeper into the cyclone of snow, only one set of footprints left behind.

☠

Ten of the coldest minutes of my life later, the dead kids stumbled through the McGriffs' tasteful off-white door and unlocked it from the inside. As soon as that lock unlatched, I followed, bringing in half the snowstorm as a puddly creek behind me. I must have looked like Goth Day at Wild Water Kingdom — my hair was dripping down my forehead, and when I wiped away the snowflakes from my cheek, it left black smudges all over my palms. But crime-solving isn't a beauty contest, right? We soldiered ahead, deep into the sinister McGriffs' lair.

Kirby tried the lights, but the snowstorm must have knocked out the power. None of the light fixtures worked, so I could see only by grace of the pale moonlight. I thought of my dad and friends at the school. Were they trapped in total darkness as well? How much longer did I have before things went totally *Lord of the Flies* and Mr. Santuzzi started running around with Principal Hamilton's head on a homemade spear? Time was of the essence!

Luckily — to continue with the time figures of speech — time was also on our side. The McGriffs had lined their front hallways and living room walls with old family photographs. The place was lousy with retro black-and-white versions of Devin and Skyler and their female equivalents. One photograph stood out for Morna: a Devin McGriff look-alike with an old military uniform and blank stare. She thrust her finger forward and howled, "Tha's him! Tha's Dr. Pain!"

The dead kids swarmed around the wall hanging, making it impossible for me to get a close look. Instead, I looked closely at the frame just over my right shoulder — a weird German needlepoint behind glass, possibly some gift from a grandmother. For some weird reason, it looked familiar.

"According to the photograph, this is Udo Schlangegriff," Kirby said, face pressed to the glass.

"So, the two are certainly the same person," Cyril confirmed.

"That's the man who killed you, Morna?" Derek asked.

The simple question reminded me of the unforgivable crime that inspired all this blizzard adventuring and breaking and entering. A man had killed my dead friend Morna when she was just thirteen, and now he had a spot of honour on some family's wall of memories. I began to feel sick as I lurched forward to see Udo Schlangegriff's portrait.

"You're sure this is him?" I asked Morna.

Morna nodded slowly. Her eyes were all red and irritated, like someone had rubbed a shedding cat across her face.

"We should search for Skyler," I decided.

"You talking to yourself?"

The search for Skyler was over. He stood menacingly before the front door, a Louisville Slugger in his hands. Somehow, these cases always seemed to end with me trapped in a dark hallway with some dude and his weapon. A baseball bat isn't a particularly complicated mechanism to operate, but Skyler Mc-Griff was varsity baseball, so he was kind of an expert in using it.

"Skyler," I said, backing into the living room slowly, "this may be strange for you to hear, but I think your ancestor Udo Schlangegriff may have killed someone."

"This garbage again?" he shouted. "My great-great-grand-father was arrested and imprisoned as a traitor to the country! They said he was a German saboteur during World War I! They dragged our name through so much dirt, we had to change it."

"Can you grab him or something?" I whispered to the dead kids.

"You know the rules," Tabetha said. "We can't hurt a livin' person."

"Take his baseball bat, at least!"

"Are you crazy?" Skyler said, advancing with his baseball bat. "I'm talking here. The government thought he was working for the Germans, but they had no idea. They didn't under-stand what he was onto."

Skyler lunged forward, swinging the bat in a sloppy arc. He missed me by a few feet, but it seemed this swing was aimed more to threaten me than cause damage. The bat slammed into the portrait of Udo Schlangegriff, which burst into hundreds of glass shards and tumbled to the carpet.

"Oh," Skyler replied, momentarily stunned. "I probably shouldn't have done that. That was actually a nice family heir-loom."

He stooped to gather the damaged picture frame and prop it against the wall, giving me a couple seconds to scheme with my dead friends.

"When he comes at me, you need to block that baseball bat. I'm going for that umbrella. But we wait for him to make the first move."

"Okay."

Returning to the standing position, Skyler passed the bat from one palm to the other, entering the living room, a pathway of glass like a slug's trail behind him.

"Why are you here, October?" he asked.

"You've been terrorizing my friend for weeks."

"That Chinese girl in the Crisparkle House?"

"Crisparkle House? Like that witch?" He was distracting me with new information. Did Yumi have something to do with a 200-year-old witch? "Yeah. She's Canadian . . . with a Japanese background, but I guess it's all the same to you."

He was trying to corner me; I started to angle myself toward the umbrella stand in the space between the living room and kitchen.

"I'm not racist."

"So you dumped yellow paint on my friend because you're culturally sensitive?"

Not a wise comeback; Skyler exploded a glass candlestick on his family coffee table with a flick of his wrist.

"You don't understand. Just like no one understood Udo. I have no beef with Asians. It was an easy means to an end."

I had *no idea* what he was talking about.

"You were trying to get your brother that radio time slot," I guessed.

"Not even close," he grinned. "You're a lousy detective, October. How much do you think I like my brother? I was trying to force your friend to leave town. What parents want their kid to be the target of harassment all through high school?"

My eyes again focused on the strange German needlepoint. Now I remembered where I'd seen it! We had the same thing at our house outside the kitchen. Sad that I'd never get to ask the McGriffs or my dad about it before being bludgeoned to death by a baseball bat.

"Why?"

"You wouldn't understand, but I needed that location. Still need it. Just like my great-great-grandfather needed that Chinese laundry. The Crisparkle property is very important to us."

The manic gleam that had been steadily growing in Skyler McGriff's eyes was starting to really freak me out. I looked to my right and left to see the dead kids equally dumbfounded by the use of "us" and frequent reference to "Crisparkle."

"Us?"

"I've said enough," he said, moving into a batter's stance, circling the bat slowly. "The key thing is, all that work wasn't for nothing. The Takeshis still think Sticksville is a terrible environment for their child. And it will only get worse when their daughter's best friend is beaten to death."

I should have asked Santa Claus for no brain damage this Christmas. My only hope was that the dead kids were prepared.

"You're the only loose end, October. How many blows to the head do you think you can take?"

Before I could answer, Skyler swung his bat, and only Derek Running Water leaping into his path deflected his blow. Derek crumpled to the floor with a loud groan.

"What the — ?"

Skyler tried again, swinging the bat overhead like a caveman — lacking all the finesse one expected of an athlete. Only Morna pushed me back and caught the bat against her forearms, keeping me from a broken skull. As another of my dead friends dropped to the living room floor in pain, Skyler became extremely confused and enraged. In his bafflement, I ran to the umbrella stand and whipped out a particularly long and sturdy one — not like those cheapo ones that collapse in a heavy rain — and held it aloft like it were a crucifix and Skyler were Count Dracula.

"I don't know how you're blocking my bat, freak, but I can go all night!"

He swung for the fences and nailed Kirby in his soft gut. I hoped Skyler wasn't right about his stamina. So far all three dead kids who'd taken a pounding had yet to stagger to their feet again. My greatest hope was his arms would get sore from all the beatings before I ran out of dead human shields. I rapped the umbrella against his knuckles to little effect.

"Stop blocking the baseball bat!" I shouted to Cyril and Tabetha. "Can't you just take it from him?!"

The two kids tried just that as my attacker flailed back and forth, trying to shake the invisible defenders like very heavy strands of hair. I continued to back away until I felt the front door's knob in the base of my spine. I'd arrived, but could I escape before Skyler reached me?

"What is this?" he said. "Are you actually talking to some phantom?" He panted. Within seconds, he'd freed himself of Cyril and Tabetha, then thrashed about with the baseball bat until he hit solid air twice more. After escaping, he took a quick breather. I took the opportunity to thrash him across the face a couple times with the umbrella. The effect was less than desired. All my dead kids were horizontal and in no shape to take another baseball bat to the face or midsection. I was on my own.

"Maybe I won't kill you right away, freak. There's something strange about you."

Skyler reared back with the bat again, and I braced myself, holding the umbrella in front of my face as I crouched down and gritted my teeth. The impact never came. Instead, the front door blew open, knocking me forward and bowling over Skyler. Scrambling back up as fast as I could, I realized the door hadn't blown open with the storm.

Mr. Santuzzi stood in the doorframe, his features (mainly his moustache) obscured by the shadows.

"Miss Schwartz?" he boomed.

"Santuzzi?" Skyler said, slowly getting his bearings. In no time, he was already primed in his imaginary batter's box. "Stay away from me. Don't think I won't bash your face in, too!"

Oddly, Mr. Santuzzi had no response to that. No *I'd like to see you try* or *curse your sudden but inevitable betrayal, teaching assistant* or *not in the face!* (as I might have screamed). Instead, he simply thrust forward, raising his right hand in a cup shape the very split-second Skyler swung his trusty bat. The end of the bat landed with a muffled thud squarely in Mr. Santuzzi's meaty palm, as if magnetized. Wasting no time, he wrenched the bat (using only one hand) free from Skyler like it were a dandelion. With his other hand, Mr. Santuzzi threw Skyler up against the wall and pinned him there.

Confronted with the full, unadulterated wrath of Mr. Santuzzi, outside the legal constraints of a public school, Skyler McGriff promptly fainted. My totally insane math teacher, still pinning the unconscious teaching assistant to the wall like a donkey tail, turned to me and announced, "Miss Schwartz, now might be a good time to call the police."

☠

Tomb for the Holidays

Your beloved narrator has returned, readers, where young October left off, with Morna and all the dead kids still lying prone on the McGriffs' living room floor, having just been the recipients of a baseball-bat beating.

If Mr. Santuzzi could see ghosts, he certainly never let on the whole time the five dead kids were scattered all over the carpet like so many heaving grape stains. October was unable to check on her battle-weary friends after calling the Sticksville Police. Instead, she and her math teacher, who was clearly dangerous — even if in a chaotic neutral kind of way — were forced to make awkward small talk with the McGriff boy still plastered to the wall by Santuzzi's massive hand. The two had discussed this past Tuesday's math lesson and October's holiday plans before the police finally arrived. Mr. Santuzzi didn't offer his holiday plans. One is safe to assume they involved repeated viewings of *Die Hard* and training his body to become immune to mistletoe's poison.

Mr. Schwartz, home a full hour before his daughter thanks to the arrival of the snow plows, was none too pleased to find October in the care of the Sticksville Police for the second time in her first semester of high school. Still, he was more relieved she'd returned from that snowstorm alive and non-frostbitten than anything else. After the police car climbed into the Schwartzes' snowy driveway with some effort and returned October safely home, Mr. Schwartz had dozens of questions for his daughter.

Namely, where had she gone while everyone else at the holiday pageant was snowed in, and why were the police bringing her back now, looking like a dampened vampire. After changing into warmer, drier clothes, and wrapping herself in the fluffiest coziest black towel she could find, October was happy to answer her dad's questions. Sort of.

Obviously, she couldn't tell her dad about old German saboteur Udo Schlangegriff, and it was probably best that she avoided discussing her whole death-defying leap through the school's skylight. Basically, any element of her story involving the dead kids — even tangentially — was edited out. In her version, she left through the back door of the music room (inexplicably clear from snow) and pursued Skyler McGriff to his home, where, when she confronted him about his campaign of harassment against Yumi, he attacked her with a baseball bat. Until Mr. Santuzzi rescued her, of course. Even without its supernatural elements, the chronicle was enough to make Mr. Schwartz seriously consider home-schooling his daughter.

If you consider things from October's dad's perspective, Sticksville Central was no place to educate a child. In October's first semester, she'd been kidnapped by her history teacher, been a victim of a hate crime, and then been menaced with a baseball bat by a teaching assistant. And classes at Sticksville Central had clearly done nothing to suppress an unhealthy vigilante impulse in his young daughter. But October's dad abandoned these concerns for a later date. The holidays were days away, and Mr. Schwartz was really just pleased to have his daughter safe.

"You left before I could compliment you on your trombone playing," he said, ruffling the black towel October was currently using as a cowl.

"Thanks, Dad," October said, bringing a mug of hot chocolate to her face. "But I really doubt you could hear me play."

"I couldn't hear you screw up," he pointed out. "So, you were at the very least a competent or quiet trombone player."

"I'm certainly not quiet."

"Seriously, pumpkin. I'm glad you're safe," Mr. Schwartz added. "And if you ever run out by yourself into a blizzard again,

I'm getting one of those tracking microchips installed in your neck."

"I understand."

"And you realize it's only fair that I ask you to join me at the volleyball regional championships in January, right? I was trapped in your school for hours because of that pageant, worrying about where you'd gone."

"Fair enough," October sighed. The dead kids would be absent until February, so at least she wouldn't miss any valuable super-sleuthing time.

October's dad, exhausted from the most exciting night of his life since Mr. Page had been arrested, made for the stairs.

"Ms. Salmons and I were both really worried."

At that point, I, your humble narrator, gagged on your behalf, dear readers.

☠

One massive disadvantage to the snowplows arriving during the winter pageant and unburying Sticksville Central was that the following morning was not heralded with news of an ever-coveted snow day on local radio stations. Beginning with the high school rescue, the Sticksville snowplows worked through the night, so that by Wednesday morning all the roadways were clear, though drifts at each side of the road reminded everyone of the feet of snow that had fallen the previous night. Blinded by sunlight reflecting off those pristine white drifts, October sauntered to school, grumbling under her breath (which was very visible that morning). At least last time she'd narrowly escaped death, she didn't have to attend school the very next day.

First order of business when October arrived at school was finding Yumi to make sure she was all right. Last October had seen her, she was doused in yellow latex paint. She hopped up the slush-covered stairs to the second floor where Yumi's and Stacey's lockers were. October found them together, and Yumi was surprisingly paint-free.

"Yumi! Are you okay?" October shouted mid-run toward her friend.

Yumi tousled her black shag of hair and grimaced. "I think so. I can still feel paint everywhere, but I think I got most of it out. Thought I'd have to cut off all my hair. I must have spent two hours in the shower last night. My dad wasn't too pleased."

"You can barely tell you were the victim of a hate crime," Stacey added, not really helping much.

"I'm so sorry I ran," October added, grabbing her friend by the shoulders.

"It's okay, October. It's okay. It was just paint. And I hear you were busy hunting down my tormentor."

October didn't want to answer that. She just glanced around the hallway.

"It's all right. We know," Yumi said.

"Does everybody know?" October asked. "They must think I'm a total freak."

Yumi nodded. The legend of October Schwartz being like some sort of vengeance demon, dashing through the snow on the hunt for high school pranksters, had filtered through the hallways nearly as soon as the doors had opened.

"So . . . Skyler McGriff," Stacey said. "I thought just the younger one hated you."

"I'm so depressed I actually had a crush on him. You have to vet all my future crushes, okay?"

"Um, I guess." The new responsibility momentarily flustered Stacey.

"Apparently, he was trying to get you to leave your house," October said, kicking her toe against a locker. "Is there something special about your house? Is it historic? Skyler seemed weirdly into it."

"I don't think so. It's a pretty new house. My parents bought it new a few years before I was born. Usually new houses aren't of much special significance, y'know?"

"No ghosts in the Takeshi household?" Though Stacey MacIsaac could be sweet like his long-ago dead ancestor Morna, he also said some dumb, insensitive things.

"Don't even," Yumi muttered.

"So," Stacey turned his focus, realizing he'd just done

something horribly wrong, if unsure of what exactly. "Mr. Santuzzi rescued you. That was unexpected."

"True," October said. "I always expected he'd somehow be the *architect* of my doom, not the . . . whatever the opposite of architect is."

"Eviction agency?"

"Guy with wrecking ball?"

"Whatever," she said as the three walked toward their first-period classes. "What I'm saying is, after being so wrong about Devin and Mr. Santuzzi, it's kind of forced me to see everyone in a different light."

Her math teacher, previously showing strong evidence of being some sort of foot soldier for Satan himself, had pursued October during a snowstorm to save her from a certain bludgeoning. Devin McGriff, while still a total weasel, was not the one being so awful to Yumi. Even Crown Attorney Salmons was showing signs of human feeling; if October's dad liked her, she had to have some positive qualities. October figured if her dad and Ashlie's mom were really going to date, she should try to see Ashlie in a different light, as well.

October, Yumi, and Stacey passed Ashlie Salmons and her insufferable friends at their lockers.

"Ashlie!" October called.

"What're you doing?" Yumi muttered. "Try *not* to draw attention to yourself."

"Ashlie, good job," October continued. "I thought you really nailed it as the Ghost of Christmas Past."

"Whatever," she responded, cinching her plaid red belt. "Not like anyone remembers the play after the sideshow that followed."

"I guess . . . sorry."

Ashlie moved closer. Never a good sign. October probably should have tried to make herself appear larger to scare her away. Like one would with a mountain lion or bear. (This book also contains helpful survival tips.)

"Listen, it looks like your dad and my mom are continuing on this misguided collision course of romance, so let me just be clear: if you and I become stepsisters — let me just stop shuddering for a second — I will make your life *very* unpleasant. Like, Cinderella will have nothing on you."

With her threat and point made, Ashlie pivoted on her flat heel and returned to her friends, their regularly scheduled giggling already in progress.

"What was that about, Schwartz?" asked Yumi.

"Nothing. My dad's love life is probably going to ruin mine. My life . . . not my love life."

"But maybe that, too," Stacey added.

What was most surprising that Wednesday was how coolly Mr. Santuzzi treated October. October imagined their shared experience evading a bat-wielding maniac would have forged some bond between them or, at least, a truce of some kind. Together they'd helped put his teaching assistant in jail (pending the results of the trial). But Mr. Santuzzi kept doing what he did best: crushing hopes and dreams (and occasionally, in the case of Skyler McGriff, collarbones). When he announced a test on polynomials the Friday before the holiday break, it was as if that night they shared defeating evil in one of Sticksville's most rotten residences had meant nothing to him. October just couldn't understand what his whole deal was.

☠

With a day of school survived and only two more to go until what October hoped would be a danger-free holiday break, our heroine returned to the Schwartz home with just three thoughts niggling in her head like loose baby teeth hanging by their nerve endings. Just before Mr. Santuzzi had frightened Skyler McGriff into a near coma, Skyler talked about "us," as if he wasn't working alone to force the Takeshis out of Sticksville. There were three masked men who had attacked her at the Crooked Arms, after all. He also mentioned Crisparkle, which was the name of the supposed witch who lived in Sticksville hundreds of years ago. Is that who had lived where Yumi's family lived now? Not the house itself, perhaps, but the property? Then there was that weird coincidence of having the same German needlepoint sampler as the McGriffs. It wasn't like two college dormmates discovering they both had the poster for Pink Floyd's *Dark Side of the Moon* on their wall. This needlepoint was handmade.

"Dad, why do we have that weird German needlepoint on our wall?" October asked between slurps of soup. The Schwartzes were enjoying Italian wedding soup for dinner, which was ironic, as they weren't Italian and Mr. Schwartz was a single dad. (Or maybe I don't understand irony.)

Mr. Schwartz, by now used to his daughter's entirely random questions, said, "Where else would I put it?"

"Where did that thing come from, anyway?" October asked.

"I don't know. It was your mother's. A family heirloom or something."

Instead of revealing secrets or, say, plot points, the needlepoint conversation was really only revealing her father's melancholy, holding onto strange family heirlooms of her mom's just to remember her by. He couldn't have been keeping it for aesthetic reasons. Still, October ventured further:

"Do you think I might be able to bring it into school?"

"Why would you want to do that?" Mr. Schwartz asked, his soup spoon frozen midway to his mouth, like a malfunctioning toll booth arm.

"For this art project I'm working on," October casually replied.

"But you don't have art this semester."

Blast my father and his engagement with my education, October thought.

"Oh, it's not for school. I'm just working on some logos for the book . . . *Two Knives, One Thousand Demons*, y'know."

"A logo."

"Yeah, that German font looks pretty wicked."

It was impossible to tell if Mr. Schwartz believed any of that or if he was just a very amenable father (save for the issue of night-time graveyard visitation). For one reason or another, he agreed.

"But take care of it, October," he said. "Remember that was your mother's. And aside from it, and your necklace, and . . . y'know, *you*, I don't have much left that belonged to her."

"I promise, Dad," October said. "I'll treat it like a kitten or something."

More soup was consumed; after talking so much about Mom, the air in the kitchen was thick with awkwardness (and the odour of soup).

"I'm glad you're safe, October," Mr. Schwartz said. "I think we're going to have a very happy holiday."

"On the topic of happy," October said, hesitating to continue. "Does Ms. Salmons make you happy?" October realized it was a loaded question, but she also wanted to make sure that if she had to make nice with Ashlie Salmons, it was for the right reasons.

"Yes," he said. "Yes, I think so."

"Good." October smiled.

☠

Though we're not quite done yet, this chapter of the chronicle of the Dead Kid Detective Agency mirrors the way our story began, friends, with October and her new history teacher, Ms. Fenstermacher, in a library. Only in this instance, they were in the school library.

On October's final day of class before the winter break, she'd asked Ms. Fenstermacher to translate "this weird art she'd found in her basement," or so she said. Ms. Fenstermacher, still working for that best teacher at Sticksville Central status because she was young and still had goals and ambitions that the world had not yet crushed, agreed to meet October during lunch period.

October left her conversation with Yumi and Stacey in the cafeteria a little early — which was unfortunate, as they were discussing Christmas film favourite *Gremlins* — to make her appointment with Ms. Fenstermacher. When October entered the hushed atmosphere of the school library, she saw Ms. Fenstermacher, her thick black glasses and western shirt standing out like a solar flare at the blandly tan round table she sat behind. October had to admit: as far as teachers went, she was kind of stellar. Having retrieved the large needlepoint from her locker, October laid it face up on the table.

"So," she huffed. "Here it is. Weird German needlepoint."

"That is unusual," Ms. Fenstermacher said, pushing her glasses up the bridge of her nose.

Intending to not just look like she was using Ms. Fenstermacher as a constant pump for information — that she, in fact, even felt a friendly vibe toward her (which she honestly did these days) — October asked her some casual personal questions while Ms. F wrote.

"Do you have any plans for the winter break, Ms. Fenstermacher?"

"Hmm? Not really," she said, scribbling onto a notepad. "I have a lot of grading to do, but I'll probably spend most of the holidays with my cat on the couch watching *Battlestar Galactica*."

Ms. Fenstermacher looked up from the paper, finished with her work. "And you said you found this in your basement?" she asked.

October nodded. "On our wall, actually. Why?"

"Just a very unusual thing to have in your house."

"What does it say?" October asked. She was almost too afraid to know.

"See for yourself," the history teacher said, and turned the notepad around so October could read what she'd scrawled. In thick black Sharpie, Ms. Fenstermacher had written:

MAY THE DARK ONE GUARD THIS HOUSE, FOR IT BELONGS TO A MEMBER OF ASPHODEL MEADOWS AND A PERSONAL FRIEND OF FAIRFAX CRISPARKLE.

A few takeaway points stood out for October:

(1) The mention of a, or rather "The," "Dark One" was troubling, to say the least, no less the fact that October's house was under his/her protection.

(2) It explained what that "Asphodel Meadows," written on the walls of the Crooked Arms, meant, but not who or what they were. They sounded like a mid-nineties British rock band. Further investigation was needed.

(3) "Crisparkle" was a name Skyler McGriff had mentioned a few times when referring to Yumi's house. It was also the name of the notorious (possibly fictional) Sticksville witch Ms. Fenstermacher had told her about.

And this needlepoint had been her mother's! The German words suggested October hadn't heard the last of the words "Asphodel Meadows." The more she learned about how the dead kids died, the more sinister Sticksville, and just life in general became. She and Ms. Fenstermacher shared a wide-eyed glance.

"I don't suppose we could just pretend you never saw this," October asked.

☠

24

Merry Crisparkle!

Realistically, it had probably been decades since the dead kids had celebrated Christmas, so I gave them a bit of a treat and we all spent Christmas Eve locked in my bedroom, while my dad and Crown Attorney Salmons watched *It's a Wonderful Life* downstairs. In a fit of rapid post-mystery errand-running, I'd bought my dad his Christmas presents — some book on rock star physicist Richard Feynman and a DVD of *Dangerous Minds*, just so he'd feel good about his career choices — and they were already wrapped. I was set for Christmas Day, so the dead kids and I made some space in my room and played (ironically, I guess) The Game of LIFE.

Remarkably, all the dead kids had made exemplary recoveries from their baseball-bat injuries. Perhaps that wasn't so remarkable: they weren't really alive and I'd seen them recover from decapitation. What *was* remarkable, though, was that Morna MacIsaac was still with us. I remembered the dead kid rules pretty well (I'd even written them down) and a crucial rule was that (6) *the dead kids will remain ghostly corpses until they somehow*

find justice for their horrible, horrible demises. I wasn't sure what we'd done wrong, but I was one hundred percent sure we'd solved Morna's murder: that creep Udo Schlangegriff (sometimes known as Dr. Alfred Pain) did it. But her continued existence was something of a relief, because I had half-expected Morna to evaporate or vanish or get beamed up to heaven overnight or something like that.

"I'm glad all that's over," Tabetha said.

"Me, too," I said. In the back of my mind, though, I knew things weren't over. Both Morna's death and Yumi's harassment were somehow connected to this Fairfax Crisparkle guy, and I knew I'd have to get to the bottom of that one day soon.

"We're just relieved you're alive and we caught the guy," Derek said. "We can handle a baseball bat to the face, but we can't handle things without you."

"Aw, thanks, guys. Even Kirby was worried about me?"

Kirby glowered. "More like I was worried your stupid face would break the bat."

"He was worried," Morna said.

"Shut up and spin the thing. It's your turn," Kirby replied.

"What is a 'computer consultant' and why is that my job?" Cyril protested from his spot on the floor, where he lay on his stomach.

"Morna, not that I'm disappointed or anything, but . . ." I wasn't really sure how to broach the topic. "Why are you still here? We solved your mystery. I thought you'd be, like, released from your ghost form by now."

"We were all expecting that," Cyril admitted, opening his palm. "Please give me another little blue man for my motorcar."

"So what happened?" I said, passing the gamepiece to him. He shrugged.

"Well, we're all ghosts because of unfinished business, right?" Derek said, taking the spinner. "We're a team now. Her unfinished business is *all* our unfinished business, maybe."

"Really?" I said. That seemed pretty vague and made up to me. I needed some hard and fast rules about the undead.

"I like it," Morna said, glancing back at my open closet. "I mean, it'd only be fair that we solve all a' our deaths. I don't want t'leave you a person short."

"So, we're keeping the Dead Kid Detective Agency together?" I asked. "I don't need to trawl the graveyard and find your replacement?"

Morna tried not to blush while nodding.

"That's kind of sweet. Maybe you can even peek in on your super-great-nephew, Stacey," I said.

"Yeah, about that," Morna said, looking back at my closet again. "Could I have tha' vest?"

"What vest?"

Morna hopped up from where she was sitting in front of the LIFE game board and disappeared into my closet. Moments later, she was standing back at the board holding up some weird purple and yellow tiger-striped polyester vest that I couldn't remember wearing or buying.

"I guess," I said. I certainly wasn't going to wear the monstrosity. "What are you going to do with it?"

"Wear it."

Kirby snorted and dropped the pile of game money he'd been holding. "Really? You've been wearing the same clothes for a hundred years."

Downstairs, my dad roared with laughter. George Bailey and Mary Hatch must have just fallen into the swimming pool under the gymnasium floor.

"Keep it down, guys," I said. Though my dad was downstairs and probably only had ears for Crown Attorney Salmons, I didn't want to be reckless.

"I'm also goin' t'need a box," Morna said, looking around my bedroom. It was so cluttered, there could have been dozens of boxes buried under the clothes and books. "Can I have one of those?"

"What is this about?" Cyril said, halting his gameplay.

"Yeah, Morna," I agreed. "What's going on?"

She looked at her hands, pulling the jungle vest in two directions at once. "I wanted t'get Stacey a Christmas present."

"What?" Tabetha was in disbelief.

"It's not weird, right?" Morna insisted. "We're related! Ye buy yer family presents!"

"It's okay, it's okay," I said, raising my hands in surrender. "Guys, stop making fun of her. This is hard. Morna, you can have the vest, a box . . . even a card if you'd like. Bring it to his house."

"Could I?" Morna asked.

"As long as he doesn't see you," I said.

Morna sat back down at the game. She shuffled through her fake money, keeping her eyes on the bills.

"Derek, can you write the card for me?" she asked, hunching up her shoulders.

"Sure, Morna," he said, propping his face up on his elbow. "What do you want it to say?"

"Make it say, *From your big sister, Morna.*"

☠

Christmas Eve had technically turned over into Christmas Day and where was I? Standing in the lobby of the Crooked Arms. In a few hours, my dad would be waking me with the smell of frying sausages and freshly brewed tea, we'd open our couple presents, and watch whatever television marathon happened to be running that day. But I decided that I needed to visit Morna's old boarding house one last time. The building was a crossroads of sorts. Though I'd never see the place as Morna did — as new, as home — it connected me to her past. I could only see the tagged furniture, the blankets of cobwebs, and the incredible damage the dead kids and three Baseball Furies had done to the furnishings, but in a way, I could also see Asphodel Meadows, that old telephone, and the spectre of Fairfax Crisparkle, whoever he was, hanging over seemingly everything in this town.

In a week, they'd start demolition, and I'd never have the chance to stand inside the Crooked Arms again. So, in the wee hours (like, really wee) of Christmas Day, I was, I guess, saying goodbye to the haunted derelict building. I'd nearly died in there at least once, and talked to a ghost (I assumed) over a telephone, so we'd forged some pretty powerful memories together.

I had thought the telephone had steered me wrong with its instruction to look at the inventor, but in the end, looking into Gideon Sundbäck had led me to Udo Schlangegriff, and to this whole Fairfax Crisparkle and Asphodel Meadows dealie. The voice on the telephone, whoever or whatever it was, had been aiding me all along. I probably should have listened to it more carefully, called more frequently. Maybe I wouldn't have ended up menaced by baseball bats so often if I had.

For what would be the final time, I stood behind former landlord Kasper Rasmussen's old desk, framed by the number 735. Taking up the candlestick telephone in my left hand, I pulled down the hood of my sweater, brought the receiver to the side of my face, and unlatched the hook. The phone was like a solid icicle in my hand. If I managed to let go of the phone without losing all the skin on my palm, I'd consider it lucky.

"Seven-three-five?" Again, I made it a question. I wasn't sure the voice on the other end of 735 wanted to talk to me again, it had been so long.

". . ."

"Hello?" I said, unsure if anyone was listening.

"You rang?" the voice asked. It really didn't sound like anyone I knew, but it felt familiar.

"Listen, I don't know who or what you are, but you helped me out a lot," I said. "You helped me figure out who killed my friend, Morna, and . . . y'know . . . I don't think we would have solved the mystery without your help. So, thank you."

". . . You're welcome . . ." the voice said, confused. I guess it wasn't expecting me to say that.

"And I'm sorry this old building is getting demolished in a few days."

"It is?"

"I'm supposed to solve four more mysteries, figure out who killed my other dead friends, and I certainly could have used your help."

The voice went quiet. The line didn't drop dead; I could hear faint breathing on the other end of the line. Rather, I guess there was nothing more to say. I wanted to know who the speaker was. If it was alive or dead or something — like my five friends — in between, but the voice had made it clear it wasn't interested in revealing its identity.

"Well, I guess this is goodbye. Hope you have a good holiday," I concluded.

"Merry Christmas, dear," the voice said.

In that moment, a hook caught onto the fish gills of my brain. I had a sudden, weird realization.

"Mom?"

☠

Appendix A: Cast of Characters

October Schwartz: she's the protagonist of the book. If you're having a hard time keeping track of her, you should probably put the book down right now. Enrol in a remedial English course or something.

Mr. (Leonard) Schwartz: October's dad and a teacher at Sticksville Central High School. He teaches auto repair and biology, and probably important life lessons to October, or whatever. He's also been clinically depressed since October's mom left the both of them when October was there.

Yumi Takeshi: October's best friend at Sticksville. She shares October's interest in black clothing, eyeliner, and horror movies. She also comes as part of a two-friend package deal with Stacey.

Yumi Takeshi's cousin: Yumi's mythical older cousin and an oracle of sorts on all matters pertaining to local Sticksville teenage gossip.

Stacey [Last Name Unknown]: friend to October and constant companion to Yumi Takeshi. A lanky boy with an affinity for mismatched vintage clothing and percussion instruments.

Ashlie Salmons: terror of the unpopular ninth grade girls at Sticksville Central High School. Loves include belts, boots, bangs, and bullying. She leads a small crew of mostly unpleasant young ladies. Salmons was left back a year for reasons unknown. (She probably just didn't study enough or something totally unmysterious.)

Devin McGriff: guitarist for Sticksville Central High School's most popular (and only) tenth grade band, Phantom Moustache, and sometime boyfriend of October's arch-nemesis, Ashlie Salmons.

Skyler McGriff: the older (university-aged) brother of Devin who helps out in Mr. Santuzzi's math classes. Former Sticksville Central High School baseball superstar. Teaching assistant of Yumi Takeshi's dreams.

Mr. Hamilton: new principal of Sticksville Central High School, he's a recent transfer from Central Tech High School in Toronto.

Ms. Fenstermacher: October's cool new history teacher (perhaps a little too cool to be a teacher), who replaced the very arrested Mr. Page (see Book One). She also works at the Sticksville Museum (former home of Cyril Cooper) and is Sticksville's biggest fan of *Battlestar Galactica*.

Mr. Terry O'Shea: October's former (and formerly living) French teacher. He coached the girls' curling team and was encouraging of October's whole writing thing and was pretty important to her. So when (spoiler alert) he died in Book One, it was très tragic.

Mrs. Eileen Tischmann: the well-meaning but somewhat flighty music teacher at Sticksville Central High School.

Mr. Santuzzi: stern mathematics teacher at Sticksville Central High School, noted for his tight leisure suits, alleged toupee, and military past. He says things like "roger" and "lock 'n' load" when teaching lessons on factoring.

Cyril Cooper: unofficial leader and oldest of the dead kids. He was from a Loyalist family who fled to Canada during the American Revolution, and had a possibly promising career in shipbuilding cut short by a mysterious assailant. Cyril is fascinated by automobiles.

Morna MacIsaac: youngest of the dead kids, Morna was a Scottish immigrant who came with her family to Canada in 1910 for work and affordable land. Instead of finding much of either, the MacIsaacs lived in squalid tenement housing until Morna was killed outside a local pub. She's the first dead kid October ever encounters and the one who leads her to the others.

Tabetha Scott: dead kid who had to escape slavery in the American South before arriving in Sticksville. She left Virginia via the Underground Railroad and settled in town with her dad. Bickers endlessly with Kirby and never hesitates to share her opinions.

Kirby LaFlamme: dead kid and one-fifth of the not-so-famous LaFlamme quintuplets. During the Depression, he and his siblings were the inspiration for the LaFlammetown theme park. He was outlived by all his brothers, and is fluent in both French and English.

Derek Running Water: the most recent of deaths among the dead kids, Derek lived with his mother in Sticksville, but became politically committed to the Mohawk Warrior cause with the 1990 stand-off in Oka, Quebec, the events of which led to his death. Derek can be relied upon to provide explanations to the other dead kids for modern technology and terminology. But he's not great with directions.

Alyosha Diamandas: one of Sticksville's most persistent realtors. Alyosha feels a healthy real estate market is indicative of a healthy democracy. He's a fan of all houses, save the haunted kind. (He's had a few run-ins with the dead kids over the years.)

Crown Attorney Salmons: mother of Ashlie Salmons who shares her daughter's taste in fashion, but also shares October's thirst for justice. (After all, she spends her days prosecuting criminals and such.)

Olivia de Kellerman: fictional heroine of October's horror opus, *Two Knives, One Thousand Demons*. Fated to fight alone (with occasional help from her wheelchair-bound Uncle Otis) against hell's hungry hordes, Olivia likes sharp things and dislikes evil. She's pretty bad news. I'd head the other way if I came across her in a darkened alley.

Dr. Lagostina: Sticksville Central High School's resident two-fer: part physician, part therapist. He, unlike most normal people, likes listening to people's problems.

Roxanne "Roxy" Wotherspoon: proto-feminist school teacher who lived in the Crooked Arms on the third floor above the MacIsaacs. The president and only member of the Sticksville Suffrage Society, as of 1914.

Sam Cheng: Chinese laundry owner and resident of the Crooked Arms. He lived on the second floor with the MacIsaacs, and in 1914 was embroiled in some sort of sabotage scandal at nearby Fort Hannover.

Dr. Alfred Pain: the only resident of the Crooked Arms with (a) a medical degree, and (b) a story about surviving the disaster of the *Titanic*.

Gideon Sundbäck: an inventor who lived in the Crooked Arms in 1914. (Did anyone not live there? That was one full boarding house!)

Boyd MacIsaac: Morna's younger brother (who was eight at the time of our Morna's death).

Rory MacIsaac: Morna's older brother (she only had two), who signed up for the Canadian military in 1914.

Appendix B: Passing References (Important Cultural History!)

Animal (from The Muppets): drummer for the house band, Dr. Teeth and The Electric Mayhem, on the classic puppet variety show (and series of movies) *The Muppets*. Animal is some sort of caveman/subhuman (it's not entirely clear), who is usually chained to the drum set and prone to violent drumming outbursts.

Archie's Pals 'n' Gals: one of the many comic books showcasing Archie, Betty, Veronica, Reggie, and Jughead, that chronicles the highs and lows of life as a clean-cut teenager in Riverdale, U.S.A.

The A-Team: the stars of a popular 1980s action television series. A group of military veterans, framed for a crime, became soldiers of fortune, and audiences fell in love with the delightful travails of Hannibal, Murdock, Faceman, and B.A. Baracus. As the title sequence says, "If you have a problem, if no one else can help, and if you can find them, maybe you can hire the A-Team."

Bad Religion: Los Angeles–based punk band known for injecting their lyrics with political commentary, their vocals with three-part harmonies, and for recording such singles as "American Jesus," "Infected," and "Los Angeles Is Burning." Their band logo was a cross with a red "no" symbol overtop.

Battlestar Galactica (BSG): a popular science-fiction television show about a fugitive fleet of humans evading and battling the Cylons, a robotic race that aims to destroy all humanity. The series referred to here is the revamp from the 2000s, not the original 1978 series.

Beyoncé: a.k.a. Sasha Fierce, one third (or fourth) of former girl group Destiny's Child, who became one of the biggest musicians of all time with such hits as "Crazy in Love," "Single Ladies (Put a Ring on It)," and personal favourite "Countdown." Also a big believer in multi-faceted shimmering hair.

The Bodyguard (1992): film starring Kevin Costner as a former Secret Service agent, now bodyguard to pop star Rachel Marron (Whitney Houston). Obviously they fall in love, but their love can never be, and it results in a massive hit soundtrack.

The Breakfast Club (1985): high school dramedy by director John Hughes about five teenagers from very different social groups who spend a Saturday detention in the school library together and learn about each other and themselves, or something like that. Mostly, it's the most quotable movie of all time: "Does Barry Manilow know that you raid his wardrobe?"

Buddy Holly: Texan musician and rock 'n' roll pioneer behind such songs as "Peggy Sue," "That'll Be the Day," and "Rave On." He died at the age of twenty-two in a tragic airplane crash. Allegedly the inspiration for Don McLean's song "American Pie" and for hip musicians' and people's eyewear for generations. (See also *Rivers Cuomo*.)

Carlos the Jackal: Ilich Ramírez Sánchez to his friends, Carlos the Jackal, one of history's most notorious political terrorists, is a Venezuelan national, convicted of killing three people, then (while in prison) sentenced again for killing 11 and injuring 150 *more* people. He is currently serving a life sentence in France.

Carrie (1974): a novel by Stephen King turned into a film by Brian De Palma (starring Sissy Spacek) about a bullied teenager with telekinetic powers and a very strict religious mother. On prom night, Carrie (spoiler alert) unleashes her incredible powers after being doused with pig's blood.

Casey Kasem: one of history's most famous radio personalities, host of *American Top 40*, and voice actor behind Shaggy on the *Scooby-Doo* television series.

Cher: actress and musician best known for her boundless (alleged) enthusiasm for plastic surgery and for hits like "If I Could Turn Back Time," "Believe," and Yumi's ringtone, "Gypsys, Tramps & Thieves."

The Craft (1996): four teenage girls dabble in witchcraft in this major motion picture; hair loss, jealousy, and wrist-cuttings ensue. Sort of like *Mean Girls*, but with more pentagrams.

The Crow (1994): staple of goth filmmaking, the movie (starring Brandon Lee, who died under mysterious circumstances during production) tells the story of a rock musician with the best name ever, Eric Draven, who is murdered, then resurrected (in goth makeup) to avenge his own and his fiancée's murders. Based on a super-goth comic book.

Dangerous Minds (1995): a retired marine (Michelle Pfeiffer) takes up a teaching position at the decidedly tough-as-nails Parkmont High School, where the students are more worried about crime and urban unrest than their GPAs. Though initially disrespected ("dissed"), Pfeiffer gains the students' trust and loyalty thanks to her trusty leather jacket and use of poetry, obviously.

Dark Shadows: long-running melodramatic soap opera about vampires that originally aired in the late 1960s and early 1970s.

The Dark Side of the Moon (1973): ever see that poster with a prism on a black background, with a light shaft entering one side and a rainbow shooting out the other? Yeah, that's actually an album cover by a band called Pink Floyd.

Die Hard (1988): only the second-greatest Christmas movie of all time. Bruce Willis, as detective John McClane, squares off against a team of terrorists led by Alan Rickman (a.k.a. Professor Snape) who have taken over the Nakatomi Plaza Building one fateful Christmas Eve.

The Electric Slide: semi-popular line dance from the 1980s, originally invented for the song "Electric Boogie" by Marcia Griffiths. Describing dance moves is difficult. Let's just say there's a lot of pitching forward and backward.

Elvira: arguably the most famous horror hostess of all time. During the 1980s, the vampire-like actress introduced low-budget horror films of the 1950s and '60s to television viewers in the Los Angeles area (and later, all of North America).

Escape from New York (1981): in the dystopian future (1997!), Manhattan Island has been converted into a maximum security prison, Air Force One has crashed inside the prison, and the President of the United States is being held hostage. It's up to the eye-patched Snake Plissken (Kurt Russell) to bring him back in one piece and escape . . . from New York! (This is a movie, by the way.)

The Exorcist (1973): perhaps one of the scariest films of all time, directed by William Friedkin and based on a book by William Peter Blatty, in which a young girl is possessed by the Devil, and an old and a young priest attempt to save her soul, through exorcism. (Hence the title.) If you don't want nightmares, don't watch this movie.

50 Cent: hip hop artist best known for surviving being shot by nine bullets, as well as hits like "In da Club" and "Candy Shop."

Final Destination (2000): horror film about a bunch of teenagers who "cheat death" by not getting on an airplane that later crashes. But Death comes for them (because they were supposed to die in that plane, right?), and the teenagers die one by one in increasingly elaborate "accidents."

Forrest Gump (1994): an Academy Award–winning film (based on a book by Winston Groom) about a slow-witted Alabama man who somehow becomes involved in most major events in American history from the '50s to the '80s. Few people can watch it from beginning to end without crying. Unfortunately spawned the crass restaurant chain Bubba Gump Shrimp Company.

Freddy Krueger: sadistic and quippy monster of the *Nightmare on Elm Street* horror movies. He wears a striped sweater, a brown fedora, and a metal glove of ten-inch razor claws. Freddy enters teenagers' dreams and kills them in their sleep. If the horror movies are too harrowing to watch, you can get a good sense of this villain from DJ Jazzy Jeff and the Fresh Prince song "Nightmare on My Street."

Gremlins (1984): the best Christmas movie of all time, because (a) it features adorable pets turning into evil monsters, (b) it co-stars Phoebe Cates (see the first Dead Kid Detective Agency book), and (c) it features a scene of a monster being shoved into a blender.

Guitar Wolf: the most amazing (and the loudest) Japanese garage rock band you've never heard of, consisting of Guitar Wolf, Bass Wolf, and Drum Wolf. Also the stars of the totally bananas zombie movie, *Wild Zero*.

Hair (1967): a rock musical about hair from the era when having long hair in North America was (for men, at least) symbolic of some sort of rebellion. Sadly, a sequel, *Nails*, was never produced.

Haley Joel Osment: actor probably best known as the child who could see dead people in M. Night Shyamalan's *The Sixth Sense*, clearly a spiritual predecessor to October Schwartz. He also played Jenny's son in *Forrest Gump!* (See also Forrest Gump.)

The Hardy Boys: Frank and Joe Hardy, two mystery-solving brothers who have appeared in dozens of books written by Franklin W. Dixon (but really a syndicate of ghost writers) since 1927. Those two brothers, it should be noted, combined their powers to produce the mystery-solving skill of a single Nancy Drew.

Hogwarts: the foremost school of Wizardry and Witchcraft in England seen in the various Harry Potter books and movies. It consists of four houses: Gryffindor, Hufflepuff, Ravenclaw, and Slytherin.

Hollow Man (2000): truly unfortunate movie that retells the story of *The Invisible Man*, with Kevin Bacon as the demented scientist who turns himself see-through.

Huey Lewis and the News: rock band popular in the 1980s, notable for their use of a horn section and doo-wop vocals. Maybe best known as "those guys who did the song for *Back to the Future*," even though they have a lot of pretty decent songs.

Indiana Jones and the Temple of Doom (1984): the second movie in the adventure serial about an extremely daring archae-ologist. Largely set in India, this installment is notable for being the grossest (chilled monkey brains, anyone?) and least cultur-ally sensitive (or flat-out racist) of the trilogy. (We'll pretend the fourth movie never existed, okay?)

Jason Bourne: main character in a series of spy novels by Robert Ludlum (later made into movies starring Matt Damon), who was turned into the ultimate covert killing-and-espionage machine through a top-secret training program.

Jedi lightsabre: the weapon of choice among the vaguely mystical cult of space samurai seen in the Star Wars movies. The sabre consists of a metal cylinder that projects a yard-long beam of plasma and makes a sound like an amplified electric razor.

John Waters: bizarre filmmaker from Baltimore, Maryland, best known for his cult films, love of kitsch, and pencil-thin moustache.

***Lord of the Flies* (1954):** you'll probably have to read this for school at some point, so I won't give too much away, but it's the story (written by William Golding) of how a bunch of boys who crash-land on a remote island attempt to govern themselves and fall into violence and chaos. You will weep for Piggy.

Kraftwerk: robotic electronic music pioneers from Düsseldorf, Germany, who popularized the use of synthesizers and minimalist, repetitive rhythm in the '70s and '80s. Look up "Tour de France" on YouTube and you'll see what I mean.

***Magic: The Gathering*:** weird and complex card game where people (pretending to be wizards) use their deck of elaborately illustrated cards to cast spells and things like that.

***The Manchurian Candidate* (1962):** classic Cold War film (and book) about the son of a U.S. political family who is brainwashed into becoming a Communist assassin (unbeknownst to him). Stars Frank Sinatra and Angela Lansbury. (See also *Murder, She Wrote*.)

Marilyn Manson: controversial rock musician who took his stage name from an actress and serial killer. Known for his angry goth-metal music ("The Dope Show," "The Beautiful People") and theatrical stage performances and costumes.

Murder, She Wrote: your mom (or grandmother) probably watches this mystery show about a lovable old mystery writer, Jessica Fletcher, who always seems able to solve crimes in her fair coastal village of Cabot Cove when the authorities can't.

Nick Cave: Australian musician and writer who has fronted bands such as The Birthday Party and Nick Cave and the Bad Seeds. Kind of like Australia's goth spirit animal.

Nine Inch Nails: industrial rock project of musician Trent Reznor that is the favourite band of countless goths around the world. Best known for songs like "Closer," "Hurt," and "Head Like a Hole," all of which have lyrics that shouldn't be listened to until you're at least sixteen. Kind of like Marilyn Manson, but with more street cred.

Northern Reflections: Since 1985, a favoured clothing brand of moms across Canada, beloved for its comfort over fashion and penchant for putting ducks and winter scenes on sweatshirts.

Ophelia: You'll probably have to read *Hamlet* in school at some point, too, but Ophelia is the daughter of Polonius and kind of Hamlet's girlfriend. The important part to remember (for this book, as well as most of art history) is that she drowns in a river.

The Parent Trap (1961): classic Disney live-action film in which twin sisters (both played by Hayley Mills) scheme to reunite their divorced parents via all sorts of identity-based shenanigans. Later remade with Lindsay Lohan in the main role.

The Price Is Right: television game show that is a perennial favourite of students trapped at home with the flu. Hosted by

Bob Barker, and later Drew Carey, the show pits contestants against one another by making them guess the retail prices of various consumer items.

Puff Daddy: a.k.a. Sean Combs, P. Diddy, Diddy, Puffy, is a hugely successful hip hop act, producer, and entertainment mogul. You might know him from such club bangers as "Bad Boy for Life," "It's All About the Benjamins," and "Coming Home."

Radiohead: British rock band that's nearly every music critic's favourite. Their first single was "Creep," which makes excellent use of crunchy guitars and well-placed F-bombs.

Richard Feynman: the one-and-only rock-star physicist. Won a Nobel Prize for his work on quantum electrodynamics, worked on the atomic bomb, and aided the team who investigated the explosion of the space shuttle *Challenger*. Basically The Fonz of theoretical physics.

Rivers Cuomo: diminutive lead singer of the band Weezer, who has written some of the best ("El Scorcho") and worst ("We Are All on Drugs") pop rock songs of the modern era. He traditionally wears horn-rimmed glasses just like Buddy Holly, as revealed in the hit single, "Buddy Holly." (See also *Buddy Holly*.)

Rodney Dangerfield: stand-up comedian who was best known for his catchphrase "I don't get no respect!" Sample joke: "I could tell my parents hated me. My bath toys were a toaster and radio."

"Rowdy" Roddy Piper: professional wrestler whose persona was an angry Scotsman. He often entered the wrestling ring in a kilt and to the tune of bagpipes. Also the star of one of the greatest films of all time, John Carpenter's *They Live*.

Runaway Bride **(1999):** a Julia Roberts–Richard Gere romantic comedy about a reporter (Gere) investigating a woman who has fled the wedding altar three times. The movie poster features Julia Roberts in a wedding gown putting on, like, New Balance sneakers, so you know it's got to be horrible.

S Club 7: Bradley. Hannah. Jo. Jon. Paul. Rachel. Tina. The seven were a British pop group with a string of hits and a TV series in the early 2000s. They also informed everyone that "there ain't no party like an S Club party," which has yet to be disproven.

***Silent Night, Deadly Night* (1984):** the first of a series of holiday-themed slasher movies, in which a deranged spree killer dressed as Santa goes a'murdering. Nightmare material, for sure.

Sun Tzu: ancient Chinese military general and strategist who put down his most strategical military thoughts in the book *The Art of War*. One such bon mot: "When torrential water tosses boulders, it is because of its momentum. When the strike of a hawk breaks the body of its prey, it is because of timing."

Swatch: Swiss watch brand most popular in the 1980s, often making use of neon, day-glo, and pastel watch bands.

***Tokyo Drift* (2006):** the third film in the Fast and the Furious series (about competitive street racing). Tokyo drift refers to "drift racing," in which drivers intentionally lose traction in the rear wheels to maintain control when turning corners. (Or something like that . . . I don't even know how to drive.)

***Twilight*:** extremely popular book (and movie) franchise about a sparkly vampire, a Native American werewolf, and one lucky, sullen lady who has to decide between romancing the two. Fans of the series are called "Twi-hards."

Tyra Banks: model and host of *America's Next Top Model*, who, among so many other life lessons, taught the world to "smize" (smile with one's eyes) and always be fierce.

Van Halen: one of the most popular American rock bands of all time, consisting of Eddie Van Halen, Alex Van Halen, Michael Anthony, and (originally) vocalist David Lee Roth. They recorded the song "Jump" and the song "Panama," which was played at high volume by the American military to drive General Noriega from the Holy See's embassy in Panama during the Panamanian invasion.

The Village People: Disco group known for songs like "YMCA," "Macho Man," and "In the Navy." They dress in costumes (Native American chief, cowboy, police officer, soldier, biker, construction worker) and are associated with the late '70s gay lifestyle in New York City.

Walkman: back before iPods and MP3 players, even back before CDs, but after vinyl records, people listened to music on cassette tapes. They could play these cassettes on a portable cassette player, more commonly referred to as a Walkman.

Evan Munday is an illustrator and the cartoonist behind the self-published comic book *Quarter-Life Crisis*, set in a post-apocalyptic Toronto. He works as a book publicist for Coach House Books. *The Dead Kid Detective Agency* is his first novel. He lives in Toronto, ON.